# *ANZIA YEZIERSKA*

(1881?–1970) was born in a village near Warsaw, in Russian Poland, one of the nine children of Pearl and Bernard Yezierska, a Talmudic scholar. In the 1890s the family sailed to America, settling in Manhattan's Lower East Side. At the age of seventeen Yezierska left home. She worked in sweatshops and laundries, then won a tuition scholarship, graduating from Columbia University in 1904. Thereafter she taught for a few years.

Around 1910 Anzia Yezierska married a laywer, Jacob Gordon, but their union was annulled a few months later. Shortly afterwards she married a teacher and textbook writer, Arnold Levitas, with whom she had a daughter. After three years she left her husband, taking the child, but financial pressures forced Yezierska to return their daughter to his care.

Denied formal teaching qualifications, Yezierska turned to John Dewey at Columbia University to assist her. He admired the writing she'd produced and gave her much encouragement. Her first story, "The Free Vacation House", appeared in the *Forum* in 1915 and in 1919 "The Fat of the Land" won the Edward J. O'Brien award for Best Short Story of the Year. But it was the collection of stories, *Hungry Hearts*, published a year later, that transformed her life. Yezierska earned instant fame and fortune when the book was bought by Samuel Goldwyn and she went to Hollywood to work on the silent film script. Yezierska then published *Salome of the Tenements* (1922, also sold for filming); *Children of Loneliness* (1923); *Bread Givers* (1925); *Arrogant Beggar* (1927); and *All I Could Never Be* (1932).

With the Depression Yezierska's luck changed: her reputation declined and poverty returned. During the 1930s she worked on the Works Progress Administration Writers Project. Her fictionalized autobiography, *Red Ribbon on a White Horse* appeared in 1950; thereafter she published short stories and contributed reviews to the *New York Times*. In 1962 and 1965 the National Institute of Arts and Letters presented Yezierska with five hundred dollars in recognition of her distinction as a writer. In her last years she left New York to live near her daughter. Yezierska died in a nursing home in Ontario, California.

VIRAGO
MODERN
CLASSIC
NUMBER

250

ANZIA YEZIERSKA

# Hungry Hearts
## and Other Stories

WITH A NEW INTRODUCTION BY
RIVA KRUT

AFTERWORD BY
LOUISE LEVITAS HENRIKSEN

First published in Great Britain by VIRAGO PRESS Limited 1987
41 William IV Street, London WC2N 4DB

First published in the United States of America by
Houghton Mifflin Company, 1920
Published, with three previously uncollected stories, by Persea Books
New York, 1985


*British Library Cataloguing in Publication Data*
Yezierska, Anzia
Hungry hearts.
I. Title
813′.52[F] PS3547.E95
ISBN 0-86068-713-9

Printed in Finland by
Werner Söderström Oy, a member of Finnprint.

# CONTENTS

# *INTRODUCTION*

*Hungry Hearts* first appeared in 1920 as a collection of ten short stories. It was the work of a little-known young author who had once lived in a squalid tenement on Hester Street in the Lower East Side of New York. Anzia Yezierska was one of many hundreds of thousands of Russian Jewish immigrants in New York, all of them striving to make a new life for themselves or their families. Like most of the Jewish writers in New York in this period, Yezierska drew heavily on her milieu for her inspiration. She described their conditions of life, their aspirations beyond the daily grind, their dream that in America would be found a new, secular "Promised Land".

What followed publication was perhaps more the stuff of a cheap dime novel than anything Yezierska could have imagined. The American Dream, which she despised because of its shallow pretensions and materialism, now became her reality. Her book was snapped up by Sam Goldwyn. Overnight, the life of the writer was transformed. She was whisked across America to Los Angeles in a private train compartment, fed roast duckling, asparagus, endive salad and strawberries and cream, ensconced in a sumptious hotel with a personal chauffeur and secretary, and wined and dined with millionaires and movie-stars. The contract earned its hitherto unknown author an overnight fortune—some $10,000. The transition "from Hester Street to Hollywood" was for Yezierska as abrupt and bewildering as American Dream mythology promised.

Anzia Yezierska was born in about 1881 in a village, a *stetl*, near Warsaw, in Russian Poland. The generation before her birth, from 1855–81, had been one of official liberalism. Under Czar Alexander II had come the momentous emancipation of the serfs. Jewish hopes, along with the aspirations of other oppressed groups, were thereby raised, and the period saw a flourishing Jewish intellectual life which briefly, and for the first time, viewed positively the possibility of integration into Russian life.

But in 1881 Alexander II was assassinated. One of those implicated in the plot was a young Jewish woman, Hessia Helfman. The combination of Nihilist activity and marginal Jewish involvement provoked renewed Czarist reaction, with the Jews as a special target. Alexander III's reign saw the introduction of policies of virulent Slavophilism and a rule of terror. Minority groups were subjected to mandatory programmes of Russification, which included a ban on non-Russian languages, educational systems and civic leadership. For Jews there was a different tactic. They were not to be forcibly yoked into the "Russian" system; they were to be rigidly excluded.

The new Minister of the Interior in charge of the "Jewish Question" was Count Ignatiev, whose brief, which he followed to the letter, was systematically to undermine the basis of Jewish economic life in Russia. Between October 1881 and May 1882, a corpus of laws was created—the so-called "May Laws"—which sought to limit Jewish life to the Pale of Settlement, a narrow strip of land on the north-west border of

Russia, which incorporated much of Russian Poland. This meant that the 40 per cent of Jews living in the interior were threatened with displacement and that Jews living in the countryside were pushed into the cities, which rapidly became overcrowded. In addition, occupational mobility was severely circumscribed. Quotas of Jews in universities were slashed, state employed doctors and lawyers were discharged and hundreds of thousands of artisans were reclassified, declared illegally resident in Russia proper, and removed to the Pale.

These vast resettlements of Russian Jewry were accompanied by outbreaks of apparently popular local feeling against Jews—pogroms—in a number of regions, which served to compound the deep insecurity of all east European Jewry. By 1900 the effects of the "May Laws" were clear: 40 per cent of Russian Jewry had become completely dependent on charity. They were, in economic terms, dying a slow and miserable death. It was a situation that was not alleviated until 1917.

Despite—perhaps because of—their oppression and abject poverty, the period 1881–1917 in Russia emerged as one of the most dynamic in modern Jewish history. Buoyed up by the cultural and intellectual life of the previous decades, these years of repression saw the birth of a variety of activist Jewish movements. Apart from Jews who now joined the Russian revolution, there were popular movements of Jewish Socialism and, even more radically, Zionism. Ideological debate was accompanied by argument over whether there was a future for Jews within Russia, then or after the revolution. Almost half of Russian Jewry not only decided that this was unlikely, they made the enormous decision to leave. And three quarters of those, some two million, went to the United States of America.

So Yezierska was born in turbulent yet exhilarating times, her move to America being part of one of the largest group migrations in recorded history. Like most of her compatriots she settled in New York City. New York, which was from the start home to over half the total American Jewish population, would soon house the largest concentration of Jews ever in one city, most of them crowded into the tenements and sweatshops of the Lower East Side.

The sheer size of the Jewish immigrant tide was to have several consequences for the developing Jewish American community, particularly in New York. Purely in terms of numbers, the Russian Jews overwhelmed not only the established Jewish community, but the city as well. In New York, it was white Protestants who struggled to maintain themselves against continual tides of immigration. By 1935 they were only the third largest population group in the city, after Catholics and Jews. Despite the anti-semitism they encountered outside of Jewish areas, in applications for jobs, club memberships, university places and apartments, America remained a country which, in theory at least, endorsed multidenominationalism and political federalism. Jews felt confident that they could be integrated into American society without surrendering their distinctiveness.

The immigrants had barely landed before they set about establishing a vibrant literary culture. By 1900 there were ninety newspapers established across America and the readership increased for as long as immigration continued. The newspaper with the largest circulation was the Yiddish daily, *Forwards*, which started life in 1897, had a circulation of twenty thousand by 1900; thirty thousand by 1918 and over two hundred thousand in the 1920s. The newspaper was a platform for politics, fiction, social analysis, lonely hearts and advertisements. *Forwards* was strongly socialist and concentrated on labour relations and industrial disputes. A minority were more Orthodox and supported the Republicans. Jewish immigrants like Sam Goldwyn were involved in the genesis of the film industry and popular immigrant themes, including Jewish ones, like the fractured family, intergenerational stress and poverty, quickly reached the screen and were eagerly devoured by the audiences of the Lower East Side.

What is distinctive about Yezierska's writing is that it is in English, not Yiddish. In this sense she was in the vanguard of an American Jewish literature that emerged after the 1930s. Her ear for the inflections of immigrant "Yinglish" recreates the sounds of a specifically Jewish world at its moment of transition, and sidesteps the caricature of immigrant life that it could so easily have become.

The rapidity with which a Jewish community was established meant that an American Jewish culture was quickly formed, drawing on America rather than Russia as its inspiration. Naturally the Russian past and the immigrant experience were major points of reference for first generation immigrants, but the nature of their connection to their roots was complex. In *Hungry Hearts*, the Russian past lurks as a backdrop, containing memories of Cossack oppression and of a patriarchal and parochial Jewish society suspicious of change and modernity. For a strong-minded woman like Yezierska, Russia did not hold warm memories. On the other hand, the turbulence of the Russian Jewish experience had generated a dynamism, a belief in change, an ambition, that the immigrants to America brought with them. In "Hunger", new immigrant Shenah Pessah confides:

> This fire in me, it's not just the hunger of a woman for a man—it's the hunger of all my people back of me, from all ages, for light, for the life higher!

For many immigrants, glad to see the last of Russia, their past and their homeland was rejected in favour of the future, "the life higher", symbolized by America.

Apart from some residual guilt which she explores in greater detail in her fictionalized autobiography, *Red Ribbon on a White Horse*, Yezierska portrays "America" as the symbol of immigrant Jewish ambition. In the original collection of *Hungry Hearts*, Shenah Pessah is instantly recognizable as a first generation immigrant. Her arrival in America is only accomplished by the painful but necessary rupture of her relationship with her parents and their tradition.

The same theme is taken up in "The Miracle". Here, Sara Reisel inveigles her parents into selling their only possessions of value—the Sabbath candles and the Torah Scrolls—for her ticket to America. The significance of a young woman making her parents convert their Orthodoxy into hard currency in order that they can help her to leave them, is not lost on the writer. But Yezierska's sympathy lies not with the parents but with the daughter who, upon her arrival in America, continues to affront Jewish tradition, consulting her heart instead of the matchmaker's lists and falling in love with a gentile.

The overwhelming attraction that immigrants felt for America is depicted as a love relationship and in "Wings", "The Miracle", "Soap and Water" and "How I Found America", the female protagonists fall in love with various White Anglo-Saxon Protestant (WASP) teachers, researchers and lecturers at night school. In "The Miracle", Yezierska investigates the contrast that she felt Russian Jews provided to middle-class American society. The teacher becomes captivated by Sara Reisel's vitality:

> We Americans are too much on earth; we need more of your power to fly. If you would only know how much you can teach us Americans. You are the promise of the centuries to come. You are the heart, the creative pulse of America to be.

The image of a fusion between the Russian Jew and the American was popular among Jewish writers in American film and fiction, who frequently expressed this possibility as a romance between individuals from both worlds. The early silent films included ones named *Abie's Irish Rose* and *The Cohens and the Kellys* which emphasized the strains put on the older generation as their children mixed and married out. However, for all that she speaks of love between Russian Jew and WASP American, and even the loss of her traditional identity, Yezierska is not clear about what America offered, apart from the promise of some nebulous freedom. It is interesting that in the last story in the original collection of *Hungry Hearts*, "How I Found America", the protagonist—again an immigrant Russian woman yearning to discover America—confesses to a teacher that "America is more far from me than it was in the old country". In fact, Yezierska, struggling to write on abstract, larger themes, was to find that inspiration would only come, and then in abundance, from "My Own People".

Independent woman and struggling artist, Yezierska herself had followed the typical pattern of emigration. Her family left the *stetl* for the New World, Yezierksa went out to work, married (twice), had a child, and then broke away to live alone and write. That decision to have a creative career, as she makes clear in the opening image of the first story, "Wings", was not made without a deep sense of loss. As Shenah Pessah explains to John Barnes:

> Since I got to work for low wages and I can't be young anymore, I'm burning to get among people where it's not against a girl if she's in years and without money.

Being "a girl in years and without money" made it difficult enough to survive, let alone as an immigrant without useful social contacts, speaking a foreign language, yet wanting to write in English. These intensely subjective stories are presented implicitly from a woman's perspective. Consequently, although her themes—poverty, labour relations and class mobility—include issues popular among other Jewish American writers in this period, Yezierska locates her stories within the world of women. A more explicitly feminist stance is taken later, in "Wild Winter Love" (1927).

"Wild Winter Love" is one of three stories written after the first publication of *Hungry Hearts* and included in this collection. It is the fictionalized biography of Rose Cohen, the successful author of *Out of the Shadows* (1918). Here, in a remarkable epitaph to a woman with whom she clearly felt deep empathy, Yezierska explores the immense difficulties for women like herself—a wife and mother—of pursuing a single-minded creative career.

*Hungry Hearts* describes scenes and emotions that were the very fibre of Jewish immigrant life. They range from the filth of tenements and the claustrophobia of life and work inside them—the kitchens, the cooking, the childcare, the "taking in" of washing and of lodgers—to conditions in the sweatshops. And always her concern is to describe not merely the conditions but the women in them, struggling, as was Yezierska, "for the life higher".

The "Hungry Hearts" were those hundreds of thousands of Jewish immigrants yearning not just for physical sustenance—although food and the getting of it was never taken lightly—but emotional and spiritual succour. In "Hunger", Shenah Pessah describes her own genesis as an artist, her early realization that she was not going to let her circumstances limit her potential. In a poignant conversation with Sam Arkin, another immigrant, typecast here as all that was homely and coarse about her Russian background, Shenah Pessah turns down his offer of marriage by explaining that she has to go her own way as a writer:

> I feel the emptiness of words—but I got to get it out. All that you suffer I have suffered, and must yet go on suffering. I see no end. But only—there is a something—a hope—a help out—it lifts me on top of my hungry body—the hunger to make from myself a person that can't be crushed by nothing nor nobody—the life higher!

Heroism in Yezierska's novels is measured simply in these terms: the ability to transcend one's environment, to sustain a vision beyond that which focuses exclusively on daily needs. This is what she admired most of all—although for herself as a writer, it was to pose special problems. The story that follows "Hunger", "The Lost 'Beautifulness'", tells just such a tale. It is wartime. Hannah Hayyeh, married to a "stoop-shouldered, care-crushed" man, has saved up all her spare money from taking in washing, to redecorate her kitchen for the return of her son Aby on leave. All the ingredients are here for a drama: the Jewish participation in America's war effort; their huge emotional investment in American promises of democracy; the vibrant yet politically powerless street life of the Lower East Side; the miserable existence in the sweatshops and tenements.

For Hannah Heyyeh, the decoration of her kitchen is explicitly in order that her son Aby can invite "even the President from America to his home" without being ashamed of it. Filled with ideas of democracy gleaned from her employer Mrs Preston, Hannah Heyyeh is inspired:

> this war is to give everybody a chance to lift up his head like a person. It is to bring together the people on top who got everything and the people on the bottom who got nothing. She's been telling me about a new word—democracy. It got me on fire. Democracy means that everybody in America is going to be with everybody alike.

Hannah Heyyeh's public are in the tenements and on the street, and she rushes out to make them all stop their selling and their shopping, to come and look at her creation. What follows is a beautiful piece of absurd theatre. Everyone troops upstairs and, for fear of dirtying such cleanliness, the admirers all crowd onto the butcher's apron which is obligingly spread on the floor, and praise Hannah Heyyeh's handiwork.

There, in the face of such artistry, even the butcher is moved to poetry:

What a whiteness! And what a cleanliness! It tears out the eyes from the head! Such a tenant the landlord ought to give out a medal or let down the rent free.

Of course, the landlord's interpretation is different, and as Hannah Heyyeh has increased the value of the property she now has to pay a higher rent. In a story that never loses its emotional hold or its narrative power, Yezierska ends with an image of a vitality broken and discarded—the greatest tragedy of all.

When Yezierska translated *Hungry Hearts* into a film script, she chose "The Lost 'Beautifulness'" as the pivot of the narrative. The script, focusing as it did on the pathos and humanity of Jewish life on the Lower East Side, was one of a new genre of films, some forty in all, produced in the early 1920s, which confronted poverty, stress and the humour of immigrant life. After the success of just such a story, *Humoresque*, based on a novel by another Jewish woman, Fannie Hurst, good writers became hot property in the studios. Of course Yezierska's plots lacked "humor", and this, to her horror, was simply added by another screenwriter, Montague Glass, whom Yezierska despised.

Unlike the movies, there is little in *Hungry Hearts* that has a happy "American" ending. More frequently, there are images of people who do not rise above their situation in life but are indelibly marked by it: of women transformed into shrieking harridans by the continual need to eke out an existence on too little money, demeaning sops from Charity, and with no support from their husbands.

State and municipal welfare, unknown to the *stetl*, emerged as a major theme in American Jewish writing. Welfare workers and institutions like "rest homes" and old age homes loomed large in the immigrant nightmare. In "The Free Vacation House", an exhausted mother is given a holiday with her children. The experience of regimentation leads her, by the end of her holiday, to appreciate her limited independence, for all her poverty.

In "My Own People", Yezierska describes Hannah Breineh, mother of six and wife of a man who "ain't no bread-giver". Her life is a continual battle against the butcher, her tenants, the landlord and the Children's Society officials, and it turns her into an unpopular neighbour, landlady and irascible mother. Quite unexpectedly, her lodger receives a food parcel from a friend and the household all gather round for the feast. For a moment, Hannah Breineh is transformed, extracting untold joy from a tiny sip of wine and showing what potential she might have had in a different setting: "How it laughs yet in me, the life, the minute I turn my head from my worries."

But if poverty can change one's character, so too can wealth, or the promise of it. In the meritocracy that was America, Yezierska was quick to point out that ambition was costly. David, an aspirant Doctor in "Where Lovers Dream", can only succeed if he sacrifices his feelings. Hannah Breineh, in "The Fat of the Land", now wealthy because her children are successful, finds herself wretched and alienated in her antiseptic apartment in 84th Street, but unwilling to return to the discomforts of the Lower East Side. And ultimately, Yezierska herself found that her single-minded pursuit of art and her attendant financial success cut her off from her family and her people.

Even during the height of her success Yezierska understood what the price was of pursuing the American Dream, not only because it contained no human value but also because it removed the lucky individuals from their roots. Just five years after *Hungry Hearts* was published, Yezierska wrote "This Is What $10,000 Did to Me", a chronicle of her life after she was "discovered" by the film studios. There is enjoyment in the luxury and comfort and the freedom to write, but a great deal of guilt at her luck compared to the misfortunes of most of the world. As she writes at the end of this piece, Yezierska found herself insulated from the very people who had given her creative sustenance: "I am alone because I left my own world."

Once she had taken the step from Hester Street to Hollywood, Yezierska discovered that there was no going back. Even when she left Hollywood in disgust and tried to live within reasonable means, the media made capital out of her story and gave her a cut. Her profits merely increased, as did demands on her purse from poor relatives and friends. As she described in *Red Ribbon on a White Horse*,

> As long as I remained with Goldwyn I was in a glasshouse with crooked mirrors. Every move I made was distorted, and every distortion exploited to further the sale of *Hungry Hearts*. The dinner parties, the invitations to speak at churches, synagogues, clubs and colleges, all that had seemed to be the spontaneous recognition of my book was but the merchandising enterprise of press agents selling a movie. Money and ballyhoo—the fruit of the struggle to write.

In the 1930s, already alienated from her work and

disenchanted with Hollywood, Yezierska lost popularity. There was a context to her decline in fortune—not only the Crash and the economic crisis of America, brilliantly chronicled in *Red Ribbon on a White Horse*, but also some specifically Jewish themes. In 1924 Jewish immigration to the United States was terminated and second generation readers were more interested in suburbia and Americanization than the poverty of the Lower East Side. In addition, the years of the Depression saw an upswing in anti-semitism and the disappearance of "Jewish" themes from view. Like a shooting star, Yezierska's public life was brilliant and brief.

Yezierska did continue to write, and won some acclaim with her fictionalized autobiography (1950) and other writings in the 1960s. By then her concerns had altered. The last piece in this collection, "One Thousand Pages of Research", was written when Yezierska was in her eighties. It is a clinically reflective piece on modern society's capacity to kill off its older members by reducing them to anthropological artefacts. This is extraordinary, especially in view of the fact, clear in this book, that Yezierska's talents grew with time—if in inverse proportion to her "success". It has only been in the 1980s that Yezierska has been rescued from obscurity by feminist research and publishing. This is a reward hugely deserved.

*Riva Krut, London, 1986*

# HUNGRY HEARTS

## WINGS

"My heart chokes in me like in a prison! I'm dying for a little love and I got nobody — nobody!" wailed Shenah Pessah, as she looked out of the dismal basement window.

It was a bright Sunday afternoon in May, and into the gray, cheerless, janitor's basement a timid ray of sunlight announced the dawn of spring.

"Oi weh! Light!" breathed Shenah Pessah, excitedly, throwing open the sash. "A little light in the room for the first time!" And she stretched out her hands hungrily for the warming bit of sun.

The happy laughter of the shopgirls standing on the stoop with their beaux and the sight of the young mothers with their husbands and babies fanned anew the consuming fire in her breast.

"I'm not jealous!" she gasped, chokingly. "My heart hurts too deep to want to tear from them their luck to happiness. But why should they live and enjoy life and why must I only *look on* how they are happy?"

She clutched at her throat like one stifled for want of air. "What is the matter with you? Are you going out of your head? For what is your crying? Who will listen to you? Who gives a care what's going to become from you?"

Crushed by her loneliness, she sank into a chair. For a long time she sat motionless, finding drear fascination in the mocking faces traced in the patches of the torn plaster. Gradually, she became aware of a tingling warmth playing upon her cheeks. And with a revived breath, she drank in the miracle of the sunlit wall.

"Ach!" she sighed. "Once a year the sun comes to light up even this dark cellar, so why should n't the High One send on me too a little brightness?"

This new wave of hope swept aside the fact that she was the "greenhorn" janitress, that she was twenty-two and dowryless, and, according to the traditions of her people, condemned to be shelved aside as an unmated thing — a creature of pity and ridicule.

"I can't help it how old I am or how poor I am!" she burst out to the deaf and dumb air. "I want a little life! I want a little joy!"

The bell rang sharply, and as she turned to answer the call, she saw a young man at the doorway — a framed picture of her innermost dreams.

The stranger spoke.

Shenah Pessah did not hear the words, she heard only the music of his voice. She gazed fascinated at his clothes — the loose Scotch tweeds, the pongee shirt, a bit open at the neck, but she did not see him or the things he wore. She only felt an irresistible presence seize her soul. It was as though the god of her innermost longings had suddenly taken shape in human form and lifted her in mid-air.

"Does the janitor live here?" the stranger repeated.

Shenah Pessah nodded.

"Can you show me the room to let?"

"Yes, right away, but wait only a minute," stammered Shenah Pessah, fumbling for the key on the shelf.

"Don't fly into the air!" She tried to reason with her wild, throbbing heart, as she walked upstairs with him. In an effort to down the chaos of emotion that shook her she began to talk nervously: "Mrs. Stein who rents out the room ain't going to be back till the evening, but I can tell you the price and anything you want to know. She's a grand cook and you can eat by her your breakfast and dinner—" She did not have the slightest notion of what she was saying, but talked on in a breathless stream lest he should hear the loud beating of her heart.

"Could I have a drop-light put in here?" the man asked, as he looked about the room.

Shenah Pessah stole a quick, shy glance at him. "Are you maybe a teacher or a writing man?"

"Yes, sometimes I teach," he said, studying her, drawn by the struggling soul of her that cried aloud to him out of her eyes.

"I could tell right away that you must be some kind of a somebody," she said, looking up with wistful worship in her eyes. "Ach, how grand it must be to live only for learning and thinking."

"Is this your home?"

"I never had a home since I was eight years old. I was living by strangers even in Russia."

"Russia?" he repeated with quickened attention. So he was in their midst, the people he had come to study. The girl with her hungry eyes and intense eagerness now held a new interest for him.

John Barnes, the youngest instructor of sociology in his university, congratulated himself at his good fortune in encountering such a splendid type for his research. He was preparing his thesis on the "Educational Problems of the Russian Jews," and in order to get into closer touch with his subject, he had determined to live on the East Side during his spring and summer vacation.

He went on questioning her, unconsciously using all the compelling power that made people open their hearts to him. "And how long have you been here?"

"Two years already."

"You seem to be fond of study. I suppose you go to night-school?"

"I never yet stepped into a night-school since I came to America. From where could I get the time? My uncle is such an old man he can't do much and he got already used to leave the whole house on me."

"You stay with your uncle, then?"

"Yes, my uncle sent for me the ticket for America when my aunt was yet living. She got herself sick. And what could an old man like him do with only two hands?"

"Was that sufficient reason for you to leave your homeland?"

"What did I have out there in Savel that I should be afraid to lose? The cows that I used to milk had it better than me. They got at least enough to eat and me slaving from morning till night went around hungry."

"You poor child!" broke from the heart of the man, the scientific inquisition of the sociologist momentarily swept away by his human sympathy.

Who had ever said "poor child" to her— and in such a voice? Tears gathered in Shenah Pessah's eyes. For the first time she mustered the courage to look straight at him. The man's face, his voice, his bearing, so different from any one she had ever known, and yet what was there about him that made her so strangely at ease with him? She went on talking, led irresistibly by the friendly glow in his eyes.

"I got yet a lot of luck. I learned myself English from a Jewish English reader, and one of the boarders left me a grand book. When I only begin to read, I forget I'm on this world. It lifts me on wings with high thoughts." Her whole face and figure lit up with animation as she poured herself out to him.

"So even in the midst of these sordid surroundings were 'wings' and 'high thoughts,' " he mused. Again the gleam of the visionary— the eternal desire to reach out and up, which was the predominant racial trait of the Russian immigrant.

"What is the name of your book?" he continued, taking advantage of this providential encounter.

"The book is 'Dreams,' by Olive Schreiner."

"H—m," he reflected. "So these are the 'wings' and 'high thoughts.' No wonder the blushes — the tremulousness. What an opportunity for a psychological test-case, and at the same time I could help her by pointing the way out of her nebulous emotionalism and place her feet firmly on earth." He made a quick, mental note of certain books that he would place in her hands and wondered how she would respond to them.

"Do you belong to a library?"

"Library? How? Where?"

Her lack of contact with Americanizing agencies appalled him.

"I'll have to introduce you to the library when I come to live here," he said.

"Ci-i! You really like it, the room?" Shenah Pessah clapped her hands in a burst of uncontrollable delight.

"I like the room very much, and I shall be

glad to take it if you can get it ready for me by next week."

Shenah Pessah looked up at the man. "Do you mean it? You really want to come and live here, in this place? The sky is falling to the earth!"

"Live here?" Most decidedly he would live here. He became suddenly enthusiastic. But it was the enthusiasm of the scientist for the specimen of his experimentation — of the sculptor for the clay that would take form under his touch.

"I'm coming here to live —" He was surprised at the eager note in his voice, the sudden leaven of joy that surged through his veins. "And I'm going to teach you to read sensible books, the kind that will help you more than your dream book."

Shenah Pessah drank in his words with a joy that struck back as fear lest this man — the visible sign of her answered prayer — would any moment be snatched up and disappear in the heavens where he belonged. With a quick leap toward him she seized his hand in both her own. "Oi, mister! Would you like to learn me English lessons too? I'll wash for you your shirts for it. If you would even only talk to me, it would be more to me than all the books in the world."

He instinctively recoiled at this outburst of demonstrativeness. His eyes narrowed and his answer was deliberate. "Yes, you ought to learn English," he said, resuming his professional tone, but the girl was too overwrought to notice the change in his manner.

"There it is," he thought to himself on his way out. "The whole gamut of the Russian Jew — the pendulum swinging from abject servility to boldest aggressiveness."

Shenah Pessah remained standing and smiling to herself after Mr. Barnes left. She did not remember a thing she had said. She only felt herself whirling in space, millions of miles beyond the earth. The god of dreams had arrived and nothing on earth could any longer hold her down.

Then she hurried back to the basement and took up the broken piece of mirror that stood on the shelf over the sink and gazed at her face trying to see herself through his eyes. "Was it only pity that made him stop to talk to me? Or can it be that he saw what's inside me?"

Her eyes looked inward as she continued to talk to herself in the mirror.

"God from the world!" she prayed. "I'm nothing and nobody now, but ach! How beautiful I would become if only the light from his eyes would fall on me!"

Covering her flushed face with her hands as if to push back the tumult of desire that surged within her, she leaned against the wall. "Who are you to want such a man?" she sobbed.

"But no one is too low to love God, the Highest One. There is no high in love and there is no low in love. Then why am I too low to love him?"

"Shenah Pessah!" called her uncle angrily. "What are you standing there like a yok, dreaming in the air? Don't you hear the tenants knocking on the pipes? They are hollering for the hot water. You let the fire go out."

At the sound of her uncle's voice all her

"high thoughts" fled. The mere reminder of the furnace with its ashes and cinders smothered her buoyant spirits and again she was weighed down by the strangling yoke of her hateful, daily round.

It was evening when she got through with her work. To her surprise she did not feel any of the old weariness. It was as if her feet danced under her. Then from the open doorway of their kitchen she overheard Mrs. Melker, the matchmaker, talking to her uncle.

"Motkeh, the fish-peddler, is looking for a wife to cook him his eating and take care on his children," she was saying in her shrill, grating voice. "So I thought to myself this is a golden chance for Shenah Pessah to grab. You know a girl in her years and without money, a single man would n't give a look on her."

Shenah Pessah shuddered. She wanted to run away from the branding torture of their low talk, but an unreasoning curiosity drew her to listen.

"Living is so high," went on Mrs. Melker, "that single men don't want to marry themselves even to *young* girls, except if they can get themselves into a family with money to start them up in business. It is Shenah Pessah's luck yet that Motkeh likes good eating and he can't stand it any more the meals in a restaurant. He heard from people what a good cook and housekeeper Shenah Pessah is, so he sent me around to tell you he would take her as she stands without a cent."

Mrs. Melker dramatically beat her breast. "I swear I should n't live to go away from here alive, I should n't live to see my own children married if I'm talking this match for the few dollars that Motkeh will pay me for it, but because I want to do something good for a poor orphan. I'm a mother, and it weeps in me my heart to see a girl in her years and not married."

"And who'll cook for me my eating, if I'll let her go?" broke out her uncle angrily. "And who'll do me my work? Did n't I spend out fifty dollars to send for her the ticket to America? Ought n't I have a little use from her for so many dollars I laid out on her?"

"Think on God!" remonstrated Mrs. Melker.

"The girl is an orphan and time is pushing itself on her. Do you want her to sit till her braids grow gray, before you'll let her get herself a man? It stands in the Talmud that a man should take the last bite away from his mouth to help an orphan get married. You'd beg yourself out a place in heaven in the next world —"

"In America a person can't live on hopes for the next world. In America everybody got to look out for himself. I'd have to give up the janitor's work to let her go, and then where would I be?"

"You lived already your life. Give her also a chance to lift up her head in the world. Could n't you get yourself in an old man's home?"

"These times you got to have money even in an old man's home. You know how they say, if you oil the wheels you can ride. With dry hands you can't get nothing in America."

"So you got no pity on an orphan and your own relation? All her young years she choked herself in darkness and now comes already a little light for her, a man that can make a good living wants her —"

"And who'll have pity on me if I'll let her out from my hands? Who is this Motkeh, anyway? Is he good off? Would I also have a place where to lay my old head? Where stands he out with his pushcart?"

"On Essex Street near Delancey."

"Oi-i! You mean Motkeh Pelz? Why, I know him yet from years ago. They say his wife died him from hunger. She had to chew the earth before she could beg herself out a cent from him. By me Shenah Pessah has at least enough to eat and shoes on her feet. I ask you only is it worth already to grab a man if you got to die from hunger for it?"

Shenah Pessah could listen no longer.

"Don't you worry yourself for me," she commanded, charging into the room. "Don't take pity on my years. I'm living in America, not in Russia. I'm not hanging on anybody's neck to support me. In America, if a girl earns her living, she can be fifty years old and without a man, and nobody pities her."

Seizing her shawl, she ran out into the street. She did not know where her feet carried her.

She had only one desire — to get away. A fierce rebellion against everything and everybody raged within her and goaded her on until she felt herself choked with hate.

All at once she visioned a face and heard a voice. The blacker, the more stifling the ugliness of her prison, the more luminous became the light of the miraculous stranger who had stopped for a moment to talk to her. It was as though inside a pit of darkness the heavens opened and hidden hopes began to sing.

Her uncle was asleep when she returned. In the dim gaslight she looked at his yellow, care-crushed face with new compassion in her heart. "Poor old man!" she thought, as she turned to her room. "Nothing beautiful never happened to him. What did he have in life outside the worry for bread and rent? Who knows, maybe if such a god of men would have shined on him —" She fell asleep and she awoke with visions opening upon visions of new, gleaming worlds of joy and hope. She leaped out of bed singing a song she had not heard since she was a little child in her mother's home.

Several times during the day, she found herself at the broken mirror, arranging and rearranging her dark mass of unkempt hair with fumbling fingers. She was all a-tremble with breathless excitement to imitate the fluffy style of the much-courted landlady's daughter.

For the first time she realized how shabby and impossible her clothes were. "Oi weh!" she wrung her hands. "I'd give away everything in the world only to have something pretty to wear for him. My whole life hangs on how I'll look in his eyes. I got to have a hat and a new dress. I can't no more wear my 'greenhorn' shawl going out with an American.

"But from where can I get the money for new clothes? Oi weh! How bitter it is not to have the dollar! Woe is me! No mother, no friend, nobody to help me lift myself out of my greenhorn rags."

"Why not pawn the feather bed your mother left you?" She jumped at the thought.

"What? Have you no heart? No feelings? Pawn the only one thing left from your dead mother?

'Why not? Nothing is too dear for him. If your mother could stand up from her grave, she'd cut herself in pieces, she'd tear the sun and stars out from the sky to make you beautiful for him."

Late one evening Zaretsky sat in his pawnshop, absorbed in counting the money of his day's sales, when Shenah Pessah, with a shawl over her head and a huge bundle over her shoulder, edged her way hesitantly into the store. Laying her sacrifice down on the counter, she stood dumbly and nervously fingered the fringes of her shawl.

The pawnbroker lifted his miserly face from the cash-box and shot a quick glance at the girl's trembling figure.

"Nu?" said Zaretsky, in his cracked voice, cutting the twine from the bundle and unfolding a feather bed. His appraising hand felt that it was of the finest down. "How much ask you for it?"

The fiendish gleam of his shrewd eyes paralyzed her with terror. A lump came in her throat and she wavered speechless.

"I'll give you five dollars," said Zaretsky.

"Five dollars?" gasped Shenah Pessah. Her hands rushed back anxiously to the feather bed and her fingers clung to it as if it were a living thing. She gazed panic-stricken at the gloomy interior of the pawnshop with its tawdry jewels in the cases; the stacks of second-hand clothing hanging overhead, back to the grisly face of the pawnbroker. The weird tickings that came from the cheap clocks on the shelves behind Zaretsky, seemed to her like the smothered heart-beats of people who like herself had been driven to barter their last precious belongings for a few dollars.

"Is it for yourself that you come?" he asked, strangely stirred by the mute anguish in the girl's eyes. This morgue of dead belongings had taken its toll of many a pitiful victim of want. But never before had Zaretsky been so affected. People bargained and rebelled and struggled with him on his own plane. But the dumb helplessness of this girl and her coming to him at such a late hour touched the man's heart.

"Is it for yourself?" he repeated, in a softened tone.

The new note of feeling in his voice made her look up. The hard, crafty expression on his face had given place to a look of sympathy.

"Yes, it's mine, from my mother," she stammered, brokenly. "The last memory from Russia. How many winters it took my mother to pick together the feathers. She began it when I was yet a little baby in the cradle — and —" She covered her face with her shawl and sobbed.

"Any one sick? Why do you got to pawn it?"

She raised her tear-stained face and mutely looked at him. How could she explain and how could he possibly understand her sudden savage desire for clothes?

Zaretsky, feeling that he had been clumsy and tactless, hastened to add, "Nu — I'll give you — a — a — a — ten dollars," he finished with a motion of his hand, as if driving from him the onrush of generosity that seized him.

"Oi, mister!" cried Shenah Pessah, as the man handed her the bill. "You're saving me my life! God will pay you for this goodness." And crumpling the money in her hand, she hurried back home elated.

The following evening, as soon as her work was over, Shenah Pessah scurried through the ghetto streets, seeking in the myriad-colored shop windows the one hat and the one dress that would voice the desire of her innermost self. At last she espied a shining straw with cherries so red, so luscious, that they cried out to her, "Bite me!" That was the hat she bought.

The magic of those cherries on her hat brought back to her the green fields and orchards of her native Russia. Yes, a green dress was what she craved. And she picked out the greenest, crispest organdie.

That night, as she put on her beloved colors, she vainly tried to see herself from head to foot, but the broken bit of a mirror that she owned could only show her glorious parts of her. Her clothes seemed to enfold her in flames of desire leaping upon desire. "Only to be beautiful! Only to be beautiful!" she murmured breathlessly. "Not for myself, but only for him."

Time stood still for Shenah Pessah as she counted the days, the hours, and the minutes for the arrival of John Barnes. At last, through her basement window, she saw him walk up the front steps. She longed to go over to him and fling herself at his feet and cry out to him with what hunger of heart she awaited his coming. But the very intensity of her longing left her faint and dumb.

He passed to his room. Later, she saw him walk out without even stopping to look at her. The next day and the day after, she watched him from her hidden corner pass in and out of the house, but still he did not come to her.

Oh, how sweet it was to suffer the very hurt of his oblivion of her! She gloried in his great height that made him so utterly unaware of her existence. It was enough for her worshiping eyes just to glimpse him from afar. What was she to him? Could she expect him to greet the stairs on which he stepped? Or take notice of the door that swung open for him? After all, she was nothing but part of the house. So why should he take notice of her? She was the steps on which he walked. She was the door that swung open for him. And he did not know it.

For four evenings in succession, ever since

John Barnes had come to live in the house, Shenah Pessah arrayed herself in her new things and waited. Was it not a miracle that he came the first time when she did not even dream that he was on earth? So why should n't the miracle happen again? This evening, however, she was so spent with the hopelessness of her longing that she had no energy left to put on her adornments.

All at once she was startled out of her apathy by a quick tap on her window-pane. "How about going to the library, to-morrow evening?" asked John Barnes.

"Oi-i-i! Yes! Thanks—" she stammered in confusion.

"Well, to-morrow night, then, at seven. Thank you." He hurried out embarrassed by the grateful look that shone to him out of her eyes. The gaze haunted him and hurt him. It was the beseeching look of a homeless dog, begging to be noticed. "Poor little immigrant," he thought, "how lonely she must be!"

"So he did n't forget," rejoiced Shenah Pessah. "How only the sound from his voice opens the sky in my heart! How the deadness and emptiness in me flames up into life! Ach! The sun is again beginning to shine!"

An hour before the appointed time, Shenah Pessah dressed herself in all her finery for John Barnes. She swung open the door and stood in readiness watching the little clock on the mantel-shelf. The ticking thing seemed to throb with the unutterable hopes compressed in her heart, all the mute years of her stifled life. Each little thud of time sang a wild song of released joy — the joy of his coming nearer.

For the tenth time Shenah Pessah went over in her mind what she would say to him when he'd come.

"It was so kind from you to take from your dear time — to —"

"No — that sounds not good. I'll begin like this — Mr. Barnes! I can't give it out in words your kindness, to stop from your high thoughts to — to —"

"No — no! Oi weh! God from the world! Why should it be so hard for me to say to him what I mean? Why should n't I be able to say to him plain out — Mr. Barnes! You are an angel from the sky! You are saving me my life to let me only give a look on you! I'm happier than a bird in the air when I think only that such goodness like you —"

The sudden ring of the bell shattered all her carefully rehearsed phrases and she met his greeting in a flutter of confusion.

"My! Have n't you blossomed out since last night!" exclaimed Mr. Barnes, startled by Shenah Pessah's sudden display of color.

"Yes," she flushed, raising to him her radiant face. "I'm through for always with old women's shawls. This is my first American dress-up."

"Splendid! So you want to be an American! The next step will be to take up some work that will bring you in touch with American people."

"Yes. You'll help me? Yes?" Her eyes sought his with an appeal of unquestioning reliance.

"Have you ever thought what kind of work you would like to take up?" he asked, when they got out into the street.

"No — I want only to get away from the basement. I'm crazy for people."

"Would you like to learn a trade in a factory?"

"Anything—anything! I'm burning to learn. Give me only an advice. What?"

"What can you do best with your hands?"

"With the hands the best? It's all the same what I do with the hands. Think you not maybe now, I could begin already something with the head? Yes?"

"We'll soon talk this over together, after you have read a book that will tell you how to find out what you are best fitted for."

When they entered the library, Shenah Pessah halted in awe. "What a stillness full from thinking! So beautiful, it comes on me like music!"

"Yes. This is quite a place," he acquiesced, seeing again the public library in a new light through her eyes. "Some of the best minds have worked to give us just this."

"How the book-ladies look so quiet like the things."

"Yes," he replied, with a tell-tale glance at her. "I too like to see a woman's face above her clothes."

The approach of the librarian cut off further comment. As Mr. Barnes filled out the application card, Shenah Pessah noted the librarian's simple attire. "What means he a woman's face above her clothes?" she wondered. And the first shadow of a doubt crossed her mind as to whether her dearly bought apparel was pleasing to his eyes. In the few brief words that passed between Mr. Barnes and the librarian, Shenah Pessah sensed that these two were of the same world and that she was different. Her first contact with him in a well-lighted room made her aware that "there were other things to the person besides the dress-up." She had noticed their well-kept hands on the desk and she became aware that her own were calloused and rough. That is why she felt her dirty finger-nails curl in awkwardly to hide themselves as she held the pen to sign her name.

When they were out in the street again, he turned to her and said, "If you don't mind, I'd prefer to walk back. The night is so fine and I've been in the stuffy office all day."

"I don't mind" — the words echoed within

her. If he only knew how above all else she wanted this walk.

"It was grand in there, but the electric lights are like so many eyes looking you over. In the street it is easier for me. The dark covers you up so good."

He laughed, refreshed by her unconscious self-revelation.

"As long as you feel in your element let's walk on to the pier."

"Like for a holiday, it feels itself in me," she bubbled, as he took her arm in crossing the street. "Now see I America for the first time!"

It was all so wonderful to Barnes that in the dirt and noise of the overcrowded ghetto, this erstwhile drudge could be transfigured into such a vibrant creature of joy. Even her clothes that had seemed so bold and garish awhile ago, were now inexplicably in keeping with the carnival spirit that he felt steal over him.

As they neared the pier, he reflected strangely upon the fact that out of the thousands of needy, immigrant girls whom he might have befriended, this eager young being at his side was ordained by some peculiar providence to come under his personal protection.

"How long did you say you have been in this country, Shenah Pessah?"

"How long?" She echoed his words as though waking from a dream. "It's two years already. But that did n't count life. From now on I live."

"And you mean to tell me that in all this time, no one has taken you by the hand and shown you the ways of our country? The pity of it!"

"I never had nothing, nor nobody. But now — it dances under me the whole earth! It feels in me grander than dreams!"

He drank in the pure joy out of her eyes. For the moment, the girl beside him was the living flame of incarnate Spring.

"He feels for me," she rejoiced, as they walked on in silence. The tenderness of his sympathy enfolded her like some blessed warmth.

When they reached the end of the pier, they paused and watched the moonlight playing on the water. In the shelter of a truck they felt benignly screened from any stray glances of the loiterers near by.

How big seemed his strength as he stood silhouetted against the blue night! For the first time Shenah Pessah noticed the splendid straightness of his shoulders. The clean glowing youth of him drew her like a spell.

"Ach! Only to keep always inside my heart the kindness, the gentlemanness that shines from his face," thought Shenah Pessah, instinctively nestling closer.

"Poor little immigrant!" murmured John Barnes. "How lonely, how barren your life must have been till—" In an impulse of compassion, his arms opened and Shenah Pessah felt her soul swoon in ecstasy as he drew her toward him.

It was three days since the eventful evening on the pier and Shenah Pessah had not seen John Barnes since. He had vanished like a dream, and yet he was not a dream. He was the only thing real in the unreal emptiness of her unlived life. She closed her eyes and she saw again his face with its joy-giving smile. She heard again his voice and felt again his arms around her as he kissed her lips. Then in the midst of her sweetest visioning a gnawing emptiness seized her and the cruel ache of withheld love sucked dry all those beautiful feelings his presence inspired. Sometimes there flashed across her fevered senses the memory of his compassionate endearments: "Poor lonely little immigrant!" And she felt his sweet words smite her flesh with their cruel mockery.

She went about her work with restlessness. At each step, at each sound, she started, "Maybe it's him! Maybe!" She could not fall asleep at night, but sat up in bed writing and tearing up letters to him. The only lull to the storm that uprooted her being was in trying to tell him how every throb within her clamored for him, but the most heart-piercing cry that she could utter only stabbed her heart with the futility of words.

In the course of the week it was Shenah Pessah's duty to clean Mrs. Stein's floor. This brought her to Mr. Barnes's den in his absence. She gazed about her, calling up his presence at the sight of his belongings.

"How fine to the touch is the feel from everything his," she sighed, tenderly resting her cheek on his dressing-gown. With a timid hand she picked up a slipper that stood beside his bed and she pressed it to her heart reverently. "I wish I was this leather thing only to hold his feet!" Then she turned to his dresser and passed her hands caressingly over the ivory things on it. "Ach! You lucky brush — smoothing his hair every day!"

All at once she heard footsteps, and before she could collect her thoughts, he entered. Her whole being lit up with the joy of his coming. But one glance at him revealed to her the changed expression that darkened his face. His arms hung limply at his side — the arms she expected to stretch out to her and enfold her. As if struck in the face by his heartless rebuff, she rushed out blindly.

"Just a minute, please," he managed to detain her. "As a gentleman, I owe you an apology. That night — it was a passing moment of forgetfulness. It's not to happen again —"

Before he had finished, she had run out scorched with shame by his words.

"Good Lord!" he ejaculated, when he found

he was alone. "Who'd ever think that she would take it so? I suppose there is no use trying to explain to her."

For some time he sat on his bed, staring ruefully. Then, springing to his feet, he threw his things together in a valise. "You'd be a cad if you did not clear out of here at once," he muttered to himself. "No matter how valuable the scientific inquiry might prove to be, you can't let the girl run away with herself."

Shenah Pessah was at the window when she saw John Barnes go out with his suitcases.

"In God's name, don't leave me!" she longed to cry out. "You are the only bit of light that I ever had, and now it will be darker and emptier for my eyes than ever before!" But no voice could rise out of her parched lips. She felt a faintness stunning her senses as though some one had cut open the arteries of her wrists and all the blood rushed out of her body.

"Oi weh!" she moaned. "Then it was all nothing to him. Why did he make bitter to me the little sweetness that was dearer to me than my life? What means he a gentleman?

"Why did he make me to shame telling me he did n't mean nothing? Is it because I 'm not a lady alike to him? Is a gentleman only a make-believe man?"

With a defiant resolve she seized hold of herself and rose to her feet. "Show him what's in you. If it takes a year, or a million years, you got to show him you're a person. From now on, you got why to live. You got to work not with the strength of one body and one brain, but with the strength of a million bodies and a million brains. By day and by night, you got to push, push yourself up till you get to him and can look him in his face eye to eye."

Spent by the fervor of this new exaltation, she sat with her head in her hands in a dull stupor. Little by little the darkness cleared from her soul and a wistful serenity crept over her. She raised her face toward the solitary ray of sunlight that stole into her basement room.

"After all, he done for you more than you could do for him. You owe it to him the deepest, the highest he waked up in you. He opened the wings of your soul."

## HUNGER

SHENAH PESSAH paused in the midst of scrubbing the stairs of the tenement. "Ach!" she sighed. "How can his face still burn so in me when he is so long gone? How the deadness in me flames up with life at the thought of him!"

The dark hallway seemed flooded with white radiance. She closed her eyes that she might see more vividly the beloved features. The glowing smile that healed all ills of life and changed her from the weary drudge into the vibrant creature of joy.

It was all a miracle — his coming, this young professor from one of the big colleges. He had rented a room in the very house where she was janitress so as to be near the people he was writing about. But more wonderful than all was the way he stopped to talk to her, to question her about herself as though she were his equal. What warm friendliness had prompted him to take her out of her dark basement to the library where there were books to read!

And then — that unforgettable night on the way home, when the air was poignant with spring! Only a moment — a kiss — a pressure of hands! And the world shone with light — the empty, unlived years filled with love!

She was lost in dreams of her one hour of romance when a woman elbowed her way through the dim passage, leaving behind her the smell of herring and onions.

Shenah Pessah gripped the scrubbing-brush with suppressed fury. "Meshugeneh! Did you not swear to yourself that you would tear his memory out from your heart? If he would have been only a man I could have forgotten him. But he was not a man! He was God Himself! On whatever I look shines his face!"

The white radiance again suffused her. The brush dropped from her hand. "He — he is the beating in my heart! He is the life in me — the hope in me — the breath of prayer in me! If not for him in me, then what am I? Deadness — emptiness — nothingness! You are going out of your head. You are living only on rainbows. He is no more real —

"What is real? These rags I wear? This pail? This black hole? Or him and the dreams of him?" She flung her challenge to the murky darkness.

"Shenah Pessah! A black year on you!" came the answer from the cellar below. It was the voice of her uncle, Moisheh Rifkin.

"Oi weh!" she shrugged young shoulders, wearied by joyless toil. "He's beginning with his hollering already." And she hurried down.

"You piece of earth! Worms should eat you! How long does it take you to wash up the stairs?" he stormed. "Yesterday, the eating was burned to coal; and to-day you forget the salt."

"What a fuss over a little less salt!"

"In the Talmud it stands a man has a right to divorce his wife for only forgetting him the salt in his soup."

"Maybe that's why Aunt Gittel went to the grave before her time — worrying how to please your taste in the mouth."

The old man's yellow, shriveled face stared up at her out of the gloom. "What has he from life? Only his pleasure in eating and going to the synagogue. How long will he live yet?" And moved by a surge of pity, "Why can't I be a little kind to him?"

"Did you chop me some herring and onions?" he interrupted harshly.

She flushed with conscious guilt. Again she wondered why ugly things and ugly smells so sickened her.

"What don't you forget?" His voice hammered upon her ears. "No care lays in your head. You're only dreaming in the air."

Her compassion was swept away in a wave of revolt that left her trembling. "I can't no more stand it from you! Get yourself somebody else!" She was surprised at her sudden spirit.

"You big mouth, you! That's your thanks for saving you from hunger."

"Two years already I'm working the nails off my fingers and you did n't give me a cent."

"Beggerin! Money yet, you want? The minute you get enough to eat you turn up your head with freshness. Are you used to anything from home? What were you out there in Savel? The dirt under people's feet. You're already forgetting how you came off from the ship — a bundle of rags full of holes. If you lived in Russia a hundred years would you have lived to wear a pair of new shoes on your feet?"

"Other girls come naked and with nothing to America and they work themselves up. Everybody gets wages in America —"

"Americanerin! Did n't I spend out enough money on your ship-ticket to have a little use from you? A thunder should strike you!"

Shenah Pessah's eyes flamed. Her broken finger-nails pierced the callous flesh of her hands. So this was the end — the awakening of her dreams of America! Her memory went back to the time her ship-ticket came. In her simple faith she had really believed that they wanted her — her father's brother and his wife who had come to the new world before ever she was born. She thought they wanted to give her a chance for happiness, for life and love. And then she came — to find the paralytic aunt — housework — janitor's drudgery. Even after her aunt's death, she had gone on uncomplainingly, till her uncle's nagging had worn down her last shred of self-control.

"It's the last time you'll holler on me!" she cried. "You'll never see my face again if I got to go begging in the street." Seizing her shawl, she rushed out. "Woe is me! Bitter is me! For what is my life? Why did n't the ship go under and drown me before I came to America?"

Through the streets, like a maddened thing, she raced, not knowing where she was going, not caring. "For what should I keep on suffering? Who needs me? Who wants me? I got nobody — nobody!"

And then the vision of the face she worshiped flashed before her. His beautiful kindness that had once warmed her into new life breathed over her again. "Why did he ever come but to lift me out of my darkness into his light?"

Instinctively her eyes sought the rift of blue above the tenement roofs and were caught by a boldly printed placard: "HANDS WANTED." It was as though the sign swung open on its hinges like a door and arms stretched out inviting her to enter. From the sign she looked to her own hands — vigorous, young hands — made strong through toil.

Hope leaped within her. "Maybe I got yet luck to have it good in this world. Ach! God from the sky! I'm so burning to live — to work myself up for a somebody! And why not?" With clenched fist she smote her bosom. "Ain't everything possible in the new world? Why is America but to give me the chance to lift up my head with everybody alike?"

Her feet scarcely touched the steps as she ran up. But when she reached the huge, iron door of Cohen Brothers, a terror seized her. "Oi weh! They'll give a look on my greenhorn rags, and down I go — For what are you afraid, you fool?" she commanded herself. "You come not to beg. They need hands. Don't the sign say so? And you got good, strong hands that can turn over the earth with their strength. America is before you. You'll begin to earn money. You'll dress yourself up like a person and men will fall on their knees to make love to you — even him — himself!"

All fear had left her. She flung open the door

and beheld the wonder of a factory — people — people — seas of bent heads and busy hands of people — the whirr of machinery — flying belts— the clicking clatter of whirling wheels — all seemed to blend and fuse into one surging song of hope — of new life — a new world — America!

A man, his arms heaped with a bundle of shirts, paused at sight of the radiant face. Her ruddy cheeks, the film of innocence shining out of eyes that knew no guile, carried him back to the green fields and open plains of his native Russia.

"Her mother's milk is still fresh on her lips," he murmured, as his gaze enveloped her.

The bundle slipped and fell to her feet. Their eyes met in spontaneous recognition of common race. With an embarrassed laugh they stooped to gather up the shirts.

"I seen downstairs hands wanted," came in a faltering voice.

"Then you're looking for work?" he questioned with keen interest. She was so different from the others he had known in his five years in this country. He was seized with curiosity to know more.

"You ain't been long in America?" His tone was an unconscious caress.

"Two years already," she confessed. "But I ain't so green like I look," she added quickly, overcome by the old anxiety.

"Trust yourself on me," Sam Arkin assured her. "I'm a feller that knows himself on a person first off. I'll take you to the office myself. Wait only till I put away these things."

Grinning with eagerness, he returned and together they sought the foreman.

"Good luck to you! I hope you'll be pushed up soon to my floor," Sam Arkin encouraged, as he hurried back to his machine.

Because of the rush of work and the scarcity of help, Shenah Pessah was hired without delay. Atremble with excitement, she tiptoed after the foreman as he led the way into the workroom.

"Here, Sadie Kranz, is another learner for you." He addressed a big-bosomed girl, the most skillful worker in the place.

"Another greenhorn with a wooden head!"

she whispered to her neighbor as Shenah Pessah removed her shawl. "Gevalt! All these greenhorn hands tear the bread from our mouths by begging to work so cheap."

But the dumb appeal of the immigrant stirred vague memories in Sadie Kranz. As she watched her run her first seam, she marveled at her speed. "I got to give it to you, you have a quick head." There was conscious condescension in her praise.

Shenah Pessah lifted a beaming face. "How kind it was from you to learn me! You good heart!"

No one had ever before called Sadie Kranz "good heart." The words lingered pleasantly.

"Ut! I like to help anybody, so long it don't cost me nothing. I get paid by the week anyhow," she half apologized.

Shenah Pessah was so thrilled with the novelty of the work, the excitement of mastering the intricacies of her machine, that she did not realize that the day was passed until the bell rang, the machines came to a halt, and the "hands" made a wild rush for the cloak-room.

"Oi weh! Is it a fire?" Shenah Pessah blanched with dread.

Loud laughter quelled her fears. "Greenie! It's six o'clock. Time to go home," chorused the voices.

"Home?" The cry broke from her. "Where will I go? I got no home." She stood bewildered, in the fast-dwindling crowd of workers. Each jostling by her had a place to go. Of them all, she alone was friendless, shelterless!

"Help me find a place to sleep!" she implored, seizing Sadie Kranz by the sleeve of her velvet coat. "I got no people. I ran away."

Sadie Kranz narrowed her eyes at the girl. A feeling of pity crept over her at sight of the outstretched, hungry hands.

"I'll fix you by me for the while." And taking the shawl off the shelf, she tossed it to the forlorn bundle of rags. "Come along. You must be starved for some eating."

As Shenah Pessah entered the dingy hall-room which Sadie Kranz called home, its chill and squalor carried her back to the janitor's basement she had left that morning. In silence she watched her companion prepare the hot dogs and potatoes on the oil-stove atop the trunk. Such pressing sadness weighed upon her that she turned from even the smell of food.

"My heart pulls me so to go back to my uncle." She swallowed hard her crust of black bread. "He's so used to have me help him. What'll he do — alone?"

"You got to look out for yourself in this world." Sadie Kranz gesticulated with a hot potato. "With your quickness, you got a chance to make money and buy clothes. You can go to shows — dances. And who knows — maybe meet a man to get married."

"Married? You know how it burns in every girl to get herself married — that's how it burns in me to work myself up for a person."

"Ut! For what need you to work yourself up. Better marry yourself up to a rich feller and you're fixed for life."

"But him I want — he ain't just a man. He is —" She paused seeking for words and a mist of longing softened the heavy peasant features. "He is the golden hills on the sky. I'm as far from him as the earth is from the stars."

"Yok! Why wills itself in you the stars?" her companion ridiculed between swallows.

Shenah Pessah flung out her hands with Jewish fervor. "Can I help it what's in my heart? It always longs in me for the higher. Maybe he has long ago forgotten me, but only one hope drives in me like madness — to make myself alike to him."

"I'll tell you the truth," laughed Sadie Kranz, fishing in the pot for the last frankfurter. "You are a little out of your head — plain mehsugeh."

"Mehsugeh?" Shenah Pessah rose to her feet vibrant with new resolve. "Mehsugeh?" she challenged, her peasant youth afire with ambition. "I'll yet show the world what's in me. I'll not go back to my uncle — till it rings with my name in America."

She entered the factory, the next day, with a light in her face, a sureness in her step that made all pause in wonder. "Look only! How high she holds herself her head! Has the matchmaker promised her a man?"

Then came her first real triumph. Shenah Pessah was raised above old hands who had been in the shop for years and made assistant to Sam Arkin, the man who had welcomed her that first day in the factory. As she was shown to the bench beside him, she waited expectantly for a word of welcome. None came. Instead, he bent the closer to his machine and the hand that held the shirt trembled as though he were cold, though the hot color flooded his face.

Resolutely, she turned to her work. She would show him how skillful she had become in those few weeks. The seams sped under her lightning touch when a sudden clatter startled her. She jumped up terror-stricken.

"The belt! The belt slipped! But it's nothing, little bird," Sam Arkin hastened to assure her. "I'll fix it." And then the quick warning, "Sh-h! The foreman is coming!"

Accustomed to her uncle's harsh bickering, this man's gentleness overwhelmed her. There was something she longed to say that trembled on her lips, but her voice refused to come.

Sam Arkin, too, was inarticulate. He felt

he must talk to her, must know more of her. Timidly he touched her sleeve. "Lunch-time — here — wait for me," he whispered, as the foreman approached.

A shrill whistle — the switch thrown — the slowing-down of the machines, then the deafening hush proclaiming noon. Followed the scraping of chairs, raucous voices, laughter, and the rush on the line to reach the steaming cauldron. One by one, as their cups of tea were filled, the hungry workers dispersed into groups. Seated on window-sills, table-tops, machines, and bales of shirts, they munched black bread and herring and sipped tea from saucers. And over all rioted the acrid odor of garlic and onions.

Rebecca Feist, the belle of the shop, pulled up the sleeve of her Georgette waist and glanced down at her fifty-nine-cent silk stocking. "A lot it pays for a girl to kill herself to dress stylish. Give only a look on Sam Arkin, how stuck he is on that new hand."

There followed a chorus of voices. "Such freshness! We been in the shop so long and she just gives a come-in and grabs the cream as if it's coming to her."

"It's her innocent-looking baby eyes that fools him in —"

"Innocent! Pfui! These make-believe innocent girls! Leave it to them! They know how to shine themselves up to a feller!"

Bleemah Levine, a stoop-shouldered, old hand, grown gray with the grayness of unrelieved drudgery, cast a furtive look in the direction of the couple. "Ach! The little bit of luck! Not looks, not smartness, but only luck, and the world falls to your feet." Her lips tightened with envy. "It's her greenhorn, red cheeks —"

Rebecca Feist glanced at herself in the mirror of her vanity bag. It was a pretty, young face, but pale and thin from undernourishment. Adroitly applying a lip-stick, she cried indignantly: "I wish I could be such a false thing like her. But only, I'm too natural — the hypocrite!"

Sadie Kranz rose to her friend's defense. "What are you falling on her like a pack of wild dogs, just because Sam Arkin gives a smile on her? He ain't marrying her yet, is he?"

"We don't say nothing against her," retorted Rebecca Feist, tapping her diamond-buckled foot, "only, she pushes herself too much. Give her a finger and she'll grab your whole hand. Is there a limit to the pushings of such a green animal? Only a while ago, she was a learner, a nobody, and soon she'll jump over all our heads and make herself for a forelady."

Sam Arkin, seated beside Shenah Pessah on the window-sill, had forgotten that it was lunch-hour and that he was savagely hungry. "It shines so from your eyes," he beamed. "What happy thoughts lay in your head?"

"Ach! When I give myself a look around on all the people laughing and talking, it makes me so happy I'm one of them."

"Ut! These Americanerins! Their heads is only on ice-cream soda and style."

"But it makes me feel so grand to be with all these hands alike. It's as if I just got out from the choking prison into the open air of my own people."

She paused for breath — a host of memories overpowering her. "I can't give it out in words," she went on. "But just as there ain't no bottom to being poor, there ain't no bottom to being lonely. Before, everything I done was alone, by myself. My heart hurt so with hunger for people. But here, in the factory, I feel I'm with everybody together. Just the sight of people lifts me on wings in the air."

Opening her bag of lunch which had lain unheeded in her lap, she turned to him with a queer, little laugh, "I don't know why I'm so talking myself out to you —"

"Only talk more. I want to know everything about yourself." An aching tenderness rushed out of his heart to her, and in his grave simplicity he told her how he had overheard one of the girls say that she, Shenah Pessah, looked like a "greeneh yenteh," just landed from the ship, so that he cried out, "Gottuniu! If only the doves from the sky were as beautiful!"

They looked at each other solemnly — the girl's lips parted, her eyes wide and serious.

"That first day I came to the shop, the minute I gave a look on you, I felt right away, here's somebody from home. I used to tremble so to talk to a man, but you — you — I could talk myself out to you like thinking in myself."

"You're all soft silk and fine velvet," he breathed reverently. "In this hard world, how could such fineness be?"

An embarrassed silence fell between them as she knotted and unknotted her colored kerchief.

"I'll take you home? Yes?" he found voice at last.

Under lowered lashes she smiled her consent.

"I'll wait for you downstairs, closing time." And he was gone.

The noon hour was not yet over, but Shenah Pessah returned to her machine. "Shall I tell him?" she mused. "Sam Arkin understands so much, shall I tell him of this man that burns in me? If I could only give out to some one about him in my heart — it would make me a little clear in the head." She glanced at Sam Arkin furtively. "He's kind, but could he understand? I only made a fool from myself trying to tell Sadie Kranz." All at once she began to sob without reason. She ran to the cloak-room and hid from prying eyes, behind the shawls and wraps. The emptiness of all for which she struggled pressed upon her like a dead weight, dragging her down, down — the reaction of her ecstasy.

As the gong sounded, she made a desperate effort to pull herself together and returned to her work.

The six o'clock whistles still reverberated when Sam Arkin hurried down the factory stairs and out to the corner where he was to meet Shenah Pessah. He cleared his throat to greet her as she came, but all he managed was a bashful grin. She was so near, so real, and he had so much to say — if he only knew how to begin.

He cracked his knuckles and bit his finger-tips, but no words came. "Ach! You yok! Why ain't you saying something?" He wrestled with his shyness in vain. The tense silence remained unbroken till they reached her house.

"I'm sorry" — Shenah Pessah colored apologetically — "But I got no place to invite you. My room is hardly big enough for a push-in of one person."

"What say you to a bite of eating with me?" he blurted.

She thought of her scant supper upstairs and would have responded eagerly, but glancing down at her clothes, she hesitated. "Could I go dressed like this in a restaurant?"

"You look grander plain, like you are, than those twisted up with style. I'll take you to the swellest restaurant on Grand Street and be proud with you!"

She flushed with pleasure. "Nu, come on, then. It's good to have a friend that knows himself on what's in you and not what's on you, but still, when I go to a place, I like to be dressed like a person so I can feel like a person."

"You'll yet live to wear diamonds that will shine up the street when you pass!" he cried.

Through streets growing black with swarming crowds of toil-released workers they made their way. Sam Arkin's thick hand rested with a lightness new to him upon the little arm tucked under his. The haggling pushcart peddlers, the newsboys screaming, "Tageblatt, Abendblatt, Herold," the roaring noises of the elevated trains resounded the pæan of joy swelling his heart.

"America was good to me, but I never guessed how good till now." The words were out before he knew it. "Tell me only, what pulled you to this country?"

"What pulls anybody here? The hope for the better. People who got it good in the old world don't hunger for the new."

A mist filled her eyes at memory of her native village. "How I suffered in Savel. I never had enough to eat. I never had shoes on my feet. I had to go barefoot even in the freezing winter. But still I love it. I was born there. I love the houses and the straw roofs, the mud streets, the cows, the chickens and the goats. My heart always hurts me for what is no more."

The brilliant lights of Levy's Café brought her back to Grand Street.

"Here is it." He led her in and over to a corner table. "Chopped herring and onions for two," he ordered with a flourish.

"Ain't there some American eating on the card?" interposed Shenah Pessah.

He laughed indulgently. "If I lived in America for a hundred years I could n't get used to the American eating. What can make the mouth so water like the taste and the smell from herring and onions?"

"There's something in me — I can't help — that so quickly takes on to the American taste. It's as if my outside skin only was Russian; the heart in me is for everything of the new world — even the eating."

"Nu, I got nothing to complain against America. I don't like the American eating, but I like the American dollar. Look only on me!" He expanded his chest. "I came to America a ragged nothing — and — see —" He exhibited a bank-book in four figures, gesticulating grandly, "And I learned in America how to sign my name!"

"Did it come hard to learn?" she asked under her breath.

"Hard?" His face purpled with excitement. "It would be easier for me to lift up this whole house on my shoulders than to make one little dot of a letter. When I took my pencil — Oi weh! The sweat would break out on my face! 'I can't, I can't!' I cried, but something in me jumped up. 'You can — you yok — you must!' — Six months, night after night, I stuck to it — and I learned to twist around the little black hooks till it means — me — Sam Arkin."

He had the rough-hewn features of the common people, but he lifted his head with the pride of a king. "Since I can write out my name, I feel I can do anything. I can sign checks, put money in the bank, or take it out without nobody to help me."

As Shenah Pessah listened, unconsciously she compared Sam Arkin, glowing with the frank conceit of the self-made man, his neglected teeth, thick, red lips, with that of the Other One — made ever more beautiful with longings and dreams.

"But in all these black years, I was always hoping to get to the golden country," Sam Arkin's voice went on, but she heard it as from afar. "Before my eyes was always the shine of the high wages and the easy money and I kept pushing myself from one city to another, and saving and saving till I saved up enough for my ship-ticket to the new world. And then when I landed here, I fell into the hands of a cockroach boss."

"A cockroach boss?" she questioned absently and reproached herself for her inattention.

"A black year on him! He was a landsman, that's how he fooled me in. He used to come to the ship with a smiling face of welcome to all the greenhorns what had nobody to go to. And then he'd put them to work in his sweatshop and sweat them into their grave."

"Don't I know it?" she cried with quickened understanding. "Just like my uncle, Moisheh Rifkin."

"The blood-sucker!" he gasped. "When I think how I slaved for him sixteen hours a day — for what? Nothing!"

She gently stroked his hand as one might a child in pain. He looked up and smiled gratefully.

"I want to forget what's already over. I got enough money now to start for myself — maybe a tailor-shop — and soon — I — I want to marry myself — but none of those crazy chickens for me." And he seemed to draw her unto himself by the intensity of his gaze.

Growing bolder, he exclaimed: "I got a grand idea. It's Monday and the bank is open yet till nine o'clock. I'll write over my bank-book on your name? Yes?"

"My name?" She fell back, dumbstruck.

"Yes — you — everything I only got — you —" he mumbled. "I'll give you dove's milk to drink — silks and diamonds to wear — you'll hold all my money."

She was shaken by this supreme proof of his devotion.

"But I — I can't — I got to work myself up for a person. I got a head. I got ideas. I can catch on to the Americans quicker'n lightning."

"My money can buy you everything. I'll buy you teachers. I'll buy you a piano. I'll make you for a lady. Right away you can stop from work." He leaned toward her, his eyes welling with tears of earnestness.

"Take your hard-earned money? Could I be such a beggerin?"

"God from the world! You are dearer to me than the eyes from my head! I'd give the blood from under my nails for you! I want only to work for you — to live for you — to die for you —" He was spent with the surge of his emotion.

Ach! To be loved as Sam Arkin loved! She covered her eyes, but it only pressed upon her the more. Home, husband, babies, a bread-giver for life!

And the Other — a dream — a madness that burns you up alive. "You might as well want to marry yourself to the President of America as to want him. But I can't help it. *Him and him only* I want."

She looked up again. "No — no!" she cried, cruel in the self-absorption of youth and ambition. "You can't make me for a person. It's not only that I got to go up higher, but I got to push myself up by myself, by my own strength —"

"Nu, nu," he sobbed. "I'll not bother you with me — only give you my everything. My bank-book is more than my flesh and blood — only take it, to do what you want with it."

Her eyes deepened with humility. "I know your goodness — but there's something like a wall around me — him in my heart."

"Him?" The word hurled itself at him like a bomb-shell. He went white with pain. And even she, immersed in her own thoughts, lowered her head before the dumb suffering on his face. She felt she owed it to him to tell him.

"I wanted to talk myself out to you about him yet before. — He ain't just a man. He is all that I want to be and am not yet. He is the hunger of me for the life that ain't just eating and sleeping and slaving for bread."

She pushed back her chair and rose abruptly. "I can't be inside walls when I talk of him. I need the earth, the whole free sky to breathe when I think of him. Come out in the air."

They walked for a time before either spoke. Sam Arkin followed where she led through the crooked labyrinth of streets. The sight of the young mothers with their nursing infants pressed to their bared bosoms stabbed anew his hurt.

Shenah Pessah, blind to all but the vision that obsessed her, talked on. "All that my mother and father and my mother's mother and father ever wanted to be is in him. This fire in me, it's not just the hunger of a woman for a man — it's the hunger of all my people back of me, from all ages, for light, for the life higher!"

A veil of silence fell between them. She felt almost as if it were a sacrilege to have spoken of that which was so deeply centered within her.

Sam Arkin's face became lifeless as clay. Bowed like an old man, he dragged his leaden feet after him. The world was dead — cold — meaningless. Bank-book, money — of what use were they now? All his years of saving could n't win her. He was suffocated in emptiness.

On they walked till they reached a deserted spot in the park. So spent was he by his sorrow that he lost the sense of time or place or that she was near.

Leaning against a tree, he stood, dumb, motionless, unutterable bewilderment in his sunken eyes.

"I lived over the hunger for bread — but this —" He clutched at his aching bosom.

"Highest One, help me!" With his face to the ground he sank, prostrate.

"Sam Arkin!" She bent over him tenderly. "I feel the emptiness of words — but I got to get it out. All that you suffer I have suffered, and must yet go on suffering. I see no end. But only — there is a something — a hope — a help out — it lifts me on top of my hungry body — the hunger to make from myself a person that can't be crushed by nothing nor nobody — the life higher!"

Slowly, he rose to his feet, drawn from his weakness by the spell of her. "With one hand you throw me down and with the other you lift me up to life again. Say to me only again, your words," he pleaded, helplessly.

"Sam Arkin! Give yourself your own strength!" She shook him roughly. "I got no pity on you, no more than I got pity on me."

He saw her eyes fill with light as though she were seeing something far beyond them both. "This," she breathed, "is only the beginning of the hunger that will make from you a person who'll yet ring in America."

## THE LOST "BEAUTIFULNESS"

"Oi weh! How it shines the beautifulness!" exulted Hanneh Hayyeh over her newly painted kitchen. She cast a glance full of worship and adoration at the picture of her son in uniform; eyes like her own, shining with eagerness, with joy of life, looked back at her.

"Aby will not have to shame himself to come back to his old home," she rejoiced, clapping her hands—hands blistered from the paintbrush and calloused from rough toil. "Now he'll be able to invite all the grandest friends he made in the army."

The smell of the paint was suffocating, but she inhaled in it huge draughts of hidden beauty. For weeks she had dreamed of it and felt in each tin of paint she was able to buy, in each stroke of the brush, the ecstasy of loving service for the son she idolized.

Ever since she first began to wash the fine silks and linens for Mrs. Preston, years ago, it had been Hanneh Hayyeh's ambition to have a white-painted kitchen exactly like that in the old Stuyvesant Square mansion. Now her own kitchen was a dream come true.

Hanneh Hayyeh ran in to her husband, a stoop-shouldered, care-crushed man who was leaning against the bed, his swollen feet outstretched, counting the pennies that totaled his day's earnings.

"Jake Safransky!" she cried excitedly, "you got to come in and give a look on my painting before you go to sleep."

"Oi, let me alone. Give me only a rest."

Too intoxicated with the joy of achievement to take no for an answer, she dragged him into the doorway. "Nu? How do you like it? Do I know what beautiful is?"

"But how much money did you spend out on that paint?"

"It was my own money," she said, wiping the perspiration off her face with a corner of her apron. "Every penny I earned myself from the extra washing."

"But you had ought save it up for the bad

times. What'll you do when the cold weather starts in and the pushcart will not wheel itself out?"

"I save and pinch enough for myself. This I done in honor for my son. I want my Aby to lift up his head in the world. I want him to be able to invite even the President from America to his home and shame himself."

"You'd pull the bananas off a blind man's pushcart to bring to your Aby. You know nothing from holding tight to a dollar and saving a penny to a penny like poor people should."

"What do I got from living if I can't have a little beautifulness in my life? I don't allow for myself the ten cents to go to a moving picture that I'm crazy to see. I never yet treated myself to an ice-cream soda even for a holiday. Shining up the house for Aby is my only pleasure."

"Yah, but it ain't your house. It's the landlord's."

"Don't I live in it? I soak in pleasure from every inch of my kitchen. Why, I could kiss the grand white color on the walls. It lights up my eyes like sunshine in the room."

Her glance traveled from the newly painted walls to the geranium on the window-sill, and back to her husband's face.

"Jake!" she cried, shaking him, "ain't you got eyes? How can you look on the way it dances the beautifulness from every corner and not jump in the air from happiness?"

"I'm only thinking on the money you spent out on the landlord's house. Look only on me! I'm black from worry, but no care lays on your head. It only dreams itself in you how to make yourself for an American and lay in every penny you got on fixing out the house like the rich."

"I'm sick of living like a pig with my nose to the earth, all the time only pinching and scraping for bread and rent. So long my Aby is with America, I want to make myself for an American. I could tear the stars out from heaven for my Aby's wish."

Her sunken cheeks were flushed and her eyes glowed with light as she gazed about her.

"When I see myself around the house how I fixed it up with my own hands, I forget I'm only a nobody. It makes me feel I'm also a person like Mrs. Preston. It lifts me with high thoughts."

"Why did n't you marry yourself to a millionaire? You always want to make yourself like Mrs. Preston who got millions laying in the bank."

"But Mrs. Preston does make me feel that I'm alike with her," returned Hanneh Hayyeh, proudly. "Don't she talk herself out to me like I was her friend? Mrs. Preston says this war is to give everybody a chance to lift up his head like a person. It is to bring together the people on top who got everything and the people on the bottom who got nothing. She's been telling me about a new word — democracy. It got me on fire. Democracy means that everybody in America is going to be with everybody alike."

"Och! Stop your dreaming out of your head. Close up your mouth from your foolishness. Women got long hair and small brains," he finished, muttering as he went to bed.

At the busy gossiping hour of the following morning when the butcher-shop was crowded with women in dressing-sacks and wrappers covered over with shawls, Hanneh Hayyeh elbowed her way into the clamorous babel of her neighbors.

"What are you so burning? What are you so flaming?"

"She's always on fire with the wonders of her son."

"The whole world must stop still to listen to what news her son writes to her."

"She thinks her son is the only one soldier by the American army."

"My Benny is also one great wonder from smartness, but I ain't such a crazy mother like she."

The voices of her neighbors rose from every corner, but Hanneh Hayyeh, deaf to all, projected herself forward.

"What are you pushing yourself so wild? You ain't going to get your meat first. Ain't it, Mr. Sopkin, all got to wait their turn?"

Mr. Sopkin glanced up in the midst of cutting apart a quarter of meat. He wiped his knife on his greasy apron and leaned across the counter.

"Nu? Hanneh Hayyeh?" his ruddy face beamed. "Have you another letter from little Aby in France? What good news have you got to tell us?"

"No — it's not a letter," she retorted, with a gesture of impatience. "The good news is that I got done with the painting of my kitchen — and you all got to come and give a look how it shines in my house like in a palace."

Mr. Sopkin resumed cutting the meat.

"Oi weh!" clamored Hanneh Hayyeh, with feverish breathlessness. "Stop with your meat already and quick come. The store ain't going to run away from you! It will take only a minute. With one step you are upstairs in my house." She flung out her hands. "And everybody got to come along."

"Do you think I can make a living from looking on the wonders you turn over in your house?" remonstrated the butcher, with a twinkle in his eye.

"Making money ain't everything in life. My new-painted kitchen will light up your heart with joy."

Seeing that Mr. Sopkin still made no move, she began to coax and wheedle, woman-fashion. "Oi weh! Mr. Sopkin! Don't be so mean. Come only. Your customers ain't going to run away from you. If they do, they only got to come back, because you ain't a skinner. You weigh the meat honest."

How could Mr. Sopkin resist such seductive flattery?

"Hanneh Hayyeh!" he laughed. "You're crazy up in the air, but nobody can say no to anything you take into your head."

He tossed his knife down on the counter. "Everybody!" he called; "let us do her the pleasure and give a look on what she got to show us."

"Oi weh! I ain't got no time," protested one. "I left my baby alone in the house locked in."

"And I left a pot of eating on the stove boiling. It must be all burned away by this time."

"But you all got time to stand around here and chatter like a box of monkeys, for hours," admonished Mr. Sopkin. "This will only take a minute. You know Hanneh Hayyeh. We can't tear ourselves away from her till we do what wills itself in her mind."

Protesting and gesticulating, they all followed Mr. Sopkin as Hanneh Hayyeh led the way. Through the hallway of a dark, ill-smelling tenement, up two flights of crooked, rickety stairs, they filed. When Hanneh Hayyeh opened the door there were exclamations of wonder and joy: "Oi! Oi!" and "Ay! Ay! Takeh! Takeh!"

"Gold is shining from every corner!"

"Like for a holiday!"

"You don't need to light up the gas, so it shines!"

"I wish I could only have it so grand!"

"You ain't got worries on your head, so it lays in your mind to make it so fancy."

Mr. Sopkin stood with mouth open, stunned with wonder at the transformation.

Hanneh Hayyeh shook him by the sleeve exultantly. "Nu? Why ain't you saying something?"

"Grand ain't the word for it! What a whiteness! And what a cleanliness! It tears out the eyes from the head! Such a tenant the landlord ought to give out a medal or let down the rent free. I saw the rooms before and I see them now. What a difference from one house to another."

"Ain't you coming in?" Hanneh Hayyeh besought her neighbors.

"God from the world! To step with our feet on this new painted floor?"

"Shah!" said the butcher, taking off his apron and spreading it on the floor. "You can all give a step on my apron. It's dirty, anyhow."

They crowded in on the outspread apron and vied with one another in their words of praise.

"May you live to see your son married from this kitchen, and may we all be invited to the wedding!"

"May you live to eat here cake and wine on the feasts of your grandchildren!"

"May you have the luck to get rich and move from here into your own bought house!"

"Amen!" breathed Hanneh Hayyeh. "May we all forget from our worries for rent!"

Mrs. Preston followed with keen delight Hanneh Hayyeh's every movement as she lifted the wash from the basket and spread it on the bed. Hanneh Hayyeh's rough, toil-worn hands lingered lovingly, caressingly over each garment. It was as though the fabrics held something subtly animate in their texture that penetrated to her very finger-tips.

"Hanneh Hayyeh! You're an artist!" There was reverence in Mrs. Preston's low voice that pierced the other woman's inmost being. "You do my laces and batistes as no one else ever has. It's as if you breathed part of your soul into it."

The hungry-eyed, ghetto woman drank in thirstily the beauty and goodness that radiated from Mrs. Preston's person. None of the cultured elegance of her adored friend escaped Hanneh Hayyeh. Her glance traveled from the exquisite shoes to the flawless hair of the well-poised head.

"Your things got so much fineness. I'm crazy for the feel from them. I do them up so light in my hands like it was thin air I was handling."

Hanneh Hayyeh pantomimed as she spoke and Mrs. Preston, roused from her habitual reserve, put her fine, white hand affectionately over Hanneh Hayyeh's gnarled, roughened ones.

"Oi-i-i-i! Mrs. Preston! You always make me feel so grand!" said Hanneh Hayyeh, a mist of tears in her wistful eyes. "When I go away from you I could just sit down and cry. I can't give it out in words what it is. It chokes me so — how good you are to me — You ain't at all like a rich lady. You're so plain from the heart. You make the lowest nobody feel he's somebody."

"You are not a 'nobody,' Hanneh Hayyeh. You are an artist — an artist laundress."

"What mean you an artist?"

"An artist is so filled with love for the beautiful that he has to express it in some way. You express it in your washing just as a painter paints it in a picture."

"Paint?" exclaimed Hanneh Hayyeh. "If you could only give a look how I painted up my kitchen! It lights up the whole tenement house for blocks around. The grocer and the butcher and all the neighbors were jumping in the air from wonder and joy when they seen how I shined up my house."

"And all in honor of Aby's home-coming?" Mrs. Preston smiled, her thoughts for a moment on her own son, the youngest captain in his regiment whose home-coming had been delayed from week to week.

"Everything I do is done for my Aby," breathed Hanneh Hayyeh, her hands clasping her bosom as if feeling again the throb of his babyhood at her heart. "But this painting was already dreaming itself in my head for years. You remember the time the hot iron fell on my foot and you came to see me and brought me a red flower-pot wrapped around with green crêpe paper? That flower-pot opened up the sky in my kitchen." The words surged from the seething soul of her. "Right away I saw before my eyes how I could shine up my kitchen like a parlor by painting the walls and sewing up new curtains for the window. It was like seeing before me your face every time I looked on your flowers. I used to talk to it like it could hear and feel and see.

And I said to it: 'I'll show you what's in me. I'll show you that I know what beautiful is.'"

Her face was aglow with an enthusiasm that made it seem young, like a young girl's face.

"I begged myself by the landlord to paint up my kitchen, but he would n't listen to me. So I seen that if I ever hoped to fix up my house, I'd have to spend out my own money. And I began to save a penny to a penny to have for the paint. And when I seen the painters, I always stopped them to ask where and how to buy it so that it should come out the cheapest. By day and by night it burned in me the picture — my kitchen shining all white like yours, till I could n't rest till I done it."

With all her breeding, with all the restraint of her Anglo-Saxon forbears, Mrs. Preston was strangely shaken by Hanneh Hayyeh's consuming passion for beauty. She looked deep into the eyes of the Russian Jewess as if drinking in the secret of their hidden glow.

"I am eager to see that wonderful kitchen of yours," she said, as Hanneh Hayyeh bade her good-bye.

Hanneh Hayyeh walked home, her thoughts in a whirl with the glad anticipation of Mrs. Preston's promised visit. She wondered how she might share the joy of Mrs. Preston's presence with the butcher and all the neighbors. "I'll bake up a shtrudel cake," she thought to herself. "They will all want to come to get a taste of the cake and then they'll give a look on Mrs. Preston."

Thus smiling and talking to herself she went about her work. As she bent over the wash-tub rubbing the clothes, she visualized the hot, steaming shtrudel just out of the oven and the exclamations of pleasure as Mrs. Preston and the neighbors tasted it. All at once there was a knock at the door. Wiping her soapy hands on the corner of her apron, she hastened to open it.

"Oi! Mr. Landlord! Come only inside," she urged. "I got the rent for you, but I want you to give a look around how I shined up my flat."

The Prince Albert that bound the protruding stomach of Mr. Benjamin Rosenblatt was no tighter than the skin that encased the smooth-shaven face. His mouth was tight. Even the small, popping eyes held a tight gleam.

"I got no time. The minutes is money," he said, extending a claw-like hand for the rent.

"But I only want you for a half a minute." And Hanneh Hayyeh dragged the owner of her palace across the threshold. "Nu? Ain't I a good painter? And all this I done while other people were sleeping themselves, after I'd come home from my day's work."

"Very nice," condescended Mr. Benjamin Rosenblatt, with a hasty glance around the room. "You certainly done a good job. But I got to go. Here's your receipt." And the fingers that seized Hanneh Hayyeh's rent-money seemed like pincers for grasping molars.

Two weeks later Jake Safransky and his wife Hanneh Hayyeh sat eating their dinner, when the janitor came in with a note.

"From the landlord," he said, handing it to Hanneh Hayyeh, and walked out.

"The landlord?" she cried, excitedly. "What for can it be?" With trembling fingers she tore open the note. The slip dropped from her hand.

Her face grew livid, her eyes bulged with terror. "Oi weh!" she exclaimed, as she fell back against the wall.

"Gewalt!" cried her husband, seizing her limp hand, "you look like struck dead."

"Oi-i-i! The murderer! He raised me the rent five dollars a month."

"Good for you! I told you to listen to me. Maybe he thinks we got money laying in the bank when you got so many dollars to give out on paint."

She turned savagely on her husband. "What are you tearing yet my flesh? Such a money-grabber! How could I imagine for myself that so he would thank me for laying in my money to painting up his house?"

She seized her shawl, threw it over her head, and rushed to the landlord's office.

"Oi weh! Mr. Landlord! Where is your heart? How could you raise me my rent when you know my son is yet in France? And even with the extra washing I take in I don't get enough when the eating is so dear?"

"The flat is worth five dollars more," answered Mr. Rosenblatt, impatiently. "I can get another tenant any minute."

"Have pity on me! I beg you! From where I can squeeze out the five dollars more for you?"

"That don't concern me. If you can't pay, somebody else will. I got to look out for myself. In America everybody looks out for himself."

"Is it nothing by you how I painted up your house with my own blood-money?"

"You did n't do it for me. You done it for yourself," he sneered. "It's nothing to me how the house looks, so long as I get my rent in time. You wanted to have a swell house, so you painted it. That's all."

With a wave of his hand he dismissed her.

"I beg by your conscience! Think on God!" Hanneh Hayyeh wrung her hands. "Ain't your house worth more to you to have a tenant clean it out and paint it out so beautiful like I done?"

"Certainly," snarled the landlord. "Because the flat is painted new, I can get more money for it. I got no more time for you."

He turned to his stenographer and resumed the dictation of his letters.

Dazedly Hanneh Hayyeh left the office. A choking dryness contracted her throat as she staggered blindly, gesticulating and talking to herself.

"Oi weh! The sweat, the money I laid into my flat and it should all go to the devil. And I should be turned out and leave all my beautifulness. And from where will I get the money for moving? When I begin to break myself up to move, I got to pay out money for the moving man, money for putting up new lines, money for new shelves and new hooks besides money for the rent. I got to remain where I am. But from where can I get together the five dollars for the robber? Should I go to Moisheh Itzek, the pawnbroker, or should I maybe ask Mrs. Preston? No — She should n't think I got her for a friend only to help me. Oi weh! Where should I turn with my bitter heart?"

Mechanically she halted at the butcher-shop. Throwing herself on the vacant bench, she buried her face in her shawl and burst out in a loud, heart-piercing wail: "Woe is me! Bitter is me!"

"Hanneh Hayyeh! What to you happened?" cried Mr. Sopkin in alarm.

His sympathy unlocked the bottom depths of her misery.

"Oi-i-i! Black is my luck! Dark is for my eyes!"

The butcher and the neighbors pressed close in upon her.

"Gewalt! What is it? Bad news from Aby in France?"

"Oi-i-i! The murderer! The thief! His gall should burst as mine is bursting! His heart should break as mine is breaking! It remains for me nothing but to be thrown out in the gutter. The landlord raised me five dollars a month rent. And he ripped yet my wounds by telling me he raised me the rent because my painted-up flat is so much more worth."

"The dogs! The blood-sucking landlords! They are the new czars from America!"

"What are you going to do?"

"What should I do? Aby is coming from France any day, and he's got to have a home to come to. I will have to take out from my eating the meat and the milk to save together the extra five dollars. People! Give me an advice! What else can I do? If a wild wolf falls on you in the black night, will crying help you?"

With a gesture of abject despair, she fell prone upon the bench. "Gottuniu! If there is any justice and mercy on this earth, then may the landlord be tortured like he is torturing me! May the fires burn him and the waters drown him! May his flesh be torn from him in pieces and his bones be ground in the teeth of wild dogs!"

Two months later, a wasted, haggard Hanneh Hayyeh stood in the kitchen, folding Mrs. Preston's wash in her basket, when the janitor — the servant of her oppressor — handed her another note.

"From the landlord," he said in his toneless voice.

Hanneh Hayyeh paled. She could tell from his smirking sneer that it was a second notice of increased rental.

It grew black before her eyes. She was too stunned to think. Her first instinct was to run to her husband; but she needed sympathy — not nagging. And then in her darkness she saw a light — the face of her friend, Mrs. Preston. She hurried to her.

"Oi — friend! The landlord raised me my rent again," she gasped, dashing into the room like a thing hounded by wild beasts.

Mrs. Preston was shocked by Hanneh Hayyeh's distraught appearance. For the first time she noticed the ravages of worry and hunger.

"Hanneh Hayyeh! Try to calm yourself. It is really quite inexcusable the way the landlords are taking advantage of the situation. There must be a way out. We'll fix it up somehow."

"How fix it up?" Hanneh Hayyeh flared.

"We'll see that you get the rent you need." There was reassurance and confidence in Mrs. Preston's tone.

Hanneh Hayyeh's eyes flamed. Too choked for utterance, her breath ceased for a moment.

"I want no charity! You think maybe I came to beg? No — I want justice!"

She shrank in upon herself, as though to ward off the raised whip of her persecutor. "You know how I feel?" Her voice came from the terrified depths of her. "It's as if the landlord pushed me in a corner and said to me: 'I want money, or I'll squeeze from you your life!' I have no money, so he takes my life.

"Last time, when he raised me my rent, I done without meat and without milk. What more can I do without?"

The piercing cry stirred Mrs. Preston as no mere words had done.

"Sometimes I get so weak for a piece of meat, I could tear the world to pieces. Hunger and bitterness are making a wild animal out of me. I ain't no more the same Hanneh Hayyeh I used to be."

The shudder that shook Hanneh Hayyeh communicated itself to Mrs. Preston. "I know the prices are hard to bear," she stammered, appalled.

"There used to be a time when poor people could eat cheap things," the toneless voice went on. "But now there ain't no more cheap things. Potatoes — rice — fish — even dry bread is dear. Look on my shoes! And I who used to be so neat with myself. I can't no more have my torn shoes fixed up. A pair of shoes or a little patch is only for millionaires."

"Something must be done," broke in Mrs. Preston, distraught for the first time in her life. "But in the meantime, Hanneh Hayyeh, you must accept this to tide you over." She spoke with finality as she handed her a bill.

Hanneh Hayyeh thrust back the money. "Ain't I hurt enough without you having to hurt me yet with charity? You want to give me hush money to swallow down an unrightness that burns my flesh? I want justice."

The woman's words were like bullets that shot through the static security of Mrs. Preston's life. She realized with a guilty pang that while strawberries and cream were being served at her table in January, Hanneh Hayyeh had doubtless gone without a square meal in months.

"We can't change the order of things overnight," faltered Mrs. Preston, baffled and bewildered by Hanneh Hayyeh's defiance of her proffered aid.

"Change things? There's got to be a change!"

cried Hanneh Hayyeh with renewed intensity. "The world as it is is not to live in any longer. If only my Aby would get back quick. But until he comes, I'll fight till all America will have to stop and listen to me. You was always telling me that the lowest nobody got something to give to America. And that's what I got to give to America — the last breath in my body for justice. I'll wake up America from its sleep. I'll go myself to the President with my Aby's soldier picture and ask him was all this war to let loose a bunch of blood-suckers to suck the marrow out from the people?"

"Hanneh Hayyeh," said Mrs. Preston, with feeling, "these laws are far from just, but they are all we have so far. Give us time. We are young. We are still learning. We're doing our best."

Numb with suffering the woman of the ghetto looked straight into the eyes of Mrs. Preston. "And you too — you too hold by the landlord's side? — Oi — I see! Perhaps you too got property out by agents."

A sigh that had in it the resignation of utter hopelessness escaped from her. "Nothing can hurt me no more — And you always stood out to me in my dreams as the angel from love and beautifulness. You always made-believe to me that you're only for democracy."

Tears came to Mrs. Preston's eyes. But she made no move to defend herself or reply and Hanneh Hayyeh walked out in silence.

A few days later the whole block was astir with the news that Hanneh Hayyeh had gone to court to answer her dispossess summons.

From the windows, the stoop, from the hallway, and the doorway of the butcher-shop the neighbors were talking and gesticulating while waiting for Hanneh Hayyeh's return.

Hopeless and dead, Hanneh Hayyeh dragged herself to the butcher-shop. All made way for her to sit on the bench. She collapsed in a heap, not uttering a single sound, nor making a single move.

The butcher produced a bottle of brandy and, hastily filling a small glass, brought it to Hanneh Hayyeh.

"Quick, take it to your lips," he commanded. Weak from lack of food and exhausted by the ordeal of the court-room, Hanneh Hayyeh obeyed like a child.

Soon one neighbor came in with a cup of hot coffee; another brought bread and herring with onion over it.

Tense, breathless, with suppressed curiosity quivering on their lips, they waited till Hanneh Hayyeh swallowed thc coffee and ate enough to regain a little strength.

"Nu? What became in the court?"

"What said the judge?"

"Did they let you talk yourself out like you said you would?"

"Was the murderer there to say something?"

Hanneh Hayyeh wagged her head and began talking to herself in a low, toneless voice as if continuing her inward thought. "The judge said the same as Mrs. Preston said: the landlord has the right to raise our rent or put us out."

"Oi weh! If Hanneh Hayyeh with her fire in her mouth could n't get her rights, then where are we?"

"To whom should we go? Who more will talk for us now?"

"Our life lays in their hands."

"They can choke us so much as they like!"

"Nobody cares. Nobody hears our cry!"

Out of this babel of voices there flashed across Hanneh Hayyeh's deadened senses the chimera that to her was the one reality of her aspiring soul — "Oi-i-i-i! My beautiful kitchen!" she sighed as in a dream.

The butcher's face grew red with wrath. His eyes gleamed like sharp, darting steel. "I would n't give that robber the satisfaction to leave your grand painted house," he said, turning to Hanneh Hayyeh. "I 'd smash down everything for spite. You got nothing to lose. Such a murderer! I would learn him a lesson! 'An eye for an eye and a tooth for a tooth.'"

Hanneh Hayyeh, hair disheveled, clothes awry, the nails of her fingers dug in her scalp, stared with the glazed, impotent stare of a madwoman. With unseeing eyes she rose and blindly made her way to her house.

As she entered her kitchen she encountered her husband hurrying in.

"Oi weh! Oi weh!" he whined. "I was always

telling you your bad end. Everybody is already pointing their fingers on me! and all because you, a meshugeneh yideneh, a starved beggerin, talked it into your head that you got to have for yourself a white-painted kitchen alike to Mrs. Preston. Now you'll remember to listen to your husband. Now, when you'll be laying in the street to shame and to laughter for the whole world."

"Out! Out from my sight! Out from my house!" shrieked Hanneh Hayyeh. In her rage she seized a flat-iron and Jake heard her hurl it at the slammed door as he fled downstairs.

It was the last night before the eviction. Hanneh Hayyeh gazed about her kitchen with tear-glazed eyes. "Some one who got nothing but only money will come in here and get the pleasure from all this beautifulness that cost me the blood from my heart. Is this already America? What for was my Aby fighting? Was it then only a dream — all these millions people from all lands and from all times, wishing and hoping and praying that America is? Did I wake myself from my dreaming to see myself back in the black times of Russia under the czar?"

Her eager, beauty-loving face became distorted with hate. "No—the landlord ain't going to get the best from me! I'll learn him a lesson. 'An eye for an eye'—"

With savage fury, she seized the chopping-axe and began to scratch down the paint, breaking the plaster on the walls. She tore up the floorboards. She unscrewed the gas-jets, turned on the gas full force so as to blacken the white-painted ceiling. The night through she raged with the frenzy of destruction.

Utterly spent she flung herself on the lounge, but she could not close her eyes. Her nerves quivered. Her body ached, and she felt her soul ache there—inside her—like a thing killed that could not die.

The first grayness of dawn filtered through the air-shaft window of the kitchen. The room was faintly lighted, and as the rays of dawn got stronger and reached farther, one by one the things she had mutilated in the night started, as it were, into consciousness. She looked at her dish-closet, once precious, that she had scratched and defaced; the uprooted geranium-box on the window-sill; the marred walls. It was unbearable all this waste and desolation that stared at her. "Can it be I who done all this?" she asked herself. "What devil got boiling in me?"

What had she gained by her rage for vengeance? She had thought to spite the landlord, but it was her own soul she had killed. These walls that stared at her in their ruin were not just walls. They were animate — they throbbed with the pulse of her own flesh. For every inch of the broken plaster there was a scar on her heart. She had destroyed that which had taken her so many years of prayer and longing to build up. But this demolished beauty like her own soul, though killed, still quivered and ached with the unstilled pain of life. "Oi weh!" she moaned, swaying to and fro. "So much lost beautifulness —"

Private Abraham Safransky, with the look in his eyes and the swing of his shoulders of all the boys who come back from overseas, edged his way through the wet Delancey Street crowds with the skill of one born to these streets and the assurance of the United States Army. Fresh from the ship, with a twenty-four-hour leave stowed safely in his pocket, he hastened to see his people after nearly two years' separation.

On Private Safransky's left shoulder was the insignia of the Statue of Liberty. The three gold service stripes on his left arm and the two wound stripes of his right were supplemented by the Distinguished Service Medal on his left breast bestowed by the United States Government.

As he pictured his mother's joy when he would surprise her in her spotless kitchen, the soldier broke into the double-quick.

All at once he stopped; on the sidewalk before their house was a heap of household things that seemed familiar and there on the curbstone a woman huddled, cowering, broken.—Good God—his mother! His own mother—and all their worldly belongings dumped there in the rain.

## THE FREE VACATION HOUSE

How came it that I went to the free vacation house was like this:

One day the visiting teacher from the school comes to find out for why don't I get the children ready for school in time; for why are they so often late.

I let out on her my whole bitter heart. I told her my head was on wheels from worrying. When I get up in the morning, I don't know on what to turn first: should I nurse the baby, or make Sam's breakfast, or attend on the older children. I only got two hands.

"My dear woman," she says, "you are about to have a nervous breakdown. You need to get away to the country for a rest and vacation."

"Gott im Himmel!" says I. "Don't I know I need a rest? But how? On what money can I go to the country?"

"I know of a nice country place for mothers

and children that will not cost you anything. It is free."

"Free! I never heard from it."

"Some kind people have made arrangements so no one need pay," she explains.

Later, in a few days, I just finished up with Masha and Mendel and Frieda and Sonya to send them to school, and I was getting Aby ready for kindergarten, when I hear a knock on the door, and a lady comes in. She had a white starched dress like a nurse and carried a black satchel in her hand.

"I am from the Social Betterment Society," she tells me. "You want to go to the country?"

Before I could say something, she goes over to the baby and pulls out the rubber nipple from her mouth, and to me, she says, "You must not get the child used to sucking this; it is very unsanitary."

"Gott im Himmel!" I beg the lady. "Please don't begin with that child, or she'll holler my head off. She must have the nipple. I'm too nervous to hear her scream like that."

When I put the nipple back again in the baby's

mouth, the lady takes herself a seat, and then takes out a big black book from her satchel. Then she begins to question me. What is my first name? How old I am? From where come I? How long I'm already in this country? Do I keep any boarders? What is my husband's first name? How old he is? How long he is in this country? By what trade he works? How much wages he gets for a week? How much money do I spend out for rent? How old are the children, and everything about them.

"My goodness!" I cry out. "For why is it necessary all this to know? For why must I tell you all my business? What difference does it make already if I keep boarders, or I don't keep boarders? If Masha had the whooping-cough or Sonya had the measles? Or whether I spend out for my rent ten dollars or twenty? Or whether I come from Schnipishock or Kovner Gubernie?"

"We must make a record of all the applicants, and investigate each case," she tells me. "There are so many who apply to the charities, we can help only those who are most worthy."

"Charities!" I scream out. "Ain't the charities those who help the beggars out? I ain't no beggar. I'm not asking for no charity. My husband, he works."

"Miss Holcomb, the visiting teacher, said that you wanted to go to the country, and I had to make out this report before investigating your case."

"Oh! Oh!" I choke and bit my lips. "Is the free country from which Miss Holcomb told me, is it from the charities? She was telling me some kind people made arrangements for any mother what needs to go there."

"If your application is approved, you will be notified," she says to me, and out she goes.

When she is gone I think to myself, I'd better knock out from my head this idea about the country. For so long I lived, I did n't know nothing about the charities. For why should I come down among the beggars now?

Then I looked around me in the kitchen. On one side was the big wash-tub with clothes, waiting for me to wash. On the table was a pile of breakfast dishes yet. In the sink was the potatoes, waiting to be peeled. The baby was beginning to cry for the bottle. Aby was hollering and pulling me to take him to kindergarten. I felt if I did n't get away from here for a little while, I would land in a crazy house, or from the window jump down. Which was worser, to land in a crazy house, jump from the window down, or go to the country from the charities?

In about two weeks later around comes the same lady with the satchel again in my house.

"You can go to the country to-morrow," she tells me. "And you must come to the charity building to-morrow at nine o'clock sharp. Here is a card with the address. Don't lose it, because you must hand it to the lady in the office."

I look on the card, and there I see my name wrote; and by it, in big printed letters, that word "CHARITY."

"Must I go to the charity office?" I ask, feeling my heart to sink. "For why must I come there?"

"It is the rule that everybody comes to the office first, and from there they are taken to the country."

I shivered to think how I would feel, suppose

somebody from my friends should see me walking into the charity office with my children. They would n't know that it is only for the country I go there. They might think I go to beg. Have I come down so low as to be seen by the charities? But what's the use? Should I knock my head on the walls? I had to go.

When I come to the office, I already found a crowd of women and children sitting on long benches and waiting. I took myself a seat with them, and we were sitting and sitting and looking on one another, sideways and crosswise, and with lowered eyes, like guilty criminals. Each one felt like hiding herself from all the rest. Each one felt black with shame in the face.

We may have been sitting and waiting for an hour or more. But every second was seeming years to me. The children began to get restless. Mendel wanted water. The baby on my arms was falling asleep. Aby was crying for something to eat.

"For why are we sittin' here like fat cats?" says the woman next to me. "Ain't we going to the country to-day yet?"

At last a lady comes to the desk and begins calling us our names, one by one. I nearly dropped to the floor when over she begins to ask: Do you keep boarders? How much do you spend out for rent? How much wages does your man get for a week?

Did n't the nurse tell them all about us already? It was bitter enough to have to tell the nurse everything, but in my own house nobody was hearing my troubles, only the nurse. But in the office there was so many strangers all around me. For why should everybody have to know my business? At every question I wanted to holler out: "Stop! Stop! I don't want no vacations! I'll better run home with my children." At every question I felt like she was stabbing a knife into my heart. And she kept on stabbing me more and more, but I could not help it, and they were all looking at me. I could n't move from her. I had to answer everything.

When she got through with me, my face was red like fire. I was burning with hurts and wounds. I felt like everything was bleeding in me.

When all the names was already called, a man

doctor with a nurse comes in, and tells us to form a line, to be examined. I wish I could ease out my heart a little, and tell in words how that doctor looked on us, just because we were poor and had no money to pay. He only used the ends from his finger-tips to examine us with. From the way he was afraid to touch us or come near us, he made us feel like we had some catching sickness that he was trying not to get on him.

The doctor got finished with us in about five minutes, so quick he worked. Then we was told to walk after the nurse, who was leading the way for us through the street to the car. Everybody what passed us in the street turned around to look on us. I kept down my eyes and held down my head and I felt like sinking into the sidewalk. All the time I was trembling for fear somebody what knows me might yet pass and see me. For why did they make us walk through the street, after the nurse, like stupid cows? Were n't all of us smart enough to find our way without the nurse? Why should the whole world have to see that we are from the charities?

When we got into the train, I opened my eyes, and lifted up my head, and straightened out my chest, and again began to breathe. It was a beautiful, sunshiny day. I knocked open the window from the train, and the fresh-smelling country air rushed upon my face and made me feel so fine! I looked out from the window and instead of seeing the iron fire-escapes with garbage-cans and bedclothes, that I always seen when from my flat I looked — instead of seeing only walls and wash-lines between walls, I saw the blue sky, and green grass and trees and flowers.

Ah, how grand I felt, just on the sky to look! Ah, how grand I felt just to see the green grass — and the free space — and no houses!

"Get away from me, my troubles!" I said. "Leave me rest a minute. Leave me breathe and straighten out my bones. Forget the unpaid butcher's bill. Forget the rent. Forget the wash-tub and the cook-stove and the pots and pans. Forget the charities!"

"Tickets, please," calls the train conductor.

I felt knocked out from heaven all at once. I

had to point to the nurse what held our tickets, and I was feeling the conductor looking on me as if to say, "Oh, you are only from the charities."

By the time we came to the vacation house I already forgot all about my knock-down. I was again filled with the beauty of the country. I never in all my life yet seen such a swell house like that vacation house. Like the grandest palace it looked. All round the front, flowers from all colors was smelling out the sweetest perfume. Here and there was shady trees with comfortable chairs under them to sit down on.

When I only came inside, my mouth opened wide and my breathing stopped still from wonder. I never yet seen such an order and such a cleanliness. From all the corners from the room, the cleanliness was shining like a looking-glass. The floor was so white scrubbed you could eat on it. You could n't find a speck of dust on nothing, if you was looking for it with eye-glasses on.

I was beginning to feel happy and glad that I come, when, Gott im Himmel! again a lady begins to ask us out the same questions what the nurse already asked me in my home and what was asked over again in the charity office. How much wages my husband makes out for a week? How much money I spend out for rent? Do I keep boarders?

We were hungry enough to faint. So worn out was I from excitement, and from the long ride, that my knees were bending under me ready to break from tiredness. The children were pulling me to pieces, nagging me for a drink, for something to eat and such like. But still we had to stand out the whole list of questionings. When she already got through asking us out everything, she gave to each of us a tag with our name written on it. She told us to tie the tag on our hand. Then like tagged horses at a horse sale in the street, they marched us into the dining-room.

There was rows of long tables, covered with pure-white oil-cloth. A vase with bought flowers was standing on the middle from each table. Each person got a clean napkin for himself. Laid out by the side from each person's plate was a silver knife and fork and spoon and teaspoon. When we only sat ourselves down, girls with white starched aprons was passing around the eatings.

I soon forgot again all my troubles. For the first time in ten years I sat down to a meal what I did not have to cook or worry about. For the first time in ten years I sat down to the table like a somebody. Ah, how grand it feels, to have handed you over the eatings and everything you need. Just as I was beginning to like it and let myself feel good, in comes a fat lady all in white, with a teacher's look on her face. I could tell already, right away by the way she looked on us, that she was the boss from this place.

"I want to read you the rules from this house, before you leave this room," says she to us.

Then she began like this: We dassen't stand on the front grass where the flowers are. We dassen't stay on the front porch. We dassen't sit on the chairs under the shady trees. We must stay always in the back and sit on those long wooden benches there. We dassen't come in the front sitting-room or walk on the front steps what have carpet on it — we must walk on tne back iron steps. Everything on the front from the house must be kept perfect for the show for visitors. We dassen't lay down on the beds in the daytime, the beds must always be made up perfect for the show for visitors.

"Gott im Himmel!" thinks I to myself; "ain't there going to be no end to the things we dassen't do in this place?"

But still she went on. The children over two years dassen't stay around by the mothers. They must stay by the nurse in the play-room. By the meal-times, they can see their mothers. The children dassen't run around the house or tear up flowers or do anything. They dassen't holler or play rough in the play-room. They must always behave and obey the nurse.

We must always listen to the bells. Bell one was for getting up. Bell two, for getting babies' bottles. Bell three, for coming to breakfast. Bell four, for bathing the babies. If we come later, after the ring from the bell, then we'll not get what we need. If the bottle bell rings and we don't come right away for the bottle, then the baby don't get no bottle. If the breakfast bell rings, and we don't come right away down to the breakfast, then there won't be no breakfast for us.

When she got through with reading the rules, I was wondering which side of the house I was to walk on. At every step was some rule what said don't move here, and don't go there, don't stand there, and don't sit there. If I tried to remember the endless rules, it would only make me dizzy in the head. I was thinking for why, with so many rules, did n't they also have already another rule, about how much air in our lungs to breathe.

On every few days there came to the house swell ladies in automobiles. It was for them that the front from the house had to be always perfect. For them was all the beautiful smelling flowers. For them the front porch, the front sitting-room, and the easy stairs with the carpet on it.

Always when the rich ladies came the fat lady, what was the boss from the vacation house, showed off to them the front. Then she took them over to the back to look on us, where we was sitting together, on long wooden benches, like prisoners. I was always feeling cheap like dirt, and mad that I had to be there, when they smiled down on us.

"How nice for these poor creatures to have a restful place like this," I heard one lady say.

The next day I already felt like going back. The children what had to stay by the nurse in the play-room did n't like it neither.

"Mamma," says Mendel to me, "I wisht I was home and out in the street. They don't let us do nothing here. It's worser than school."

"Ain't it a play-room?" asks I. "Don't they let you play?"

"Gee wiss! play-room, they call it! The nurse hollers on us all the time. She don't let us do nothing."

The reason why I stayed out the whole two weeks is this: I think to myself, so much shame in the face I suffered to come here, let me at least make the best from it already. Let me at least save up for two weeks what I got to spend out for grocery and butcher for my back bills to pay out. And then also think I to myself, if I go back on Monday, I got to do the big washing; on Tuesday waits for me the ironing; on Wednesday, the scrubbing and cleaning, and so goes it on. How bad it is already in this place, it's a change from the very same sameness of what I'm having day in and day out at home. And so I stayed out this vacation to the bitter end.

But at last the day for going out from this prison came. On the way riding back, I kept thinking to myself: "This is such a beautiful vacation house. For why do they make it so hard for us? When a mother needs a vacation, why must they tear the insides out from her first, by making her come down to the charity office? Why drag us from the charity office through the streets? And when we live through the shame of the charities and when we come already to the vacation house, for why do they boss the life out of us with so many rules and bells? For why don't they let us lay down our heads on the bed when we are tired? For why must we always stick in the back, like dogs what have got to be chained in one spot? If they would let us walk around free, would we bite off something from the front part of the house?

"If the best part of the house what is comfortable is made up for a show for visitors, why ain't they keeping the whole business for a show for visitors? For why do they have to fool in worn-out mothers, to make them think they'll give them a rest? Do they need the worn-out mothers as part of the show? I guess that is it, already."

When I got back in my home, so happy and thankful I was I could cry from thankfulness. How good it was feeling for me to be able to move around my own house, like I pleased. I was always kicking that my rooms was small and narrow, but now my small rooms seemed to grow so big like the park. I looked out from my window on the fire-escapes, full with bedding and garbage-cans, and on the wash-lines full with the clothes. All these ugly things was grand in my eyes. Even the high brick walls all around made me feel like a bird what just jumped out from a cage. And I cried out, "Gott sei dank! Gott sei dank!"

## THE MIRACLE

LIKE all people who have nothing, I lived on dreams. With nothing but my longing for love, I burned my way through stone walls till I got to America. And what happened to me when I became an American is more than I can picture before my eyes, even in a dream.

I was a poor Melamid's daughter in Savel, Poland. In my village, a girl without a dowry was a dead one. The only kind of a man that would give a look on a girl without money was a widower with a dozen children, or some one with a hump or on crutches.

There was the village water-carrier with red, teary eyes, and warts on his cracked lip. There was the janitor of the bath-house, with a squash nose, and long, black nails with all the dirt of the world under them. Maybe one of these uglinesses might yet take pity on me and do me the favor to marry me. I shivered and grew cold through all my bones at the thought of them.

Like the hunger for bread was my hunger for love. My life was nothing to me. My heart was empty. Nothing I did was real without love. I used to spend nights crying on my pillow, praying to God: "I want love! I want love! I can't live — I can't breathe without love!"

And all day long I'd ask myself: "Why was I born? What is the use of dragging on day after day, wasting myself eating, sleeping, dressing? What is the meaning of anything without love?" And my heart was so hungry I could n't help feeling and dreaming that somehow, somewhere, there must be a lover waiting for me. But how and where could I find my lover was the one longing that burned in my heart by day and by night.

Then came the letter from Hanneh Hayyeh, Zlata's daughter, that fired me up to go to America for my lover.

"America is a lover's land," said Hanneh Hayyeh's letter. "In America millionaires fall in love with poorest girls. Matchmakers are out of style, and a girl can get herself married to a man without the worries for a dowry."

"God from the world!" began knocking my heart. "How grand to live where the kind of a man you get don't depend on how much money your father can put down! If I could only go to America! There—there waits my lover for me."

That letter made a holiday all over Savel. The butcher, the grocer, the shoemaker, everybody stopped his work and rushed to our house to hear my father read the news from the Golden Country.

"Stand out your ears to hear my great happiness," began Hanneh Hayyeh's letter. "I, Hanneh Hayyeh, will marry myself to Solomon Cohen, the boss from the shirtwaist factory, where all day I was working sewing on buttons. If you could only see how the man is melting away his heart for me! He kisses me after each step I walk. The only wish from his heart is to make me for a lady. Think only, he is buying me a piano! I should learn piano lessons as if I were from millionaires."

Fire and lightning burst through the crowd. "Hanneh Hayyeh a lady!" They nudged and winked one to the other as they looked on the loose fatness of Zlata, her mother, and saw before their eyes Hanneh Hayyeh, with her thick, red lips, and her shape so fat like a puffed-out barrel of yeast.

"In America is a law called 'ladies first,'" the letter went on. "In the cars the men must get up to give their seats to the women. The men hold the babies on their hands and carry the bundles for the women, and even help with the dishes. There are not enough women to go around in America. And the men run after the women, and not like in Poland, the women running after the men."

Gewalt! What an excitement began to burn through the whole village when they heard of Hanneh Hayyeh's luck!

The ticket agents from the ship companies seeing how Hanneh Hayyeh's letter was working like yeast in the air for America, posted up big signs by all the market fairs: "Go to America, the New World. Fifty rubles a ticket."

"Fifty rubles! Only fifty rubles! And there waits your lover!" cried my heart.

Oi weh! How I was hungering to go to America after that! By day and by night I was tearing and turning over the earth, how to get to my lover on the other side of the world.

"Nu, Zalmon?" said my mother, twisting my father around to what I wanted. "It's not so far from sense what Sara Reisel is saying. In Savel, without a dowry, she had no chance to get a man, and if we got to wait much longer she will be too old to get one anywhere."

"But from where can we get together the fifty rubles?" asked my father. "Why don't it will itself in you to give your daughter the moon?"

I could no more think on how to get the money than they. But I was so dying to go, I felt I could draw the money out from the sky.

One night I could not fall asleep. I lay in the darkness and stillness, my wild, beating heart on fire with dreams of my lover. I put out my hungry hands and prayed to my lover through the darkness: "Oh, love, love! How can I get the fifty rubles to come to you?"

In the morning I got up like one choking for

air. We were sitting down to eat breakfast, but I could n't taste nothing. I felt my head drop into my hands from weakness.

"Why don't you try to eat something?" begged my mother, going over to me.

"Eat?" I cried, jumping up like one mad. "How can I eat? How can I sleep? How can I breathe in this deadness? I want to go to America. I *must* go, and I *will* go!"

My mother began wringing her hands. "Oi weh! Mine heart! The knife is on our neck. The landlord is hollering for the unpaid rent, and it wills itself in you America?"

"Are you out of your head?" cried my father. "What are you dreaming of golden hills on the sky? How can we get together the fifty rubles for a ticket?"

I stole a look at Yosef, my younger brother. Nothing that was sensible ever laid in his head to do; but if there was anything wild, up in the air that willed itself in him, he could break through stone walls to get it. Yosef gave a look around the house. Everything was old and poor, and not a thing to get money on — nothing except father's Saifer Torah — the Holy Scrolls — and mother's silver candlesticks, her wedding present from our grandmother.

"Why not sell the Saifer Torah and the candlesticks?" said Yosef.

Nobody but my brother would have dared to breathe such a thing.

"What? A Jew sell the Saifer Torah or the Sabbath candlesticks?" My father fixed on us his burning eyes like flaming wells. His hands tightened over his heart. He could n't speak. He just looked on the Saifer Torah, and then on us with a look that burned like live coals on our naked bodies. "What?" he gasped. "Should I sell my life, my soul from generation and generation? Sell my Saifer Torah? Not if the world goes under!"

There was a stillness of thunder about to break. Everybody heard everybody's heart beating.

"Did I live to see this black day?" moaned my father, choking from quick breathing. "Mine own son, mine Kadish — mine Kadish tells me to sell the Holy Book that our forefathers shed rivers of blood to hand down to us."

"What are you taking it so terrible?" said my brother. "Does n't it stand in the Talmud that to help marry his daughter a man may sell the holiest thing — even the Holy Book?"

"*Are there miracles in America?* Can she yet get there a man at her age and without a dowry?"

"If Hanneh Hayyeh, who is older than Sara Reisel and not half as good-looking," said my brother, "could get a boss from a factory, then whom cannot Sara Reisel pick out? And with her luck all of us will be lifted over to America."

My father did not answer. I waited, but still he did not answer.

At last I burst out with all the tears choking in me for years: "Is your old Saifer Torah that hangs on the wall dearer to you than that I should marry? The Talmud tells you to sell the holiest thing to help marry your daughter, but you — you love yourself more than your own child!"

Then I turned to my mother. I hit my hands on the table and cried in a voice that made her tremble and grow frightened: "Maybe you love your silver candlesticks more than your daughter's happiness? To whom can I marry myself here, I ask you, only — to the bath janitor, to the water-carrier? I tell you I'll kill myself if you don't help me get away! I can't stand no more this deadness here. I must get away. And you must give up everything to help me get away. All I need is a chance. I can do a million times better than Hanneh Hayyeh. I got a head. I got brains. I feel I can marry myself to the greatest man in America."

My mother stopped crying, took up the candlesticks from the mantelpiece and passed her hands over them. "It's like a piece from my flesh," she said. "We grew up with this, you children and I, and my mother and my mother's mother. This and the Saifer Torah are the only things that shine up the house for the Sabbath."

She could n't go on, her words choked in her so. I am seeing yet how she looked, holding the candlesticks in her hands, and her eyes that she turned on us. But then I did n't see anything but to go to America.

She walked over to my father, who sat with his head in his hands, stoned with sadness. "Zalmon!" she sobbed. "The blood from under my nails I'll give away, only my child should have a chance to marry herself well. I'll give away my candlesticks —"

Even my brother Yosef's eyes filled with tears, so he quick jumped up and began to whistle and move around. "You don't have to sell them," he cried, trying to make it light in the air. "You can pawn them by Moisheh Itzek, the usurer, and as soon as Sara Reisel will get herself married, she'll send us the money to get them out again, and we'll yet live to take them over with us to America."

I never saw my father look so sad. He looked like a man from whom the life is bleeding away. "I'll not stand myself against your happiness," he said, in a still voice. "I only hope this will be to your luck and that you'll get married quick, so we could take out the Saifer Torah from the pawn."

In less than a week the Saifer Torah and the candlesticks were pawned and the ticket bought. The whole village was ringing with the news that I am going to America. When I walked in the street people pointed on me with their fingers as if I were no more the same Sara Reisel.

Everybody asked me different questions.

"Tell me how it feels to go to America? Can you yet sleep nights like other people?"

"When you 'll marry yourself in America, will you yet remember us?"

God from the world! That last Friday night before I went to America! Maybe it is the last time we are together was in everybody's eyes. Everything that happened seemed so different from all other times. I felt I was getting ready to tear my life out from my body.

Without the Saifer Torah the house was dark and empty. The sun, the sky, the whole heaven shined from that Holy Book on the wall, and when it was taken out it left an aching emptiness on the heart, as if something beautiful passed out of our lives.

I yet see before me my father in the Rabbi's

cap, with eyes that look far away into things; the way he sang the prayer over the wine when he passed around the glass for every one to give a sip. The tears rolled out from my little sister's eyes down her cheeks and fell into the wine. On that my mother, who was all the time wiping her tears, burst out crying. "Shah! Shah!" commanded my father, rising up from his chair and beginning to walk around the room. "It's Sabbath night, when every Jew should be happy. Is this the way you give honor to God on His one day that He set aside for you?"

On the next day, that was Sabbath, father as if held us up in his hands, and everybody behaved himself. A stranger coming in could n't see anything that was going on, except that we walked so still and each one by himself, as if somebody dying was in the air over us.

On the going-away morning, everybody was around our house waiting to take me to the station. Everybody wanted to give a help with the bundles. The moving along to the station was like a funeral. Nobody could hold in their feelings any longer. Everybody fell on my neck to kiss me, as if it was my last day on earth.

"Remember you come from Jews. Remember to pray every day," said my father, putting his hands over my head, like in blessing on the day of Atonement.

"Only try that we should be together soon again," were the last words from my mother as she wiped her eyes with the corner of her shawl.

"Only don't forget that I want to study, and send for me as quick as you marry yourself," said Yosef, smiling good-bye with tears in his eyes.

As I saw the train coming, what would n't I have given to stay back with the people in Savel forever! I wanted to cry out: "Take only away my ticket! I don't want any more America! I don't want any more my lover!"

But as soon as I got into the train, although my eyes were still looking back to the left-behind faces, and my ears were yet hearing the good-byes and the partings, the thoughts of America began stealing into my heart. I was thinking how soon I'd have my lover and be rich like

Hanneh Hayyeh. And with my luck, everybody was going to be happy in Savel. The dead people will stop dying and all the sorrows and troubles of the world will be wiped away with my happiness.

I did n't see the day. I did n't see the night. I did n't see the ocean. I did n't see the sky. I only saw my lover in America, coming nearer and nearer to me, till I could feel his eyes bending on me so near that I got frightened and began to tremble. My heart ached so with the joy of his nearness that I quick drew back and turned away, and began to talk to the people that were pushing and crowding themselves on the deck.

Nu, I got to America.

Ten hours I pushed a machine in a shirt-waist factory, when I was yet lucky to get work. And always my head was drying up with saving and pinching and worrying to send home a little from the little I earned. All that my face saw all day long was girls and machines — and nothing else. And even when I came already home from work, I could only talk to the girls in the working-girls' boarding-house, or shut myself up in my dark, lonesome bedroom. No family, no friends, nobody to get me acquainted with nobody! The only men I saw were what passed me by in the street and in cars.

"Is this 'lovers' land'?" was calling in my heart. "Where are my dreams that were so real to me in the old country?"

Often in the middle of the work I felt like stopping all the machines and crying out to the world the heaviness that pressed on my heart. Sometimes when I walked in the street I felt like goingover to the first man I met and cry out to him: "Oh, I'm so lonely! I'm so lonely!"

One day I read in the Jewish "Tageblatt" the advertisement from Zaretzky, the matchmaker. "What harm is it if I try my luck?" I said to myself. "I can't die away an old maid. Too much love burns in my heart to stand back like a stone and only see how other people are happy. I want to tear myself out from my deadness. I'm in a living grave. I've got to lift myself up. I have nobody to try for me, and maybe the matchmaker will help."

As I walked up Delancey Street to Mr. Zaretzky, the street was turning with me. I did n't see the crowds. I did n't see the pushcart peddlers with their bargains. I did n't hear the noises or anything. My eyes were on the sky, praying: "Gottuniu! Send me only the little bit of luck!"

"Nu? Nu? What need you?" asked Mr. Zaretzky when I entered.

I got red with shame in the face the way he looked at me. I turned up my head. I was too proud to tell him for what I came. Before I walked in I thought to tell him everything. But when I looked on his face and saw his hard eyes, I could n't say a word. I stood like a yok unable to move my tongue. I went to the matchmaker with my heart, and I saw before me a stone. The stone was talking to me — but — but — he was a stone!

"Are you looking for a shidduch?" he asked.

"Yes," I said, proud, but crushed.

"You know I charge five dollars for the stepping in," he bargained.

It got cold by my heart. It was n't only to give him the five dollars, nearly a whole week's wages, but his thick-skinness for being only after the money. But I could n't help myself — I was like in his fists hypnotized. And I gave him the five dollars.

I let myself go to the door, but he called me back.

"Wait, wait. Come in and sit down. I did n't question you yet."

"About what?"

"I got to know how much money you got saved before I can introduce you to anybody."

"Oh—h—h! Is it only depending on the *money?*"

"Certainly. No move in this world without money," he said, taking a pinch of snuff in his black, hairy fingers and sniffing it up in his nose.

I glanced on his thick neck and greasy, red face. "And to him people come looking for love," I said to myself, shuddering. Oh, how it burned in my heart, but still I went on, "Can't I get a man in America without money?"

He gave a look on me with his sharp eyes. Gottuniu! What a look! I thought I was sinking into the floor.

"There are plenty of *young* girls with money that are begging themselves the men to take them. So what can you expect? *Not young, not lively, and without money, too?* But, anyhow, I'll see what I can do for you."

He took out a little book from his vest-pocket and looked through the names.

"What trade do you go on your hands?" he asked, turning to me. "Sometimes a dressmaker or a hairdresser that can help make a living for a man, maybe —"

I could n't hear any more. It got black before my eyes, my voice stopped inside of me.

"If you want to listen to sense from a friend, so I have a good match for you," he said, following me to the door. "I have on my list a widower with not more than five or six children. He has a grand business, a herring-stand on Hester Street. He don't ask for no money, and he don't make an objection if the girl is in years, so long as she knows how to cook well for him."

How I got myself back to my room I don't know. But for two days and for two nights I lay still on my bed, unable to move. I looked around on my empty walls, thinking, thinking, "Where am I? Is this the world? Is this America?"

Suddenly I sprang up from bed. "What can come from pitying yourself?" I cried. "If the world kicks you down and makes nothing of you, you bounce yourself up and make something of yourself." A fire blazed up in me to rise over the world because I was downed by the world.

"Make a person of yourself," I said. "Begin to learn English. Make yourself for an American if you want to live in America. American girls don't go to matchmakers. American girls don't run after a man: if they don't get a husband they don't think the world is over; they turn their mind to something else.

"Wake up!" I said to myself. "You want love to come to you? Why don't you give it out to other people? Love the women and children, everybody in the street and the shop. Love the rag-picker and the drunkard, the bad and the ugly. All those whom the world kicks down you pick up and press to your heart with love."

As I said this I felt wells of love that choked in me all my life flowing out of me and over me. A strange, wonderful light like a lover's smile melted over me, and the sweetness of lover's arms stole around me.

The first night I went to school I felt like falling on everybody's neck and kissing them. I felt like kissing the books and the benches. It was such great happiness to learn to read and write the English words.

Because I started a few weeks after the beginning of the term, my teacher said I might stay after the class to help me catch up with my back lessons. The minute I looked on him I felt that grand feeling: "Here is a person! Here is America!" His face just shined with high thoughts. There was such a beautiful light in his eyes that it warmed my heart to steal a look on him.

At first, when it came my turn to say something in the class, I got so excited the words stuck and twisted in my mouth and I could n't give out my thoughts. But the teacher did n't see my nervousness. He only saw that I had something to say, and he helped me say it. How or what he did I don't know. I only felt his look of understanding flowing into me like draughts of air to one who is choking.

Long after I already felt free and easy to talk to him alone after the class, I looked at all the books on his desk. "Oi weh!" I said to him, "if I only knew half of what is in your books, I could n't any more sit still in the chair like you. I'd fly in the air with the joy of so much knowledge."

"Why are you so eager for learning?" he asked me.

"Because I want to make a person of myself," I answered. "Since I got to work for low wages and I can't be young any more, I'm burning to get among people where it's not against a girl if she is in years and without money."

His hand went out to me. "I'll help you," he said. "But you must first learn to get hold of yourself."

Such a beautiful kindness went out of his heart to me with his words! His voice, and the goodness that shone from his eyes, made me want to burst out crying, but I choked back my tears till I got home. And all night long I wept on my pillow: "Fool! What is the matter with you? Why are you crying?" But I said, "I can't help it. He is so beautiful!"

My teacher was so much above me that he was n't a man to me at all. He was a God. His face lighted up the shop for me, and his voice sang itself in me everywhere I went. It was like healing medicine to the flaming fever within me to listen to his voice. And then I'd repeat to myself his words and live in them as if they were religion.

Often as I sat at the machine sewing the waists I'd forget what I was doing. I'd find myself dreaming in the air. "Ach!" I asked myself, "what was that beautifulness in his eyes that made the lowest nobody feel like a somebody? What was that about him that when his smile fell on me I felt lifted up to the sky away from all the coldness and the ugliness of the world? Gottunui!" I prayed, "if I could only always hold on to the light of high thoughts that shined from him. If I could only always hear in my heart the sound of his voice I would need nothing more in life. I would be happier than a bird in the air.

"Friend," I said to him once, "if you could but teach me how to get cold in the heart and clear in the head like you are!"

He only smiled at me and looked far away. His calmness was like the sureness of money in the bank. Then he turned and looked on me, and said: "I am not so cold in the heart and clear in the head as I make-believe. I am bound. I am a prisoner of convention."

"You make-believe — you bound?" I burst out. "You who do not have foreladies or bosses — you who do not have to sell yourself for wages — you who only work for love and truth — you a prisoner?"

"True, I do not have bosses just as you do," he said. "But still I am not free. I am bound by formal education and conventional traditions. Though you work in a shop, you are really freer than I. You are not repressed as I am by the fear and shame of feeling. You could teach me more than I could teach you. You could teach me how to be natural."

"I'm not so natural like you think," I said. "I 'm afraid."

He smiled at me out of his eyes. "What are you afraid of?"

"I'm afraid of my heart," I said, trying to hold back the blood rushing to my face. "I'm burning to get calm and sensible like the born Americans. But how can I help it? My heart flies away from me like a wild bird. How can I learn to keep myself down on earth like the born Americans?"

"But I don't want you to get down on earth like the Americans. That is just the beauty and the wonder of you. We Americans are too much on earth; we need more of your power to fly. If you would only know how much you can teach us Americans. You are the promise of the centuries to come. You are the heart, the creative pulse of America to be."

I walked home on wings. My teacher said that I could help him; that I had something to give to Americans. "But how could I teach him?" I wondered; "I who had never had a chance to learn anything except what he taught me. And what had I to give to the Americans, I who am nothing but dreams and longings and hunger for love?"

When school closed down for vacation, it seemed to me all life stopped in the world. I had no more class to look forward to, no more chance of seeing my teacher. As I faced the emptiness of my long vacation, all the light went out of my eyes, and all the strength out of my arms and fingers.

For nearly a week I was like without air. There was no school. One night I came home from the shop and threw myself down on the bed. I wanted to cry, to let out the heavy weight that pressed on my heart, but I could n't cry. My tears felt like hot, burning sand in my eyes.

"Oi-i-i! I can't stand it no more, this emptiness," I groaned. "Why don't I kill myself? Why don't something happen to me? No consumption, no fever, no plague or death ever comes to save me from this terrible world. I have to go on suffering and choking inside myself till I grow mad."

I jumped up from the bed, threw open the window, and began fighting with the deaf-and-dumb air in the air-shaft.

"What is the matter with you?" I cried. "You are going out of your head. You are sinking back into the old ways from which you dragged yourself out with your studies. Studies! What did I get from all my studies? Nothing. Nothing. I am still in the same shop with the same shirt-waists. A lot my teacher cares for me once the class is over."

A fire burned up in me that he was already forgetting me. And I shot out a letter to him:

"You call yourself a teacher? A friend? How can you go off in the country and drop me out of your heart and out of your head like a read-over book you left on the shelf of your shut-down classroom? How can you enjoy your vacation in the country while I'm in the sweatshop? You learned me nothing. You only broke my heart. What good are all the books you ever gave me? They don't tell me how to be happy in a factory. They don't tell me how to keep alive in emptiness, or how to find something beautiful in the dirt and ugliness in which I got to waste away. I want life. I want people. I can't live inside my head as you do."

I sent the letter off in the madness in which I wrote it, without stopping to think; but the minute after I dropped it in the mail-box my reason came again to my head. I went back tearing my hair. "What have I done? Meshugeneh!"

Walking up the stairs I saw my door open. I went in. The sky is falling to the earth! Am I dreaming? There was my teacher sitting on my trunk! My teacher come to see me? Me, in my dingy room? For a minute it got blind before my eyes, and I did n't know where I was any more.

"I had to come," he said, the light of heaven shining on me out of his eyes. "I was so desolate without you. I tried to say something to you before I left for my vacation, but the words would n't come. Since I have been away I have written you many letters, but I did not mail them, for they were like my old self from which I want to break away."

He put his cool, strong hand into mine. "You can save me," he said. "You can free me from the bondage of age-long repressions. You can lift me out of the dead grooves of sterile intellectuality. Without you I am the dry dust of hopes unrealized. You are fire and sunshine and desire. You make life changeable and beautiful and full of daily wonder."

I could n't speak. I was so on fire with his words. Then, like whirlwinds in my brain, rushed out the burning words of the matchmaker: "Not young, not lively, and without money, too!"

"You are younger than youth," he said, kissing my hands. "Every day of your unlived youth shall be relived with love, but such a love as youth could never know."

And then how it happened I don't know; but his arms were around me. "Sara Reisel, tell me, do you love me," he said, kissing me on my hair and on my eyes and on my lips.

I could only weep and tremble with joy at his touch. "The miracle!" cried my heart; "the miracle of America come true!"

## WHERE LOVERS DREAM

FOR years I was saying to myself — Just so you will act when you meet him. Just so you will stand. So will you look on him. These words you will say to him.

I wanted to show him that what he had done to me could not down me; that his leaving me the way he left me, that his breaking my heart the way he broke it, did n't crush me; that his grand life and my pinched-in life, his having learning and my not having learning — that the difference did n't count so much like it seemed; that on the bottom I was the same like him.

But he came upon me so sudden, all my plannings for years smashed to the wall. The sight of him was like an earthquake shaking me to pieces.

I can't yet see nothing in front of me and can't get my head together to anything, so torn up I am from the shock.

It was at Yetta Solomon's wedding I met him again. She was after me for weeks I should only come.

"How can I come to such a swell hall?" I told her. "You know I ain't got nothing decent to wear."

"Like you are without no dressing-up, I want you to come. You are the kind what people look in your eyes and not on what you got on. Ain't you yourself the one what helped me with my love troubles? And now, when everything is turning out happy, you mean to tell me that you ain't going to be there?"

She gave me a grab over and kissed me in a way that I could n't say "No" to her.

So I shined myself up in the best I had and went to the wedding.

I was in the middle from giving my congratulations to Yetta and her new husband, when — Gott! Gott im Himmel! The sky is falling to the earth! I see him — him, and his wife leaning on his arm, coming over.

I gave a fall back, like somcthing sharp hit me. My head got dizzy, and my eyes got blind.

I wanted to run away from him, but, ach! everything in me rushed to him.

I was feeling like struck deaf, dumb, and blind all in one.

He must have said something to me, and I must have answered back something to him, but how? What? I only remember like in a dream my getting to the cloakroom. Such a tearing, grinding pain was dragging me down to the floor that I had to hold on to the wall not to fall.

All of a sudden I feel a pull on my arm. It was the janitor with the broom in his hand.

"Lady, are you sick? The wedding people is all gone, and I swept up already."

But I could n't wake up from myself.

"Lady, the lights is going out," he says, looking on me queer.

"I think I ain't well," I said. And I went out.

Ach, I see again the time when we was lovers! How beautiful the world was then!

"Maybe there never was such love like ours, and never will be," we was always telling one another.

When we was together there was like a light shining around us, the light from his heart on mine, and from my heart on his. People began to look happy just looking on us.

When we was walking we did n't feel we was touching the earth but flying high up through the air. We looked on the rest of the people with pity, because it was seeming to us that we was the only two persons awake, and all the rest was hurrying and pushing and slaving and crowding one on the other without the splendidness of feeling for what it was all for, like we was feeling it.

David was learning for a doctor. Daytimes he went to college, and nights he was in a drugstore. I was working in a factory on shirt-waists. We was poor. But we did n't feel poor. The waists I was sewing flyed like white birds through my fingers, because his face was shining out of everything I touched.

David was always trying to learn me how to make myself over for an American. Sometimes he would spend out fifteen cents to buy me the "Ladies' Home Journal" to read about American life, and my whole head was put away on how to look neat and be up-to-date like the American girls. Till long hours in the night I used to stay up brushing and pressing my plain blue suit with the white collar what David liked, and washing my waists, and fixing up my hat like the pattern magazines show you.

On holidays he took me out for a dinner by a restaurant, to learn me how the Americans eat, with napkins, and use up so many plates — the butter by itself, and the bread by itself, and the meat by itself, and the potatoes by itself.

Always when the six o'clock whistle blowed, he was waiting for me on the corner from the shop to take me home.

"Ut, there waits Sara's doctor feller," the girls were nudging one to the other, as we went out from the shop. "Ain't she the lucky one!"

All the way as we walked along he was learning me how to throw off my greenhorn talk, and say out the words in the American.

He used to stop me in the middle of the pavement and laugh from me, shaking me: "No t'ink or t'ank or t'ought, now. You're an American," he would say to me. And then he would fix my tongue and teeth together and make me say after him: "th-think, th-thank, th-thought; this, that, there." And if I said the words right, he kissed me in the hall when we got home. And if I said them wrong, he kissed me anyhow.

He moved next door to us, so we should n't lose the sweetness from one little minute that we could be together. There was only the thin wall between our kitchen and his room, and the first thing in the morning, we would knock in one to the other to begin the day together.

"See what I got for you, Hertzele," he said to me one day, holding up a grand printed card.

I gave a read. It was the ticket invitation for his graduation from college. I gave it a touch, with pride melting over in my heart.

"Only one week more, and you'll be a doctor for the world!"

"And then, heart of mine," he said, drawing me over to him and kissing me on the lips, "when I get my office fixed up, you will marry me?"

"Ach, such a happiness," I answered, "to be

together all the time, and wait on you and cook for you, and do everything for you, like if I was your mother!"

"Uncle Rosenberg is coming special from Boston for my graduation."

"The one what helped out your chance for college?" I asked.

"Yes, and he's going to start me up the doctor's office, he says. Like his son he looks on me, because he only got daughters in his family."

"Ach, the good heart! He'll yet have joy and good luck from us! What is he saying about me?" I ask.

"I want him to see you first, darling. You can't help going to his heart, when he'll only give a look on you."

"Think only, Mammele — David is graduating for a doctor in a week!" I gave a hurry in to my mother that night. "And his Uncle Rosenberg is coming special from Boston and says he'll start him up in his doctor's office."

"Oi weh, the uncle is going to give a come, you say? Look how the house looks! And the children in rags and no shoes on their feet!"

The whole week before the uncle came, my mother and I was busy nights buying and fixing up, and painting the chairs, and nailing together solid the table, and hanging up calendar pictures to cover up the broken plaster on the wall, and fixing the springs from the sleeping lounge so it did n't sink in, and scrubbing up everything, and even washing the windows, like before Passover.

I stopped away from the shop, on the day David was graduating. Everything in the house was like for a holiday. The children shined up like rich people's children, with their faces washed clean and their hair brushed and new shoes on their feet. I made my father put away his black shirt and dress up in an American white shirt and starched collar. I fixed out my mother in a new white waist and a blue checked apron, and I blowed myself to dress up the baby in everything new, like a doll in a window. Her round, laughing face lighted up the house, so beautiful she was.

By the time we got finished the rush to fix ourselves out, the children's cheeks was red with excitement and our eyes was bulging bright, like ready to start for a picnic.

When David came in with his uncle, my father and mother and all the children gave a stand up.

But the "Boruch Chabo" and the hot words of welcome, what was rushing from us to say, froze up on our lips by the stiff look the uncle throwed on us.

David's uncle did n't look like David. He had a thick neck and a red face and the breathing of a man what eats plenty. — But his eyes looked smart like David's.

He would n't take no seat and did n't seem to want to let go from the door.

David laughed and talked fast, and moved around nervous, trying to cover up the ice. But he did n't get no answers from nobody. And he did n't look in my eyes, and I was feeling myself ashamed, like I did something wrong which I did n't understand.

My father started up to say something to the uncle — "Our David —" But I quick pulled him by the sleeve to stop. And nobody after that could say nothing, nobody except David.

I could n't get up the heart to ask them to give a taste from the cake and the wine what we made ready special for them on the table.

The baby started crying for a cake, and I quick went over to take her up, because I wanted to hide myself with being busy with her. But only the crying and nothing else happening made my heart give a shiver, like bad luck was in the air.

And right away the uncle and him said good-bye and walked out.

When the door was shut the children gave a rush for the cakes, and then burst out in the street.

"Come, Schmuel," said my mother, "I got to say something with you." And she gave my father a pull in the other room and closed the door.

I felt they was trying not to look on me, and was shrinking away from the shame that was throwed on me.

"Och, what's the matter with me! Nothing can come between David and me. His uncle ain't everything," I said, trying to pull up my head.

I sat myself down by the table to cool down my nervousness. "Brace yourself up," I said to myself, jumping up from the chair and beginning to walk around again. "Nothing has happened. Stop off nagging yourself."

Just then I hear loud voices through the wall. I go nearer. Ut, it's his uncle!

The plaster from the wall was broken on our side by the door. "Lay your ear in this crack, and you can hear plain the words," I say to myself.

"What's getting over you? You ain't that kind to do such a thing," I say. But still I do it.

Oi weh, I hear the uncle plainly! "What's all this mean, these neighbors? Who's the pretty girl what made such eyes on you?"

"Ain't she beautiful? Do you like her?" I hear David.

"What? What's that matter to you?"

"I'll marry myself to her," says David.

"Marry! Marry yourself into that beggar house! Are you crazy?"

"A man could get to anywhere with such a beautiful girl."

"Koosh! Pretty faces is cheap like dirt. What has she got to bring you in for your future? An empty pocketbook? A starving family to hang over your neck?"

"You don't know nothing about her. You don't know what you're saying. She comes from fine people in Russia. You can see her father is a learned man."

"Ach! You make me a disgust with your calf talk! Poverty winking from every corner of the house! Hunger hollering from all their starved faces! I got too much sense to waste my love on beggars. And all the time I was planning for you an American family, people which are somebodies in this world, which could help you work up a practice! For why did I waste my good dollars on you?"

"Gott! Ain't David answering?" my heart cries out. "Why don't he throw him out of the house?"

"Perhaps I can't hear him," I think, and with my finger-nails I pick thinner the broken plaster.

I push myself back to get away and not to do it. But it did itself with my hands. "Don't let me hear nothing," I pray, and yet I strain more to hear.

The uncle was still hollering. And David was n't saying nothing for me.

"Gazlen! You want to sink your life in a family of beggars?"

"But I love her. We're so happy together. Don't that count for something? I can't live without her."

"Koosh! Love her! Do you want to plan your future with your heart or with your head? Take for your wife an ignorant shopgirl without a cent! Can two dead people start up a dance together?"

"So you mean not to help me with the office?"

"Yah-yah-yah! I'll run on all fours to do it! The impudence from such penniless nobodies wanting to pull in a young man with a future for a doctor! Nobody but such a yok like you would be such an easy mark."

"Well, I got to live my own life, and I love her."

"That's all I got to say. — Where's my hat? Throw yourself away on the pretty face, make yourself to shame and to laughter with a ragged Melamid for a father-in-law, and I wash my hands from you for the rest of your life."

A change came over David from that day. For the first time we was no more one person together. We could n't no more laugh and talk like we used to. When I tried to look him in the eyes, he gave them a turn away from me.

I used to lie awake nights turning over in my head David's looks, David's words, and it made me frightened like something black rising over me and pushing me out from David's heart. I could feel he was blaming me for something I could n't understand.

Once David asked me, "Don't you love me no more?"

I tried to tell him that there was n't no change in my love, but I could n't no more talk out to him what was in my mind, like I used.

"I did n't want to worry you before with my worries," he said to me at last.

"Worry me, David! What am I here for?"

"My uncle is acting like a stingy grouch," he answered me, "and I can't stand no more his bossing me."

"Why did n't you speak yourself out to me what was on your mind, David?" I asked him.

"You don't know how my plans is smashed to pieces," he said, with a worried look on his face. "I don't see how I'll ever be able to open my doctor's office. And how can we get married with your people hanging on for your wages?"

"Ah, David, don't you no longer feel that love can find a way out?"

He looked on me, down and up, and up and down, till I drawed myself back, frightened.

But he grabbed me back to him. "I love you. I love you, heart of mine," he said, kissing me on the neck, on my hair and my eyes. "And nothing else matters, does it, does it?" and he kissed me again and again, as if he wanted to swallow me up.

Next day I go out from the shop and down the steps to meet him, like on every day.

I give a look around.

"Gott! Where is he? He was n't never late before," gave a knock my heart.

I waited out till all the girls was gone, and the streets was getting empty, but David did n't come yet.

"Maybe an accident happened to him, and I standing round here like a dummy," and I gave a quick hurry home.

But nobody had heard nothing.

"He's coming! He *must* come!" I fighted back my fear. But by evening he had n't come yet.

I sent in my brother next door to see if he could find him.

"He moved to-day," comes in my brother to tell me.

"My God! David left me? It ain't possible!"

I walk around the house, waiting and listening. "Don't let nobody see your nervousness. Don't let yourself out. Don't break down."

It got late and everybody was gone to bed.

I could n't take my clothes off. Any minute he'll come up the steps or knock on the wall. Any minute a telegram will come.

It's twelve o'clock. It's one. Two!

Every time I hear footsteps in the empty street, I am by the window—"Maybe it's him."

It's beginning the day.

The sun is rising. Oi weh, how can the sun rise and he not here?

Mein Gott! He ain't coming!

I sit myself down on the floor by the window with my head on the sill.

Everybody is sleeping. I can't sleep. And I'm so tired.

Next day I go, like pushed on, to the shop, glad to be swallowed up by my work.

The noise of the knocking machines is like a sleeping-medicine to the cryings inside of me. All day I watched my hands push the waists up and down the machine. I was n't with my hands. It was like my breathing stopped and I was sitting inside of myself, waiting for David.

The six o'clock whistle blowed. I go out from the shop.

I can't help it — I look for him.

"Oi, Gott! Do something for me once! Send him only!"

I hold on to the iron fence of the shop, because I feel my heart bleeding away.

I can't go away. The girls all come out from the shops, and the streets get empty and still. But at the end of the block once in a while somebody crosses and goes out from sight.

I watch them. I begin counting, "One, two, three — "

Underneath my mind is saying, "Maybe it's him. Maybe the next one!"

My eyes shut themselves. I feel the end from everything.

"Ah, David! David! Gott! Mein Gott!"

I fall on the steps and clinch the stones with the twistings of my body. A terrible cry breaks out from me — "David! David!" My soul is tearing itself out from my body. It is gone.

Next day I got news — David opened a doctor's office uptown.

Nothing could hurt me no more. I did n't hope for nothing. Even if he wanted me back, I could n't go to him no more. I was like something dying what wants to be left alone in darkness.

But still something inside of me wanted to see for itself how all is dead between us, and I write him:

"David Novak: You killed me. You killed my love. Why did you leave me yet living? Why must I yet drag on the deadness from me?"

I don't know why I wrote him. I just wanted to give a look on him. I wanted to fill up my eyes with him before I turned them away forever.

I was sitting by the table in the kitchen, wanting to sew, but my hands was lying dead on the table, when the door back of me burst open.

"O God! What have I done? Your face is like ashes! You look like you are dying!" David gave a rush in.

His hair was n't combed, his face was n't shaved, his clothes was all wrinkled. My letter he was holding crushed in his hand.

"I killed you! I left you! But I did n't rest a minute since I went away! Heart of mine, forgive me!"

He gave a take my hand, and fell down kneeling by me.

"Sarale, speak to me!"

"False dog! Coward!" cried my father, breaking in on us. "Get up! Get out! Don't dare touch my child again! May your name and memory be blotted out!"

David covered up his head with his arm and fell back to the wall like my father had hit him.

"You yet listen to him?" cried my father, grabbing me by the arm and shaking me. "Did n't I tell you he's a Meshumid, a denier of God?"

"Have pity! Speak to me! Give me only a word!" David begged me.

I wanted to speak to him, to stretch out my hands to him and call him over, but I could n't move my body. No voice came from my lips no more than if I was locked in my grave.

I was dead, and the David I loved was dead.

I married Sam because he came along and wanted me, and I did n't care about nothing no more.

But for long after, even when the children

began coming, my head was still far away in the dream of the time when love was. Before my eyes was always his face, drawing me on. In my ears was always his voice, but thin, like from far away.

I was like a person following after something in the dark.

For years when I went out into the street or got into a car, it gave a knock my heart — "Maybe I'll see him yet to-day."

When I heard he got himself engaged, I hunted up where she lived, and with Sammy in the carriage and the three other children hanging on to my skirts, I stayed around for hours to look up at the grand stone house where she lived, just to take a minute's look on her.

When I seen her go by, it stabbed awake in me the old days.

It ain't that I still love him, but nothing don't seem real to me no more. For the little while when we was lovers I breathed the air from the high places where love comes from, and I can't no more come down.

## SOAP AND WATER

WHAT I so greatly feared, happened! Miss Whiteside, the dean of our college, withheld my diploma. When I came to her office, and asked her why she did not pass me, she said that she could not recommend me as a teacher because of my personal appearance.

She told me that my skin looked oily, my hair unkempt, and my finger-nails sadly neglected. She told me that I was utterly unmindful of the little niceties of the well-groomed lady. She pointed out that my collar did not set evenly, my belt was awry, and there was a lack of freshness in my dress. And she ended with: "Soap and water are cheap. Any one can be clean."

In those four years while I was under her supervision, I was always timid and diffident. I shrank and trembled when I had to come near her. When I had to say something to her, I mumbled and stuttered, and grew red and white in the face with fear.

Every time I had to come to the dean's office for a private conference, I prepared for the ordeal of her cold scrutiny, as a patient prepares for a surgical operation. I watched her gimlet eyes searching for a stray pin, for a spot on my dress, for my unpolished shoes, for my uncared-for finger-nails, as one strapped on the operating table watches the surgeon approaching with his tray of sterilized knives.

She never looked into my eyes. She never perceived that I had a soul. She did not see how I longed for beauty and cleanliness. How I strained and struggled to lift myself from the dead toil and exhaustion that weighed me down. She could see nothing in people like me, except the dirt and the stains on the outside.

But this last time when she threatened to withhold my diploma, because of my appearance, this last time when she reminded me that "Soap and water are cheap. Any one can be clean," this last time, something burst within me.

I felt the suppressed wrath of all the unwashed of the earth break loose within me. My eyes blazed fire. I did n't care for myself, nor the dean, nor the whole laundered world. I had suffered the cruelty of their cleanliness and the tyranny of their culture to the breaking point. I was too frenzied to know what I said or did. But I saw clean, immaculate, spotless Miss Whiteside shrivel and tremble and cower before me, as I had shriveled and trembled and cowered before her for so many years.

Why did she give me my diploma? Was it pity? Or can it be that in my outburst of fury, at the climax of indignities that I had suffered, the barriers broke, and she saw into the world below from where I came?

Miss Whiteside had no particular reason for hounding and persecuting me. Personally, she did n't give a hang if I was clean or dirty. She was merely one of the agents of clean society, delegated to judge who is fit and who is unfit to teach.

While they condemned me as unfit to be a teacher, because of my appearance, I was slaving to keep them clean. I was slaving in a laundry from five to eight in the morning, before going to college, and from six to eleven at night, after coming from college. Eight hours of work a day, outside my studies. Where was the time and the strength for the "little niceties of the well-groomed lady"?

At the time when they rose and took their morning bath, and put on their fresh-laundered linen that somebody had made ready for them, when they were being served with their breakfast, I had already toiled for three hours in a laundry.

When college hours were over, they went for a walk in the fresh air. They had time to rest, and bathe again, and put on fresh clothes for dinner. But I, after college hours, had only time to bolt a soggy meal, and rush back to the grind of the laundry till eleven at night.

At the hour when they came from the theater or musicale, I came from the laundry. But I was so bathed in the sweat of exhaustion that I could not think of a bath of soap and water. I had only strength to drag myself home, and fall down on the bed and sleep. Even if I had had the desire and the energy to take a bath, there were no such things as bathtubs in the house where I lived.

Often as I stood at my board at the laundry, I thought of Miss Whiteside, and her clean world, clothed in the snowy shirt-waists I had ironed. I was thinking — I, soaking in the foul vapors of the steaming laundry, I, with my dirty, tired hands, I am ironing the clean, immaculate shirt-waists of clean, immaculate society. I, the unclean one, am actually fashioning the pedestal of their cleanliness, from which they reach down, hoping to lift me to the height that I have created for them.

I look back at my sweatshop childhood. One day, when I was about sixteen, some one gave me Rosenfeld's poem, "The Machine," to read. Like a spark thrown among oily rags, it set my whole being aflame with longing for self-expression. But I was dumb. I had nothing but blind, aching feeling. For days I went about with agonies of feeling, yet utterly at sea how to fathom and voice those feelings — birth-throes of infinite worlds, and yet dumb.

Suddenly, there came upon me this inspiration. I can go to college! There I shall learn to express myself, to voice my thoughts. But I was not prepared to go to college. The girl in the cigar factory, in the next block, had gone first to a preparatory school. Why should n't I find a way, too?

Going to college seemed as impossible for me, at that time, as for an ignorant Russian shop-girl to attempt to write poetry in English. But I was sixteen then, and the impossible was a magnet to draw the dreams that had no outlet. Besides, the actual was so barren, so narrow, so strangling, that the dream of the unattainable was the only air in which the soul could survive.

The ideal of going to college was like the birth of a new religion in my soul. It put new fire in my eyes, and new strength in my tired arms and fingers.

For six years I worked daytimes and went at night to a preparatory school. For six years I went about nursing the illusion that college was a place where I should find self-expression, and vague, pent-up feelings could live as thoughts and grow as ideas.

At last I came to college. I rushed for it with the outstretched arms of youth's aching hunger to give and take of life's deepest and highest, and I came against the solid wall of the well-fed, well-dressed world — the frigid whitewashed wall of cleanliness.

Until I came to college I had been unconscious of my clothes. Suddenly I felt people looking at me at arm's length, as if I were crooked or crippled, as if I had come to a place where I did n't belong, and would never be taken in.

How I pinched, and scraped, and starved myself, to save enough to come to college! Every cent of the tuition fee I paid was drops of sweat and blood from underpaid laundry work. And what did I get for it? A crushed spirit, a broken heart, a stinging sense of poverty that I never felt before.

The courses of study I had to swallow to get my diploma were utterly barren of interest to me. I did n't come to college to get dull learning from dead books. I did n't come for that dry, inanimate stuff that can be hammered out in lectures. I came because I longed for the larger life, for the stimulus of intellectual associations. I came because my whole being clamored for more vision, more light. But everywhere I went I saw big fences put up against me, with the brutal signs: "No trespassing. Get off the grass."

I experienced at college the same feeling of years ago when I came to this country, when after months of shut-in-ness, in dark tenements and stifling sweatshops, I had come to Central Park for the first time. Like a bird just out from a cage, I stretched out my arms, and then flung myself in ecstatic abandon on the grass. Just as I began to breathe in the fresh-smelling earth, and lift up my eyes to the sky, a big, fat policeman with a club in his hand, seized me, with: "Can't you read the sign? Get off the grass!" Miss Whiteside, the dean of the college, the representative of the clean, the educated world, for all her external refinement, was to me like that big, brutal policeman, with the club in his hand, that drove me off the grass.

The death-blows to all aspiration began when

I graduated from college and tried to get a start at the work for which I had struggled so hard to fit myself. I soon found other agents of clean society, who had the power of giving or withholding the positions I sought, judging me as Miss Whiteside judged me. One glance at my shabby clothes, the desperate anguish that glazed and dulled my eyes and I felt myself condemned by them before I opened my lips to speak.

Starvation forced me to accept the lowest-paid substitute position. And because my wages were so low and so unsteady, I could never get the money for the clothes to make an appearance to secure a position with better pay. I was tricked and foiled. I was considered unfit to get decent pay for my work because of my appearance, and it was to the advantage of those who used me that my appearance should damn me, so as to get me to work for the low wages I was forced to accept. It seemed to me the whole vicious circle of society's injustices was thrust like a noose around my neck to strangle me.

The insults and injuries I had suffered at

college had so eaten into my flesh that I could not bear to get near it. I shuddered with horror whenever I had to pass the place blocks away. The hate which I felt for Miss Whiteside spread like poison inside my soul, into hate for all clean society. The whole clean world was massed against me. Whenever I met a well-dressed person, I felt the secret stab of a hidden enemy.

I was so obsessed and consumed with my grievances that I could not get away from myself and think things out in the light. I was in the grip of that blinding, destructive, terrible thing — righteous indignation. I could not rest. I wanted the whole world to know that the college was against democracy in education, that clothes form the basis of class distinctions, that after graduation the opportunities for the best positions are passed out to those who are best-dressed, and the students too poor to put up a front are pigeon-holed and marked unfit and abandoned to the mercy of the wind.

A wild desire raged in the corner of my brain. I knew that the dean gave dinners to the faculty at regular intervals. I longed to burst in at one of those feasts, in the midst of their grand speech-making, and tear down the fine clothes from these well-groomed ladies and gentlemen, and trample them under my feet, and scream like a lunatic: "Soap and water are cheap! Soap and water are cheap! Look at me! See how cheap it is!"

There seemed but three avenues of escape to the torments of my wasted life, madness, suicide, or a heart-to-heart confession to some one who understood. I had not energy enough for suicide. Besides, in my darkest moments of despair, hope clamored loudest. Oh, I longed so to live, to dream my way up on the heights, above the unreal realities that ground me and dragged me down to earth.

Inside the ruin of my thwarted life, the *unlived* visionary immigrant hungered and thirsted for America. I had come a refugee from the Russian pogroms, aflame with dreams of America. I did not find America in the sweatshops, much less in the schools and colleges. But for hundreds of years the persecuted races all over the world were nurtured on hopes of America. When a little baby in my mother's arms, before I was old enough to speak, I saw all around me weary faces light up with thrilling tales of the far-off "golden country." And so, though my faith in this so-called America was shattered, yet underneath, in the sap and roots of my soul, burned the deathless faith that America is, must be, somehow, somewhere. In the midst of my bitterest hates and rebellions, visions of America rose over me, like songs of freedom of an oppressed people.

My body was worn to the bone from overwork, my footsteps dragged with exhaustion, but my eyes still sought the sky, praying, ceaselessly praying, the dumb, inarticulate prayer of the lost immigrant: "America! Ach, America! Where is America?"

It seemed to me if I could only find some human being to whom I could unburden my heart, I would have new strength to begin again my insatiable search for America.

But to whom could I speak? The people in the laundry? They never understood me. They had a grudge against me because I left them when I tried to work myself up. Could I speak to the college people? What did these icebergs of convention know about the vital things of the heart?

And yet, I remembered, in the freshman year, in one of the courses in chemistry, there was an instructor, a woman, who drew me strangely. I felt she was the only real teacher among all the teachers and professors I met. I did n't care for the chemistry, but I liked to look at her. She gave me life, air, the unconscious emanation of her beautiful spirit. I had not spoken a word to her, outside the experiments in chemistry, but I knew her more than the people around her who were of her own class. I felt in the throb of her voice, in the subtle shading around the corner of her eyes, the color and texture of her dreams.

Often in the midst of our work in chemistry I felt like crying out to her: "Oh, please be my friend. I'm so lonely." But something choked me. I could n't speak. The very intensity of my longing for her friendship made me run away from her in confusion the minute she approached me. I was so conscious of my shabbiness that I was afraid maybe she was only trying to be kind. I could n't bear kindness. I wanted from her love, understanding, or nothing.

About ten years after I left college, as I walked the streets bowed and beaten with the shame of having to go around begging for work, I met Miss Van Ness. She not only recognized me, but stopped to ask how I was, and what I was doing.

I had begun to think that my only comrades in this world were the homeless and abandoned cats and dogs of the street, whom everybody gives another kick, as they slam the door on them. And here was one from the clean world human enough to be friendly. Here was one of the well-dressed, with a look in her eyes and a sound in her voice that was like healing oil over the bruises of my soul. The mere touch of that woman's hand in mine so overwhelmed me, that I burst out crying in the street.

The next morning I came to Miss Van Ness

at her office. In those ten years she had risen to a professorship. But I was not in the least intimidated by her high office. I felt as natural in her presence as if she were my own sister. I heard myself telling her the whole story of my life, but I felt that even if I had not said a word she would have understood all I had to say as if I had spoken. It was all so unutterable, to find one from the other side of the world who was so simply and naturally that miraculous thing — a friend. Just as contact with Miss Whiteside had tied and bound all my thinking processes, so Miss Van Ness unbound and freed me and suffused me with light.

I felt the joy of one breathing on the mountain-tops for the first time. I looked down at the world below. I was changed and the world was changed. My past was the forgotten night. Sunrise was all around me.

I went out from Miss Van Ness's office, singing a song of new life: "America! I found America."

## "THE FAT OF THE LAND"

In an air-shaft so narrow that you could touch the next wall with your bare hands, Hanneh Breineh leaned out and knocked on her neighbor's window.

"Can you loan me your wash-boiler for the clothes?" she called.

Mrs. Pelz threw up the sash.

"The boiler? What's the matter with yours again? Did n't you tell me you had it fixed already last week?"

"A black year on him, the robber, the way he fixed it! If you have no luck in this world, then it's better not to live. There I spent out fifteen cents to stop up one hole, and it runs out another. How I ate out my gall bargaining with him he should let it down to fifteen cents! He wanted yet a quarter, the swindler. Gottuniu! My bitter heart on him for every penny he took from me for nothing!"

"You got to watch all those swindlers, or

they'll steal the whites out of your eyes," admonished Mrs. Pelz. "You should have tried out your boiler before you paid him. Wait a minute till I empty out my dirty clothes in a pillow-case; then I'll hand it to you."

Mrs. Pelz returned with the boiler and tried to hand it across to Hanneh Brcineh, but the soap-box refrigerator on the window-sill was in the way.

"You got to come in for the boiler yourself," said Mrs. Pelz.

"Wait only till I tie my Sammy on to the high-chair he should n't fall on me again. He's so wild that ropes won't hold him."

Hanneh Breineh tied the child in the chair, stuck a pacifier in his mouth, and went in to her neighbor. As she took the boiler Mrs. Pelz said:

"Do you know Mrs. Melker ordered fifty pounds of chicken for her daughter's wedding? And such grand chickens! Shining like gold! My heart melted in me just looking at the flowing fatness of those chickens."

Hanneh Breineh smacked her thin, dry lips, a hungry gleam in her sunken eyes.

"Fifty pounds!" she gasped. "It ain't possible. How do you know?"

"I heard her with my own ears. I saw them with my own eyes. And she said she will chop up the chicken livers with onions and eggs for an appetizer, and then she will buy twenty-five pounds of fish, and cook it sweet and sour with raisins, and she said she will bake all her shtrudels on pure chicken fat."

"Some people work themselves up in the world," sighed Hanneh Breineh. "For them is America flowing with milk and honey. In Savel Mrs. Melker used to get shriveled up from hunger. She and her children used to live on potato-peelings and crusts of dry bread picked out from the barrels; and in America she lives to eat chicken, and apple shtrudels soaking in fat."

"The world is a wheel always turning," philosophized Mrs. Pelz. "Those who were high go down low, and those who've been low go up higher. Who will believe me here in America that in Poland I was a cook in a banker's house? I handled ducks and geese every day. I used to bake coffee-cake with cream so thick you could cut it with a knife."

"And do you think I was a nobody in Poland?" broke in Hanneh Breineh, tears welling in her eyes as the memories of her past rushed over her. "But what's the use of talking? In America money is everything. Who cares who my father or grandfather was in Poland? Without money I'm a living dead one. My head dries out worrying how to get for the children the eating a penny cheaper."

Mrs. Pelz wagged her head, a gnawing envy contracting her features.

"Mrs. Melker had it good from the day she came," she said, begrudgingly. "Right away she sent all her children to the factory, and she began to cook meat for dinner every day. She and her children have eggs and buttered rolls for breakfast each morning like millionaires."

A sudden fall and a baby's scream, and the boiler dropped from Hanneh Breineh's hands as she rushed into her kitchen, Mrs. Pelz after her. They found the high-chair turned on top of the baby.

"Gewalt! Save me! Run for a doctor!" cried Hanneh Breineh, as she dragged the child from under the high-chair. "He's killed! He's killed! My only child! My precious lamb!" she shrieked as she ran back and forth with the screaming infant.

Mrs. Pelz snatched little Sammy from the mother's hands.

"Meshugneh! What are you running around like a crazy, frightening the child? Let me see. Let me tend to him. He ain't killed yet." She hastened to the sink to wash the child's face, and discovered a swelling lump on his forehead. "Have you a quarter in your house?" she asked.

"Yes, I got one," replied Hanneh Breineh, climbing on a chair. "I got to keep it on a high shelf where the children can't get it."

Mrs. Pelz seized the quarter Hanneh Breineh handed down to her.

"Now pull your left eyelid three times while I'm pressing the quarter, and you'll see the swelling go down."

Hanneh Breineh took the child again in her arms, shaking and cooing over it and caressing it.

"Ah-ah-ah, Sammy! Ah-ah-ah-ah, little lamb! Ah-ah-ah, little bird! Ah-ah-ah-ah, precious heart! Oh, you saved my life; I thought he was killed," gasped Hanneh Breineh, turning to Mrs. Pelz. "Oi-i!" she sighed, "a mother's heart! Always in fear over her children. The minute anything happens to them all life goes out of me. I lose my head and I don't know where I am any more."

"No wonder the child fell," admonished Mrs. Pelz. "You should have a red ribbon or red beads on his neck to keep away the evil eye. Wait. I got something in my machine-drawer."

Mrs. Pelz returned, bringing the boiler and a red string, which she tied about the child's neck while the mother proceeded to fill the boiler.

A little later Hanneh Breineh again came into Mrs. Pelz's kitchen, holding Sammy in one arm and in the other an apronful of potatoes. Putting the child down on the floor, she seated herself on the unmade kitchen-bed and began to peel the potatoes in her apron.

"Woe to me!" sobbed Hanneh Breineh. "To my bitter luck there ain't no end. With all my other troubles, the stove got broke. I lighted the fire to boil the clothes, and it's to get choked with smoke. I paid rent only a week ago, and the agent don't want to fix it. A thunder should strike him! He only comes for the rent, and if anything has to be fixed, then he don't want to hear nothing.

"Why comes it to me so hard?" went on Hanneh Breineh, the tears streaming down her cheeks. "I can't stand it no more. I came into you for a minute to run away from my troubles. It's only when I sit myself down to peel potatoes or nurse the baby that I take time to draw a breath, and beg only for death."

Mrs. Pelz, accustomed to Hanneh Breineh's bitter outbursts, continued her scrubbing.

"Ut!" exclaimed Hanneh Breineh, irritated at her neighbor's silence, "what are you tearing up the world with your cleaning? What's the use to clean up when everything only gets dirty again?"

"I got to shine up my house for the holidays."

"You've got it so good nothing lays on your

mind but to clean your house. Look on this little blood-sucker," said Hanneh Breineh, pointing to the wizened child, made prematurely solemn from starvation and neglect. "Could anybody keep that brat clean? I wash him one minute, and he is dirty the minute after." Little Sammy grew frightened and began to cry. "Shut up!" ordered the mother, picking up the child to nurse it again. "Can't you see me take a rest for a minute?"

The hungry child began to cry at the top of its weakened lungs.

"Na, na, you glutton." Hanneh Breineh took out a dirty pacifier from her pocket and stuffed it into the baby's mouth. The grave, pasty-faced infant shrank into a panic of fear, and chewed the nipple nervously, clinging to it with both his thin little hands.

"For what did I need yet the sixth one?" groaned Hanneh Breineh, turning to Mrs. Pelz. "Was n't it enough five mouths to feed? If I did n't have this child on my neck, I could turn myself around and earn a few cents." She wrung her hands in a passion of despair. "Gottuniu! The earth should only take it before it grows up!"

"Shah! Shah!" reproved Mrs. Pelz. "Pity yourself on the child. Let it grow up already so long as it is here. See how frightened it looks on you." Mrs. Pelz took the child in her arms and petted it. "The poor little lamb! What did it done you should hate it so?"

Hanneh Breineh pushed Mrs. Pelz away from her.

"To whom can I open the wounds of my heart?" she moaned. "Nobody has pity on me. You don't believe me, nobody believes me until I'll fall down like a horse in the middle of the street. Oi weh! Mine life is so black for my eyes! Some mothers got luck. A child gets run over by a car, some fall from a window, some burn themselves up with a match, some get choked with diphtheria; but no death takes mine away."

"God from the world, stop cursing!" admonished Mrs. Pelz. "What do you want from the poor children? Is it their fault that their father makes small wages? Why do you let it all out on them?" Mrs. Pelz sat down beside Hanneh Breineh. "Wait only till your children get old enough to go to the shop and earn money," she consoled. "Push only through those few years while they are yet small; your sun will begin to shine; you will live on the fat of the land, when they begin to bring you in the wages each week."

Hanneh Breineh refused to be comforted.

"Till they are old enough to go to the shop and earn money they'll eat the head off my bones," she wailed. "If you only knew the fights I got by each meal. Maybe I gave Abe a bigger piece of bread than Fanny. Maybe Fanny got a little more soup in her plate than Jake. Eating is dearer than diamonds. Potatoes went up a cent on a pound, and milk is only for millionaires. And once a week, when I buy a little meat for the Sabbath, the butcher weighs it for me like gold, with all the bones in it. When I come to lay the meat out on a plate and divide it up, there ain't nothing to it but bones. Before, he used to throw me in a piece of fat extra or a piece of lung, but now you got to pay for everything, even for a bone to the soup."

"Never mind; you'll yet come out from all your troubles. Just as soon as your children get old enough to get their working papers the more children you got, the more money you'll have."

"Why should I fool myself with the false shine of hope? Don't I know it's already my black luck not to have it good in this world? Do you think American children will right away give everything they earn to their mother?"

"I know what is with you the matter," said Mrs. Pelz. "You did n't eat yet to-day. When it is empty in the stomach, the whole world looks black. Come, only let me give you something good to taste in the mouth; that will freshen you up." Mrs. Pelz went to the cupboard and brought out the saucepan of gefülte fish that she had cooked for dinner and placed it on the table in front of Hanneh Breineh. "Give a taste my fish," she said, taking one slice on a spoon, and handing it to Hanneh Breineh with a piece of bread. "I would n't give it to you on a plate because I just cleaned up my house, and I don't want to dirty up more dishes."

"What, am I a stranger you should have to serve me on a plate yet!" cried Hanneh Breineh, snatching the fish in her trembling fingers.

"Oi weh! How it melts through all the bones!" she exclaimed, brightening as she ate. "May it be for good luck to us all!" she exulted, waving aloft the last precious bite.

Mrs. Pelz was so flattered that she even ladled up a spoonful of gravy.

"There is a bit of onion and carrot in it," she said, as she handed it to her neighbor.

Hanneh Breineh sipped the gravy drop by drop, like a connoisseur sipping wine.

"Ah-h-h! A taste of that gravy lifts me up to heaven!" As she disposed leisurely of the slice of onion and carrot she relaxed and expanded and even grew jovial. "Let us wish all our troubles on the Russian Czar! Let him burst with our worries for rent! Let him get shriveled with our hunger for bread! Let his eyes dry out of his head looking for work!

"Shah! I'm forgetting from everything," she exclaimed, jumping up. "It must be eleven or soon twelve, and my children will be right away out of school and fall on me like a pack of wild wolves. I better quick run to the market and see what cheaper I can get for a quarter."

Because of the lateness of her coming, the stale bread at the nearest bakeshop was sold out, and Hanneh Breineh had to trudge from shop to shop in search of the usual bargain, and spent nearly an hour to save two cents.

In the meantime the children returned from school, and, finding the door locked, climbed through the fire-escape, and entered the house through the window. Seeing nothing on the table, they rushed to the stove. Abe pulled a steaming potato out of the boiling pot, and so scalded his fingers that the potato fell to the floor; where upon the three others pounced on it.

"It was my potato," cried Abe, blowing his burned fingers, while with the other hand and his foot he cuffed and kicked the three who were struggling on the floor. A wild fight ensued, and the potato was smashed under Abe's foot amid shouts and screams. Hanneh Breineh, on the stairs, heard the noise of her famished brood, and topped their cries with curses and invectives.

"They are here already, the savages! They are here already to shorten my life! They heard you all over the hall, in all the houses around!"

The children, disregarding her words, pounced on her market-basket, shouting ravenously: "Mamma, I'm hungry! What more do you got to eat?"

They tore the bread and herring out of Hanneh Breineh's basket and devoured it in starved savagery, clamoring for more.

"Murderers!" screamed Hanneh Breineh, goaded beyond endurance. "What are you tearing from me my flesh? From where should I steal to give you more? Here I had already a pot of potatoes and a whole loaf of bread and two herrings, and you swallowed it down in the wink of an eye. I have to have Rockefeller's millions to fill your stomachs."

All at once Hanneh Breineh became aware that Benny was missing. "Oi weh!" she burst out, wringing her hands in a new wave of woe, "where is Benny? Did n't he come home yet from school?"

She ran out into the hall, opened the grime-coated window, and looked up and down the street; but Benny was nowhere in sight.

"Abe, Jake, Fanny, quick, find Benny!" entreated Hanneh Breineh, as she rushed back into the kitchen. But the children, anxious to snatch a few minutes' play before the school-call, dodged past her and hurried out.

With the baby on her arm, Hanneh Breineh hastened to the kindergarten.

"Why are you keeping Benny here so long?" she shouted at the teacher as she flung open the door. "If you had my bitter heart, you would send him home long ago and not wait till I got to come for him."

The teacher turned calmly and consulted her record-cards.

"Benny Safron? He was n't present this morning."

"Not here?" shrieked Hanneh Breineh. "I pushed him out myself he should go. The children did n't want to take him, and I had no time. Woe is me! Where is my child?" She began pulling her hair and beating her breast as she ran into the street.

Mrs. Pelz was busy at a pushcart, picking over some spotted apples, when she heard the clamor of an approaching crowd. A block off she recognized Hanneh Breineh, her hair disheveled, her clothes awry, running toward her with her yelling baby in her arms, the crowd following.

"Friend mine," cried Hanneh Breineh, falling on Mrs. Pelz's neck, "I lost my Benny, the best child of all my children." Tears streamed down her red, swollen eyes as she sobbed. "Benny! mine heart, mine life! Oi-i-i!"

Mrs. Pelz took the frightened baby out of the mother's arms.

"Still yourself a little! See how you're frightening your child."

"Woe to me! Where is my Benny? Maybe he's killed already by a car. Maybe he fainted away from hunger. He did n't eat nothing all day long. Gottuniu! Pity yourself on me!"

She lifted her hands full of tragic entreaty.

"People, my child! Get me my child! I'll go crazy out of my head! Get me my child, or I'll take poison before your eyes!"

"Still yourself a little!" pleaded Mrs. Pelz.

"Talk not to me!" cried Hanneh Breineh, wringing her hands. "You 're having all your children. I lost mine. Every good luck comes to other people. But I did n't live yet to see a good day in my life. Mine only joy, mine Benny, is lost away from me."

The crowd followed Hanneh Breineh as she wailed through the streets, leaning on Mrs. Pelz. By the time she returned to her house the children were back from school; but seeing that Benny was not there, she chased them out in the street, crying:

"Out of here, you robbers, gluttons! Go find Benny!" Hanneh Breineh crumpled into a chair in utter prostration. "Oi weh! he's lost! Mine life; my little bird; mine only joy! How many nights I spent nursing him when he had the measles! And all that I suffered for weeks and months when he had the whooping-cough! How the eyes went out of my head till I learned him how to walk, till I learned him how to talk! And such a smart child! If I lost all the others, it would n't tear me so by the heart."

She worked herself up into such a hysteria, crying, and tearing her hair, and hitting her head with her knuckles, that at last she fell into a faint. It took some time before Mrs. Pelz, with the aid of neighbors, revived her.

"Benny, mine angel!" she moaned as she opened her eyes.

Just then a policeman came in with the lost Benny.

"Na, na, here you got him already!" said Mrs. Pelz. "Why did you carry on so for nothing? Why did you tear up the world like a crazy?"

The child's face was streaked with tears as he cowered, frightened and forlorn. Hanneh Breineh sprang toward him, slapping his cheeks, boxing his ears, before the neighbors could rescue him from her.

"Woe on your head!" cried the mother. "Where did you lost yourself? Ain't I got enough worries on my head than to go around looking for you? I did n't have yet a minute's peace from that child since he was born!"

"See a crazy mother!" remonstrated Mrs.

Pelz, rescuing Benny from another beating. "Such a mouth! With one breath she blesses him when he is lost, and with the other breath she curses him when he is found."

Hanneh Breineh took from the window-sill a piece of herring covered with swarming flies, and putting it on a slice of dry bread, she filled a cup of tea that had been stewing all day, and dragged Benny over to the table to eat.

But the child, choking with tears, was unable to touch the food.

"Go eat!" commanded Hanneh Breineh. "Eat and choke yourself eating!"

"Maybe she won't remember me no more. Maybe the servant won't let me in," thought Mrs. Pelz, as she walked by the brownstone house on Eighty-Fourth Street where she had been told Hanneh Breineh now lived. At last she summoned up enough courage to climb the steps. She was all out of breath as she rang the bell with trembling fingers. "Oi weh! even the outside smells riches and plenty! Such curtains! And shades on all windows like by millionaires!

Twenty years ago she used to eat from the pot to the hand, and now she lives in such a palace."

A whiff of steam-heated warmth swept over Mrs. Pelz as the door opened, and she saw her old friend of the tenements dressed in silk and diamonds like a being from another world.

"Mrs. Pelz, is it you!" cried Hanneh Breineh, overjoyed at the sight of her former neighbor. "Come right in. Since when are you back in New York?"

"We came last week," mumbled Mrs. Pelz, as she was led into a richly carpeted reception-room.

"Make yourself comfortable. Take off your shawl," urged Hanneh Breineh.

But Mrs. Pelz only drew her shawl more tightly around her, a keen sense of her poverty gripping her as she gazed, abashed by the luxurious wealth that shone from every corner.

"This shawl covers up my rags," she said, trying to hide her shabby sweater.

"I'll tell you what; come right into the kitchen," suggested Hanneh Breineh. "The servant is away for this afternoon, and we can feel more comfortable there. I can breathe like a free person in my kitchen when the girl has her day out."

Mrs. Pelz glanced about her in an excited daze. Never in her life had she seen anything so wonderful as a white-tiled kitchen, with its glistening porcelain sink and the aluminum pots and pans that shone like silver.

"Where are you staying now?" asked Hanneh Breineh, as she pinned an apron over her silk dress.

"I moved back to Delancey Street, where we used to live," replied Mrs. Pelz, as she seated herself cautiously in a white enameled chair.

"Oi weh! What grand times we had in that old house when we were neighbors!" sighed Hanneh Breineh, looking at her old friend with misty eyes.

"You still think on Delancey Street? Haven't you more high-class neighbors uptown here?"

"A good neighbor is not to be found every day," deplored Hanneh Breineh. "Uptown here, where each lives in his own house, nobody cares if the person next door is dying or going crazy from loneliness. It ain't anything like we used to have it in Delancey Street, when we could walk into one another's rooms without knocking, and borrow a pinch of salt or a pot to cook in."

Hanneh Breineh went over to the pantry-shelf.

"We are going to have a bite right here on the kitchen-table like on Delancey Street. So long there's no servant to watch us we can eat what we please."

"Oi! How it waters my mouth with appetite, the smell of the herring and onion!" chuckled Mrs. Pelz, sniffing the welcome odors with greedy pleasure.

Hanneh Breineh pulled a dish-towel from the rack and threw one end of it to Mrs. Pelz.

"So long there's no servant around, we can use it together for a napkin. It's dirty, anyhow. How it freshens up my heart to see you!" she rejoiced as she poured out her tea into a saucer. "If you would only know how I used to beg my daughter to write for me a letter to you; but these American children, what is to them a mother's feelings?"

"What are you talking!" cried Mrs. Pelz. "The whole world rings with you and your children. Everybody is envying you. Tell me how began your luck?"

"You heard how my husband died with consumption," replied Hanneh Breineh. "The five hundred dollars lodge money gave me the first lift in life, and I opened a little grocery store. Then my son Abe married himself to a girl with a thousand dollars. That started him in business, and now he has the biggest shirtwaist factory on West Twenty-Ninth Street."

"Yes, I heard your son had a factory." Mrs. Pelz hesitated and stammered; "I'll tell you the truth. What I came to ask you — I thought maybe you would beg your son Abe if he would give my husband a job."

"Why not?" said Hanneh Breineh. "He keeps more than five hundred hands. I'll ask him if he should take in Mr. Pelz."

"Long years on you, Hanneh Breineh! You'll save my life if you could only help my husband get work."

"Of course my son will help him. All my

children like to do good. My daughter Fanny is a milliner on Fifth Avenue, and she takes in the poorest girls in her shop and even pays them sometimes while they learn the trade." Hanneh Breineh's face lit up, and her chest filled with pride as she enumerated the successes of her children. "And my son Benny he wrote a play on Broadway and he gave away more than a hundred free tickets for the first night."

"Benny? The one who used to get lost from home all the time? You always did love that child more than all the rest. And what is Sammy your baby doing?"

"He ain't a baby no longer. He goes to college and quarterbacks the football team. They can't get along without him.

"And my son Jake, I nearly forgot him. He began collecting rent in Delancey Street, and now he is boss of renting the swellest apartment-houses on Riverside Drive."

"What did I tell you? In America children are like money in the bank," purred Mrs. Pelz, as she pinched and patted Hanneh Breineh's silk sleeve. "Oi weh! How it shines from you!

You ought to kiss the air and dance for joy and happiness. It is such a bitter frost outside; a pail of coal is so dear, and you got it so warm with steam heat. I had to pawn my feather bed to have enough for the rent, and you are rolling in money."

"Yes, I got it good in some ways, but money ain't everything," sighed Hanneh Breineh.

"You ain't yet satisfied?"

"But here I got no friends," complained Hanneh Breineh.

"Friends?" queried Mrs. Pelz. "What greater friend is there on earth than the dollar?"

"Oi! Mrs. Pelz; if you could only look into my heart! I'm so choked up! You know they say a cow has a long tongue, but can't talk." Hanneh Breineh shook her head wistfully, and her eyes filmed with inward brooding. "My children give me everything from the best. When I was sick, they got me a nurse by day and one by night. They bought me the best wine. If I asked for dove's milk, they would buy it for me; but—but—I can't talk myself out in their language. They want to make me over for an American lady, and I'm different." Tears cut their way under her eyelids with a pricking pain as she went on: "When I was poor, I was free, and could holler and do what I like in my own house. Here I got to lie still like a mouse under a broom. Between living up to my Fifth-Avenue daughter and keeping up with the servants, I am like a sinner in the next world that is thrown from one hell to another." The doorbell rang, and Hanneh Breineh jumped up with a start.

"Oi weh! It must be the servant back already!" she exclaimed, as she tore off her apron. "Oi weh! Let's quickly put the dishes together in a dish-pan. If she sees I eat on the kitchen table, she will look on me like the dirt under her feet."

Mrs. Pelz seized her shawl in haste.

"I better run home quick in my rags before your servant sees me."

"I'll speak to Abe about the job," said Hanneh Breineh, as she pushed a bill into the hand of Mrs. Pelz, who edged out as the servant entered.

"I'm having fried potato lotkes special for

you, Benny," said Hanneh Breineh, as the children gathered about the table for the family dinner given in honor of Benny's success with his new play. "Do you remember how you used to lick the fingers from them?"

"Oh, mother!" reproved Fanny. "Any one hearing you would think we were still in the pushcart district."

"Stop your nagging, sis, and let ma alone," commanded Benny, patting his mother's arm affectionately. "I'm home only once a month. Let her feed me what she pleases. My stomach is bomb-proof."

"Do I hear that the President is coming to your play?" said Abe, as he stuffed a napkin over his diamond-studded shirt-front.

"Why should n't he come?" returned Benny. "The critics say it's the greatest antidote for the race hatred created by the war. If you want to know, he is coming to-night; and what's more, our box is next to the President's."

"Nu, mammeh," sallied Jake, "did you ever dream in Delancey Street that we should rub sleeves with the President?"

"I always said that Benny had more head than the rest of you," replied the mother.

As the laughter died away, Jake went on:

"Honor you are getting plenty; but how much mezummen does this play bring you? Can I invest any of it in real estate for you?"

"I'm getting ten per cent royalties of the gross rcceipts," replied the youthful playwright.

"How much is that?" queried Hanneh Breineh.

"Enough to buy up all your fish-markets in Delancey Street," laughed Abe in good-natured raillery at his mother.

Her son's jest cut like a knife-thrust in her heart. She felt her heart ache with the pain that she was shut out from their successes. Each added triumph only widened the gulf. And when she tried to bridge this gulf by asking questions, they only thrust her back upon herself.

"Your fame has even helped me get my hat trade solid with the Four Hundred," put in Fanny. "You bet I let Mrs. Van Suyden know that our box is next to the President's. She said she would drop in to meet you. Of course she let on to me that she had n't seen the play yet, though my designer said she saw her there on the opening night."

"Oh, Gosh, the toadies!" sneered Benny. "Nothing so sickens you with success as the way people who once shoved you off the sidewalk come crawling to you on their stomachs begging you to dine with them."

"Say, that leading man of yours he's some class!" cried Fanny. "That's the man I'm looking for. Will you invite him to supper after the theater?"

The playwright turned to his mother.

"Say, ma," he said, laughingly, "how would you like a real actor for a son-in-law?"

"She should worry," mocked Sam. "She'll be discussing with him the future of the Greek drama. Too bad it does n't happen to be Warfield, or mother could give him tips on the 'Auctioneer.'"

Jake turned to his mother with a covert grin.

"I guess you'd have no objection if Fanny got next to Benny's leading man. He makes at least fifteen hundred a week. That would n't be such a bad addition to the family, would it?"

Again the bantering tone stabbed Hanneh Breineh. Everything in her began to tremble and break loose.

"Why do you ask me?" she cried, throwing her napkin into her plate. "Do I count for a person in this house? If I'll say something, will you even listen to me? What is to me the grandest man that my daughter could pick out? Another enemy in my house! Another person to shame himself from me!" She swept in her children in one glance of despairing anguish as she rose from the table. "What worth is an old mother to American children? The President is coming to-night to the theater, and none of you asked me to go." Unable to check the rising tears, she fled toward the kitchen and banged the door.

They all looked at one another guiltily.

"Say, sis," Benny called out sharply, "what sort of frame-up is this? Have n't you told mother that she was to go with us to-night?"

"Yes — I —" Fanny bit her lips as she fumbled evasively for words. "I asked her if she would n't mind my taking her some other time."

"Now you have made a mess of it!" fumed Benny. "Mother'll be too hurt to go now."

"Well, I don't care," snapped Fanny. "I can't appear with mother in a box at the theater. Can I introduce her to Mrs. Van Suyden? And suppose your leading man should ask to meet me?"

"Take your time, sis. He has n't asked yet," scoffed Benny.

"The more reason I should n't spoil my chances. You know mother. She'll spill the beans that we come from Delancey Street the minute we introduce her anywhere. Must I always have the black shadow of my past trailing after me?"

"But have you no feelings for mother?" admonished Abe.

"I've tried harder than all of you to do my duty. I've *lived* with her." She turned angrily upon them. "I've borne the shame of mother while you bought her off with a present and a treat here and there. God knows how hard I tried to civilize her so as not to have to blush with shame when I take her anywhere. I dressed her in the most stylish Paris models, but Delancey Street sticks out from every inch of her. Whenever she opens her mouth, I'm done for. You fellows had your chance to rise in the world because a man is free to go up as high as he can reach up to; but I, with all my style and pep, can't get a man my equal because a girl is always judged by her mother."

They were silenced by her vehemence, and unconsciously turned to Benny.

"I guess we all tried to do our best for mother," said Benny, thoughtfully. "But wherever there is growth, there is pain and heartbreak. The trouble with us is that the ghetto of the Middle Ages and the children of the twentieth century have to live under one roof, and —"

A sound of crashing dishes came from the kitchen, and the voice of Hanneh Breineh resounded through the dining-room as she wreaked her pent-up fury on the helpless servant.

"Oh, my nerves! I can't stand it any more! There will be no girl again for another week!" cried Fanny.

"Oh, let up on the old lady," protested Abe. "Since she can't take it out on us any more, what harm is it if she cusses the servants?"

"If you fellows had to chase around employment agencies, you would n't see anything funny about it. Why can't we move into a hotel that will do away with the need of servants altogether?"

"I got it better," said Jake, consulting a notebook from his pocket. "I have on my list an apartment on Riverside Drive where there's only a small kitchenette; but we can do away with the cooking, for there is a dining service in the building."

The new Riverside apartment to which Hanneh Breineh was removed by her socially ambitious children was for the habitually active mother an empty desert of enforced idleness. Deprived of her kitchen, Hanneh Breineh felt robbed of the last reason for her existence.

Cooking and marketing and puttering busily with pots and pans gave her an excuse for living and struggling and bearing up with her children. The lonely idleness of Riverside Drive stunned all her senses and arrested all her thoughts. It gave her that choked sense of being cut off from air, from life, from everything warm and human. The cold indifference, the each-for-himself look in the eyes of the people about her were like stinging slaps in the face. Even the children had nothing real or human in them. They were starched and stiff miniatures of their elders.

But the most unendurable part of the stifling life on Riverside Drive was being forced to eat in the public dining-room. No matter how hard she tried to learn polite table manners, she always found people staring at her, and her daughter rebuking her for eating with the wrong fork or guzzling the soup or staining the cloth.

In a fit of rebellion Hanneh Breineh resolved never to go down to the public dining-room again, but to make use of the gas-stove in the kitchenette to cook her own meals. That very day she rode down to Delancey Street and purchased a new market-basket. For some time she walked among the haggling pushcart venders, relaxing and swimming in the warm waves of her old familiar past.

A fish-peddler held up a large carp in his black, hairy hand and waved it dramatically:

"Women! Women! Fourteen cents a pound!"

He ceased his raucous shouting as he saw Hanneh Breineh in her rich attire approach his cart.

"How much?" she asked, pointing to the fattest carp.

"Fifteen cents, lady," said the peddler, smirking as he raised his price.

"Swindler! Did n't I hear you call fourteen cents?" shrieked Hanneh Breineh, exultingly, the spirit of the penny chase surging in her blood. Diplomatically, Hanneh Breineh turned as if to go, and the fisherman seized her basket in frantic fear.

"I should live; I'm losing money on the fish, lady," whined the peddler. "I'll let it down to thirteen cents for you only."

"Two pounds for a quarter, and not a penny more," said Hanneh Breineh, thrilling again with the rare sport of bargaining, which had been her chief joy in the good old days of poverty.

"Nu, I want to make the first sale for good luck." The peddler threw the fish on the scale.

As he wrapped up the fish, Hanneh Breineh saw the driven look of worry in his haggard eyes, and when he counted out the change from her dollar, she waved it aside. "Keep it for your luck," she said, and hurried off to strike a new bargain at a pushcart of onions.

Hanneh Breineh returned triumphantly with her purchases. The basket under her arm gave forth the old, homelike odors of herring and garlic, while the scaly tail of a four-pound carp protruded from its newspaper wrapping. A gilded placard on the door of the apartment-house proclaimed that all merchandise must be delivered through the trade entrance in the rear; but Hanneh Breineh with her basket strode proudly through the marble-paneled hall and rang nonchalantly for the elevator.

The uniformed hall-man, erect, expressionless, frigid with dignity, stepped forward:

"Just a minute, madam. I'll call a boy to take up your basket for you."

Hanneh Breineh, glaring at him, jerked the basket savagely from his hands. "Mind your own business!" she retorted. "I'll take it up myself. Do you think you're a Russian policeman to boss me in my own house?"

Angry lines appeared on the countenance of the representative of social decorum.

"It is against the rules, madam," he said, stiffly.

"You should sink into the earth with all your rules and brass buttons. Ain't this America? Ain't this a free country? Can't I take up in my own house what I buy with my own money?" cried Hanneh Breineh, reveling in the opportunity to shower forth the volley of invectives that had been suppressed in her for the weeks of deadly dignity of Riverside Drive.

In the midst of this uproar Fanny came in with Mrs. Van Suyden. Hanneh Breineh rushed over to her, crying:

"This bossy policeman won't let me take up my basket in the elevator."

The daughter, unnerved with shame and confusion, took the basket in her white-gloved hand and ordered the hall-boy to take it around to the regular delivery entrance.

Hanneh Breineh was so hurt by her daughter's apparent defense of the hall-man's rules that she utterly ignored Mrs. Van Suyden's greeting and walked up the seven flights of stairs out of sheer spite.

"You see the tragedy of my life?" broke out Fanny, turning to Mrs. Van Suyden.

"You poor child! You go right up to your dear, old lady mother, and I'll come some other time."

Instantly Fanny regretted her words. Mrs. Van Suyden's pity only roused her wrath the more against her mother.

Breathless from climbing the stairs, Hanneh Breineh entered the apartment just as Fanny tore the faultless millinery creation from her head and threw it on the floor in a rage.

"Mother, you are the ruination of my life!

You have driven away Mrs. Van Suyden, as you have driven away all my best friends. What do you think we got this apartment for but to get rid of your fish smells and your brawls with the servants? And here you come with a basket on your arm as if you just landed from steerage! And this afternoon, of all times, when Benny is bringing his leading man to tea. When will you ever stop disgracing us?"

"When I'm dead," said Hanneh Breineh, grimly. "When the earth will cover me up, then you'll be free to go your American way. I'm not going to make myself over for a lady on Riverside Drive. I hate you and all your swell friends. I'll not let myself be choked up here by you or by that hall-boss policeman that is higher in your eyes than your own mother."

"So that's your thanks for all we've done for you?" cried the daughter.

"All you've done for me!" shouted Hanneh Breineh. "What have you done for me? You hold me like a dog on a chain! It stands in the Talmud; some children give their mothers dry bread and water and go to heaven for it, and some give their mother roast duck and go to Gehenna because it's not given with love."

"You want me to love you yet?" raged the daughter. "You knocked every bit of love out of me when I was yet a kid. All the memories of childhood I have is your everlasting cursing and yelling that we were gluttons."

The bell rang sharply, and Hanneh Breineh flung open the door.

"Your groceries, ma'am," said the boy.

Hanneh Breineh seized the basket from him, and with a vicious fling sent it rolling across the room, strewing its contents over the Persian rugs and inlaid floor. Then seizing her hat and coat, she stormed out of the apartment and down the stairs.

Mr. and Mrs. Pelz sat crouched and shivering over their meager supper when the door opened, and Hanneh Breineh in fur coat and plumed hat charged into the room.

"I come to cry out to you my bitter heart," she sobbed. "Woe is me! It is so black for my eyes!"

"What is the matter with you, Hanneh

Breineh?" cried Mrs. Pelz in bewildered alarm.

"I am turned out of my own house by the brass-buttoned policeman that bosses the elevator. Oi-i-i-i! Weh-h-h-h! What have I from my life? The whole world rings with my son's play. Even the President came to see it, and I, his mother, have not seen it yet. My heart is dying in me like in a prison," she went on wailing. "I am starved out for a piece of real eating. In that swell restaurant is nothing but napkins and forks and lettuce-leaves. There are a dozen plates to every bite of food. And it looks so fancy on the plate, but it's nothing but straw in the mouth. I'm starving, but I can't swallow down their American eating."

"Hanneh Breineh," said Mrs. Pelz, "you are sinning before God. Look on your fur coat; it alone would feed a whole family for a year. I never had yet a piece of fur trimming on a coat, and you are in fur from the neck to the feet. I never had yet a piece of feather on a hat, and your hat is all feathers."

"What are you envying me?" protested Hanneh Breineh. "What have I from all my fine furs and feathers when my children are strangers to me? All the fur coats in the world can't warm up the loneliness inside my heart. All the grandest feathers can't hide the bitter shame in my face that my children shame themselves from me."

Hanneh Breineh suddenly loomed over them like some ancient, heroic figure of the Bible condemning unrighteousness.

"Why should my children shame themselves from me? From where did they get the stuff to work themselves up in the world? Did they get it from the air? How did they get all their smartness to rise over the people around them? Why don't the children of born American mothers write my Benny's plays? It is I, who never had a chance to be a person, who gave him the fire in his head. If I would have had a chance to go to school and learn the language, what could n't I have been? It is I and my mother and my mother's mother and my father and father's father who had such a black life in Poland; it is our choked thoughts and feelings that are flaming up in my children and making them great in America. And yet they shame themselves from me!"

For a moment Mr. and Mrs. Pelz were hypnotized by the sweep of her words. Then Hanneh Breineh sank into a chair in utter exhaustion. She began to weep bitterly, her body shaking with sobs.

"Woe is me! For what did I suffer and hope on my children? A bitter old age — my end. I'm so lonely!"

All the dramatic fire seemed to have left her. The spell was broken. They saw the Hanneh Breineh of old, ever discontented, ever complaining even in the midst of riches and plenty.

"Hanneh Breineh," said Mrs. Pelz, "the only trouble with you is that you got it too good. People will tear the eyes out of your head because you're complaining yet. If I only had your fur coat! If I only had your diamonds! I have nothing. You have everything. You are living on the fat of the land. You go right back home and thank God that you don't have my bitter lot."

"You got to let me stay here with you," insisted Hanneh Breineh. "I'll not go back to my children except when they bury me. When they will see my dead face, they will understand how they killed me."

Mrs. Pelz glanced nervously at her husband. They barely had enough covering for their one bed; how could they possibly lodgc a visitor?

"I don't want to take up your bed," said Hanneh Breineh. "I don't care if I have to sleep on the floor or on the chairs, but I'll stay here for the night."

Seeing that she was bent on staying, Mr. Pelz prepared to sleep by putting a few chairs next to the trunk, and Hanneh Breineh was invited to share the rickety bed with Mrs. Pelz.

The mattress was full of lumps and hollows. Hanneh Breineh lay cramped and miserable, unable to stretch out her limbs. For years she had been accustomed to hair mattresses and ample woolen blankets, so that though she covered herself with her fur coat, she was too cold to sleep. But worse than the cold were the creeping things on the wall. And as the lights were turned low, the mice came through the broken plaster and raced across the floor. The foul odors of the kitchen-sink added to the night of horrors.

"Are you going back home?" asked Mrs. Pelz, as Hanneh Breineh put on her hat and coat the next morning.

"I don't know where I'm going," she replied, as she put a bill into Mrs. Pelz's hand.

For hours Hanneh Breineh walked through the crowded ghetto streets. She realized that she no longer could endure the sordid ugliness of her past, and yet she could not go home to her children. She only felt that she must go on and on.

In the afternoon a cold, drizzling rain set in. She was worn out from the sleepless night and hours of tramping. With a piercing pain in her heart she at last turned back and boarded the subway for Riverside Drive. She had fled from the marble sepulcher of the Riverside apartment to her old home in the ghetto; but now she knew that she could not live there again. She had outgrown her past by the habits of years of physical comforts, and these material comforts that she could no longer do without choked and crushed the life within her.

A cold shudder went through Hanneh Breineh as she approached the apartment-house. Peering through the plate glass of the door she saw the face of the uniformed hall-man. For a hesitating moment she remained standing in the drizzling rain, unable to enter, and yet knowing full well that she would have to enter.

Then suddenly Hanneh Breineh began to laugh. She realized that it was the first time she had laughed since her children had become rich. But it was the hard laugh of bitter sorrow. Tears streamed down her furrowed cheeks as she walked slowly up the granite steps.

"The fat of the land!" muttered Hanneh Breineh, with a choking sob as the hall-man with immobile face deferentially swung open the door — "the fat of the land!"

## MY OWN PEOPLE

With the suitcase containing all her worldly possessions under her arm, Sophie Sapinsky elbowed her way through the noisy ghetto crowds. Pushcart peddlers and pullers-in shouted and gesticulated. Women with market-baskets pushed and shoved one another, eyes straining with the one thought — how to get the food a penny cheaper. With the same strained intentness, Sophie scanned each tenement, searching for a room cheap enough for her dwindling means.

In a dingy basement window a crooked sign, in straggling, penciled letters, caught Sophie's eye: "Room to let, a bargain, cheap."

The exuberant phrasing was quite in keeping with the extravagant dilapidation of the surroundings. "This is the very place," thought Sophie. "There could n't be nothing cheaper in all New York."

At the foot of the basement steps she knocked.

"Come in!" a voice answered.

As she opened the door she saw an old man bending over a pot of potatoes on a shoemaker's bench. A group of children in all degrees of rags surrounded him, greedily snatching at the potatoes he handed out.

Sophie paused for an instant, but her absorption in her own problem was too great to halt the question: "Is there a room to let?"

"Hanneh Breineh, in the back, has a room." The old man was so preoccupied filling the hungry hands that he did not even look up.

Sophie groped her way to the rear hall. A gaunt-faced woman answered her inquiry with loquacious enthusiasm. "A grand room for the money. I'll let it down to you only for three dollars a month. In the whole block is no bigger bargain. I should live so."

As she talked, the woman led her through the dark hall into an airshaft room. A narrow window looked out into the bottom of a chimney-like pit, where lay the accumulated refuse from a score of crowded kitchens.

"Oi weh!" gasped Sophie, throwing open the

sash. "No air and no light. Outside shines the sun and here it's so dark."

"It ain't so dark. It's only a little shady. Let me only turn up the gas for you and you'll quick see everything like with sunshine."

The claw-fingered flame revealed a rusty, iron cot, an inverted potato barrel that served for a table, and two soap-boxes for chairs.

Sophie felt of the cot. It sagged and flopped under her touch. "The bed has only three feet!" she exclaimed in dismay.

"You can't have Rockefeller's palace for three dollars a month," defended Hanneh Breineh, as she shoved one of the boxes under the legless corner of the cot. "If the bed ain't so steady, so you got good neighbors. Upstairs lives Shprintzeh Gittle, the herring-woman. You can buy by her the biggest bargains in fish, a few days older. . . . What she got left over from the Sabbath, she sells to the neighbors cheap. . . . In the front lives Shmendrik, the shoemaker. I'll tell you the truth, he ain't no real shoemaker. He never yet made a pair of whole shoes in his life. He's a learner from the old country

— a tzadik, a saint; but every time he sees in the street a child with torn feet, he calls them in and patches them up. His own eating, the last bite from his mouth, he divides up with them."

"Three dollars," deliberated Sophie, scarcely hearing Hanneh Breineh's chatter. "I will never find anything cheaper. It has a door to lock and I can shut this woman out . . . I'll take it," she said, handing her the money.

Hanneh Breineh kissed the greasy bills gloatingly. "I'll treat you like a mother! You'll have it good by me like in your own home."

"Thanks — but I got no time to shmoos. I got to be alone to get my work done."

The rebuff could not penetrate Hanneh Breineh's joy over the sudden possession of three dollars.

"Long years on you! May we be to good luck to one another!" was Hanneh Breineh's blessing as she closed the door.

Alone in her room — *her* room, securely hers — yet with the flash of triumph, a stab of bitterness. All that was hers — so wretched and so ugly! Had her eager spirit, eager to give and give, no claim to a bit of beauty — a shred of comfort?

Perhaps her family was right in condemning her rashness. Was it worth while to give up the peace of home, the security of a regular job — suffer hunger, loneliness, and want — for what? For something she knew in her heart was beyond her reach. Would her writing ever amount to enough to vindicate the uprooting of her past? Would she ever become articulate enough to express beautifully what she saw and felt? What had she, after all, but a stifling, sweatshop experience, a meager, night-school education, and this wild, blind hunger to release the dumbness that choked her?

Sophie spread her papers on the cot beside her. Resting her elbows on the potato barrel, she clutched her pencil with tense fingers. In the notebook before her were a hundred beginnings, essays, abstractions, outbursts of chaotic moods. She glanced through the titles: "Believe in Yourself," "The Quest of the Ideal."

Meaningless tracings on the paper, her words seemed to her now — a restless spirit pawing at the air. The intensity of experience, the surge of emotion that had been hers when she wrote — where were they? The words had failed to catch the life-beat — had failed to register the passion she had poured into them.

Perhaps she was not a writer, after all. Had the years and years of night-study been in vain? Choked with discouragement, the cry broke from her, "O — God — God help me! I feel — I see, but it all dies in me — dumb!"

Tedious days passed into weeks. Again Sophie sat staring into her notebook. "There's nothing here that's alive. Not a word yet says what's in me . . .

"But it *is* in me!" With clenched fist she smote her bosom. "It must be in me! I believe in it! I got to get it out — even if it tears my flesh in pieces — even if it kills me! . . .

"But these words—these flat, dead words . . .

"Whether I can write or can't write — I can't stop writing. I can't rest. I can't breathe. There's no peace, no running away for me on earth except in the struggle to give out what's in me. The beat from my heart — the blood from my veins — must flow out into my words."

She returned to her unfinished essay, "Believe in Yourself." Her mind groping — clutching at the misty incoherence that clouded her thoughts — she wrote on.

"These sentences are yet only wood — lead; but I can't help it — I'll push on — on — I'll not eat — I'll not sleep — I'll not move from this spot till I get it to say on the paper what I got in my heart!"

Slowly the dead words seemed to begin to breathe. Her eyes brightened. Her cheeks flushed. Her very pencil trembled with the eager onrush of words.

Then a sharp rap sounded on her door. With a gesture of irritation Sophie put down her pencil and looked into the burning, sunken eyes of her neighbor, Hanneh Breineh.

"I got yourself a glass of tea, good friend. It ain't much I got to give away, but it's warm even if it's nothing."

Sophie scowled. "You must n't bother yourself with me. I'm so busy — thanks."

"Don't thank me yet so quick. I got no sugar." Hanneh Breineh edged herself into the room confidingly. "At home, in Poland, I not only had sugar for tea—but even jelly—a jelly that would lift you up to heaven. I thought in America everything would be so plenty, I could drink the tea out from my sugar-bowl. But ach! Not in Poland did my children starve like in America!"

Hanneh Breineh, in a friendly manner, settled herself on the sound end of the bed, and began her jeremiad.

"Yosef, my man, ain't no bread-giver. Already he got consumption the second year. One week he works and nine weeks he lays sick."

In despair Sophie gathered her papers, wondering how to get the woman out of her room. She glanced through the page she had written, but Hanneh Breineh, unconscious of her indifference, went right on.

"How many times it is tearing the heart out from my body—should I take Yosef's milk to give to the baby, or the baby's milk to give to Yosef? If he was dead the pensions they give to widows would help feed my children. Now I got only the charities to help me. A black year on them! They should only have to feed their own children on what they give me."

Resolved not to listen to the intruder, Sophie debated within herself: "Should I call my essay 'Believe in Yourself,' or would n't it be stronger to say, 'Trust Yourself'? But if I say, 'Trust Yourself,' would n't they think that I got the words from Emerson?"

Hanneh Breineh's voice went on, but it sounded to Sophie like a faint buzzing from afar. "Gotteniu! How much did it cost me my life to go and swear myself that my little Fannie — only skin and bones — that she is already fourteen! How it chokes me the tears every morning when I got to wake her and push her out to the shop when her eyes are yet shutting themselves with sleep!"

Sophie glanced at her wrist-watch as it ticked away the precious minutes. She must get rid of the woman! Had she not left her own sister, sacrificed all comfort, all association, for solitude and its golden possibilities? For the first time in her life she had the chance to be by herself and think. And now, the thoughts which a moment ago had seemed like a flock of fluttering birds had come so close — and this woman with her sordid wailing had scattered them.

"I'm a savage, a beast, but I got to ask her to get out — this very minute," resolved Sophie. But before she could summon the courage to do what she wanted to do, there was a timid knock at the door, and the wizened little Fannie, her face streaked with tears, stumbled in.

"The inspector said it's a lie. I ain't yet fourteen," she whimpered.

Hanneh Breineh paled. "Woe is me! Sent back from the shop? God from the world — is there no end to my troubles? Why did n't you hide yourself when you saw the inspector come?"

"I was running to hide myself under the table, but she caught me and she said she'll take me to the Children's Society and arrest me and my mother for sending me to work too soon."

"Arrest me?" shrieked Hanneh Breineh, beating her breast. "Let them only come and arrest me! I'll show America who I am! Let them only begin themselves with me!... Black is for my eyes... the groceryman will not give us another bread till we pay him the bill!"

"The inspector said..." The child's brow puckered in an effort to recall the words.

"What did the inspector said? Gotteniu!" Hanneh Breineh wrung her hands in passionate entreaty. "Listen only once to my prayer! Send on the inspector only a quick death! I only wish her to have her own house with twenty-four rooms and each of the twenty-four rooms should be twenty-four beds and the chills and the fever should throw her from one bed to another!"

"Hanneh Breineh, still yourself a little," entreated Sophie.

"How can I still myself without Fannie's wages? Bitter is me! Why do I have to live so long?"

"The inspector said..."

"What did the inspector said? A thunder should strike the inspector! Ain't I as good a mother as other mothers? Would n't I better send my children to school? But who'll give us to eat? And who'll pay us the rent?"

Hanneh Breineh wiped her red-lidded eyes with the corner of her apron.

"The president from America should only come to my bitter heart. Let him go fighting himself with the pushcarts how to get the eating a penny cheaper. Let him try to feed his children on the money the charities give me and we'd see if he would n't better send his littlest ones to the shop better than to let them starve before his eyes. Woe is me! What for did I come to America? What's my life — nothing but one terrible, never-stopping fight with the grocer and the butcher and the landlord . . ."

Suddenly Sophie's resentment for her lost morning was forgotten. The crying waste of Hanneh Breineh's life lay open before her eyes like pictures in a book. She saw her own life in Hanneh Breineh's life. Her efforts to write were like Hanneh Breineh's efforts to feed her children. Behind her life and Hanneh Breineh's life she saw the massed ghosts of thousands upon thousands beating—beating out their hearts against rock barriers.

"The inspector said . . ." Fannie timidly attempted again to explain.

"The inspector!" shrieked Hanneh Breineh, as she seized hold of Fannie in a rage. "Hell-fire should burn the inspector! Tell me again about the inspector and I'll choke the life out from you—"

Sophie sprang forward to protect the child from the mother. "She's only trying to tell you something."

"Why should she yet throw salt on my wounds? If there was enough bread in the house would I need an inspector to tell me to send her to school? If America is so interested in poor people's children, then why don't they give them to eat till they should go to work? What learning can come into a child's head when the stomach is empty?"

A clutter of feet down the creaking cellar steps, a scuffle of broken shoes, and a chorus of shrill voices, as the younger children rushed in from school.

"Mamma — what's to eat?"

"It smells potatoes!"

"Pfui! The pot is empty! It smells over from Cohen's."

"Jake grabbed all the bread!"

"Mamma — he kicked the piece out from my hands!"

"Mamma — it's so empty in my stomach! Ain't there nothing?"

"Gluttons — wolves — thieves!" Hanneh Breineh shrieked. "I should only live to bury you all in one day!"

The children, regardless of Hanneh Breineh's invectives, swarmed around her like hungry bees, tearing at her apron, her skirt. Their voices rose in increased clamor, topped only by their mother's imprecations. "Gotteniu! Tear me away from these leeches on my neck! Send on them only a quick death!... Only a minute's peace before I die!"

"Hanneh Breineh — children! What's the matter?" Shmendrik stood at the door. The sweet quiet of the old man stilled the raucous voices as the coming of evening stills the noises of the day.

"There's no end to my troubles! Hear them hollering for bread, and the grocer stopped to give till the bill is paid. Woe is me! Fannie sent home by the inspector and not a crumb in the house!"

"I got something." The old man put his hands over the heads of the children in silent benediction. "All come in by me. I got sent me a box of cake."

"Cake!" The children cried, catching at the kind hands and snuggling about the shabby coat.

"Yes. Cake and nuts and raisins and even a bottle of wine."

The children leaped and danced around him in their wild burst of joy.

"Cake and wine — a box — to you? Have the charities gone crazy?" Hannch Breineh's eyes sparkled with light and laughter.

"No — no," Shmendrik explained hastily. "Not from the charities — from a friend — for the holidays."

Shmendrik nodded invitingly to Sophie, who was standing in the door of her room. "The roomerkeh will also give a taste with us our party?"

"Sure will she!" Hanneh Breineh took Sophie by the arm. "Who'll say no in this black life to cake and wine?"

Young throats burst into shrill cries: "Cake and wine — wine and cake — raisins and nuts — nuts and raisins!" The words rose in a triumphant chorus. The children leaped and danced in time to their chant, almost carrying the old man bodily into his room in the wildness of their joy.

The contagion of this sudden hilarity erased from Sophie's mind the last thought of work and she found herself seated with the others on the cobbler's bench.

From under his cot the old man drew forth a wooden box. Lifting the cover he held up before wondering eyes a large frosted cake embedded in raisins and nuts.

Amid the shouts of glee Shmendrik now waved aloft a large bottle of grape-juice.

The children could contain themselves no longer and dashed forward.

"Shah—shah! Wait only!" He gently halted their onrush and waved them back to their seats.

"The glasses for the wine!" Hanneh Breineh rushed about hither and thither in happy confusion. From the sink, the shelf, the window-sill, she gathered cracked glasses, cups without handles — anything that would hold even a few drops of the yellow wine.

Sacrificial solemnity filled the basement as the children breathlessly watched Shmendrik cut the precious cake. Mouths — even eyes — watered with the intensity of their emotion.

With almost religious fervor Hanneh Breineh poured the grape-juice into the glasses held in the trembling hands of the children. So overwhelming was the occasion that none dared to taste till the ritual was completed. The suspense was agonizing as one and all waited for Shmendrik's signal.

"Hanneh Breineh — you drink from my Sabbath wine-glass!"

Hanneh Breineh clinked glasses with Schmendrik. "Long years on you — long years on us all!" Then she turned to Sophie, clinked glasses once more. "May you yet marry yourself from our basement to a millionaire!" Then she lifted the glass to her lips.

The spell was broken. With a yell of triumph the children gobbled the cake in huge mouthfuls and sucked the golden liquid. All the traditions of wealth and joy that ever sparkled from the bubbles of champagne smiled at Hanneh Breineh from her glass of California grape-juice.

"Ach!" she sighed. "How good it is to forget your troubles, and only those that's got troubles have the chance to forget them!"

She sipped the grape-juice leisurely, thrilled into ecstacy with each lingering drop. "How it laughs yet in me, the life, the minute I turn my head from my worries!"

With growing wonder in her eyes, Sophie watched Hanneh Breineh. This ragged wreck of a woman — how passionately she clung to every atom of life! Hungrily, she burned through the depths of every experience. How she flared against wrongs — and how every tiny spark of pleasure blazed into joy!

Within a half-hour this woman had touched the whole range of human emotions, from bitterest agony to dancing joy. The terrible despair at the onrush of her starving children when she cried out, "O that I should only bury you all in one day!" And now the leaping light of the words: "How it laughs yet in me, the life, the minute I turn my head from my worries."

"Ach, if I could only write like Hanneh Breineh talks!" thought Sophie. "Her words dance with a thousand colors. Like a rainbow it flows from her lips." Sentences from her own essays marched before her, stiff and wooden. How clumsy, how unreal, were her most labored phrases compared to Hanneh Breineh's spontaneity. Fascinated, she listened to Hanneh Breineh, drinking her words as a thirst-perishing man drinks water. Every bubbling phrase filled her with a drunken rapture to create.

"Up till now I was only trying to write from my head. It was n't real — it was n't life. Hanneh Breineh is real. Hanneh Breineh is life."

"Ach! What do the rich people got but dried-up dollars? Pfui on them and their money!" Hanneh Breineh held up her glass to be refilled. "Let me only win a fortune on the lotteree and move myself in my own bought house. Let me only have my first hundred dollars in the bank and I'll lift up my head like a person and tell the charities to eat their own cornmeal. I'll get myself an automobile like the kind rich ladies and ride up to their houses on Fifth Avenue and feed them only once on the eating they like so good for me and my children."

With a smile of benediction Shmendrik refilled the glasses and cut for each of his guests another slice of cake. Then came the handful of nuts and raisins.

As the children were scurrying about for hammers and iron lasts with which to crack their nuts, the basement door creaked. Unannounced, a woman entered — the "friendly visitor" of the charities. Her look of awful amazement swept the group of merrymakers.

"Mr. Shmendrik!—Hanneh Breineh!" Indignation seethed in her voice. "What's this? A feast—a birthday?"

Gasps—bewildered glances—a struggle for utterance!

"I came to make my monthly visit—evidently I'm not needed."

Shmendrik faced the accusing eyes of the "friendly visitor." "Holiday eating . . ."

"Oh—I'm glad you're so prosperous."

Before any one had gained presence of mind enough to explain things, the door had clanked. The "friendly visitor" had vanished.

"Pfui!" Hanneh Breineh snatched up her glass and drained its contents. "What will she do now? Will we get no more dry bread from the charities because once we ate cake?"

"What for did she come?" asked Sophie.

"To see that we don't over-eat ourselves!" returned Hanneh Breineh. "She's a 'friendly visitor'! She learns us how to cook cornmeal. By pictures and lectures she shows us how the poor people should live without meat, without milk, without butter, and without eggs. Always it's on the end of my tongue to ask her, 'You learned us to do without so much, why can't you yet learn us how to eat without eating?'"

The children seized the last crumbs of cake that Shmendrik handed them and rushed for the street.

"What a killing look was on her face," said Sophie. "Could n't she be a little glad for your gladness?"

"Charity ladies — gladness?" The joy of the grape-wine still rippled in Hanneh Breineh's laughter. "For poor people is only cornmeal. Ten cents a day — to feed my children!"

Still in her rollicking mood Hanneh Breineh picked up the baby and tossed it like a Bacchante. "Could you be happy a lot with ten cents in your stomach? Ten cents — half a can of condensed milk — then fill yourself the rest with water! . . . Maybe yet feed you with all water and save the ten-cent pieces to buy you a carriage like the Fifth Avenue babies! . . ."

The soft sound of a limousine purred through the area grating and two well-fed figures in sealskin coats, led by the "friendly visitor," appeared at the door.

"Mr. Bernstein, you can see for yourself." The "friendly visitor" pointed to the table.

The merry group shrank back. It was as if a gust of icy wind had swept all the joy and laughter from the basement.

"You are charged with intent to deceive and obtain assistance by dishonest means," said Mr. Bernstein.

"Dishonest?" Shmendrik paled.

Sophie's throat strained with passionate protest, but no words came to her release.

"A friend — a friend" — stammered Shmendrik — "sent me the holiday eating."

The superintendent of the Social Betterment Society faced him accusingly. "You told us that you had no friends when you applied to us for assistance."

"My friend — he knew me in my better time." Shmendrik flushed painfully. "I was once a scholar — respected. I wanted by this one friend to hold myself like I was."

Mr. Bernstein had taken from the bookshelf

a number of letters, glanced through them rapidly and handed them one by one to the deferential superintendent.

Shmendrik clutched at his heart in an agony of humiliation. Suddenly his bent body straightened. His eyes dilated. "My letters — my life — you dare?"

"Of course we dare!" The superintendent returned Shmendrik's livid gaze, made bold by the confidence that what he was doing was the only scientific method of administering philanthropy. "These dollars, so generously given, must go to those most worthy. . . . I find in these letters references to gifts of fruit and other luxuries you did not report at our office."

"He never kept nothing for himself!" Hanneh Breineh broke in defensively. "He gave it all for the children."

Ignoring the interruption Mr. Bernstein turned to the "friendly visitor." "I'm glad you brought my attention to this case. It's but one of the many impositions on our charity . . . Come . . ."

"Kossacks! Pogromschiks!" Sophie's rage

broke at last. "You call yourselves Americans? You dare call yourselves Jews? You bosses of the poor! This man Shmendrik, whose house you broke into, whom you made to shame like a beggar — he is the one Jew from whom the Jews can be proud! He gives all he is — all he has — as God gives. *He is* charity.

"But you — you are the greed — the shame of the Jews! *All-right-niks* — fat bellies in fur coats! What do you give from yourselves? You may eat and bust eating! Nothing you give till you've stuffed yourselves so full that your hearts are dead!"

The door closed in her face. Her wrath fell on indifferent backs as the visitors mounted the steps to the street.

Shmendrik groped blindly for the Bible. In a low, quavering voice, he began the chant of the oppressed — the wail of the downtrodden. "I am afraid, and a trembling taketh hold of my flesh. Wherefore do the wicked live, become old, yea, mighty in power?"

Hanneh Breineh and the children drew close around the old man. They were weeping —

unconscious of their weeping — deep-buried memories roused by the music, the age-old music of the Hebrew race.

Through the grating Sophie saw the limousine pass. The chant flowed on: "Their houses are safe from fear; neither is the rod of God upon them."

Silently Sophie stole back to her room. She flung herself on the cot, pressed her fingers to her burning eyeballs. For a long time she lay rigid, clenched — listening to the drumming of her heart like the sea against rock barriers. Presently the barriers burst. Something in her began pouring itself out. She felt for her pencil — paper — and began to write. Whether she reached out to God or man she knew not, but she wrote on and on all through that night.

The gray light entering her grated window told her that beyond was dawn. Sophie looked up: "Ach! At last it writes itself in me!" she whispered triumphantly. "It's not me — it's their cries — my own people — crying in me! Hanneh Breineh, Shmendrik, they will not be stilled in me, till all America stops to listen."

## HOW I FOUND AMERICA

### Part I

Every breath I drew was a breath of fear, every shadow a stifling shock, every footfall struck on my heart like the heavy boot of the Cossack.

On a low stool in the middle of the only room in our mud hut sat my father — his red beard falling over the Book of Isaiah open before him. On the tile stove, on the benches that were our beds, even on the earthen floor, sat the neighbors' children, learning from him the ancient poetry of the Hebrew race.

As he chanted, the children repeated:

"The voice of him that crieth in the wilderness,
Prepare ye the way of the Lord.
Make straight in the desert a highway for our God

"Every valley shall be exalted,
And every mountain and hill shall be made low,
And the crooked shall be made straight,
And the rough places plain.

"And the glory of the Lord shall be revealed,
And all flesh shall see it together."

Undisturbed by the swaying and chanting of teacher and pupils, old Kakah, our speckled hen, with her brood of chicks, strutted and pecked at the potato-peelings which fell from my mother's lap, as she prepared our noon meal.

I stood at the window watching the road, lest the Cossack come upon us unawares to enforce the ukaz of the Czar, which would tear the bread from our mouths: "No Chadir [Hebrew school] shall be held in a room used for cooking and sleeping."

With one eye I watched ravenously my mother cutting chunks of black bread. At last the potatoes were ready. She poured them out of the iron pot into a wooden bowl and placed them in the center of the table.

Instantly the swaying and chanting ceased, the children rushed forward. The fear of the Cossacks was swept away from my heart by the fear that the children would get my potato.

The sentry deserted his post. With a shout of joy I seized my portion and bit a huge mouthful of mealy delight.

At that moment the door was driven open by the blow of an iron heel. The Cossack's whip swished through the air. Screaming, we scattered.

The children ran out — our livelihood gone with them.

"Oi weh," wailed my mother, clutching her breast, "is there a God over us — and sees all this?"

With grief-glazed eyes my father muttered a broken prayer as the Cossack thundered the ukaz: "A thousand rubles fine or a year in prison if you are ever found again teaching children where you're eating and sleeping."

"Gottuniu!" pleaded my mother, "would you tear the last skin from our bones? Where else can we be eating and sleeping? Or should we keep chadir in the middle of the road? Have we houses with separate rooms like the Czar?"

Ignoring my mother's entreaties the Cossack strode out of the hut. My father sank into a chair, his head bowed in the silent grief of the helpless.

"God from the world" — my mother wrung

her hands — "is there no end to our troubles? When will the earth cover me and my woes?"

I watched the Cossack disappear down the road. All at once I saw the whole village running toward us. I dragged my mother to the window to see the approaching crowd.

"Gewalt! What more is falling over our heads?" she cried in alarm.

Masheh Mindel, the water-carrier's wife, headed a wild procession. The baker, the butcher, the shoemaker, the tailor, the goatherd, the workers of the fields, with their wives and children, pressed toward us through a cloud of dust.

Masheh Mindel, almost fainting, fell in front of the doorway. "A letter from America!" she gasped.

"A letter from America!" echoed the crowd, as they snatched the letter from her and thrust it into my father's hands.

"Read! Read!" they shouted tumultuously.

My father looked through the letter, his lips uttering no sound. In breathless suspense the crowd gazed at him. Their eyes shone with wonder and reverence for the only man in the village who could read.

Masheh Mindel crouched at his feet, her neck stretched toward him to catch each precious word of the letter.

"To my worthy wife, Masheh Mindel, and to my loving son, Susha Feifel, and to my precious darling daughter, the apple of my eye, the pride of my life, Tzipkeleh!

"Long years and good luck on you! May the blessings from heaven fall over your beloved heads and save you from all harm!

"First I come to tell you that I am well and in good health. May I hear the same from you.

"Secondly, I am telling you that my sun is beginning to shine in America. I am becoming a person — a business man.

"I have for myself a stand in the most crowded part of America, where people are as thick as flies and every day is like market-day by a fair. My business is from bananas and apples. The day begins with my pushcart full of fruit, and the day never ends before I count up at least $2.00 profit — that means four rubles.

Stand before your eyes . . . I . . . Gedalyeh Mindel, four rubles a day, twenty-four rubles a week!"

"Gedalyeh Mindel, the water-carrier, twenty-four roubles a week . . ." The words leaped like fire in the air.

We gazed at his wife, Masheh Mindel — a dried-out bone of a woman.

"Masheh Mindel, with a husband in America — Masheh Mindel, the wife of a man earning twenty-four rubles a week!"

We looked at her with new reverence. Already she was a being from another world. The dead, sunken eyes became alive with light. The worry for bread that had tightened the skin of her cheek-bones was gone. The sudden surge of happiness filled out her features, flushing her face as with wine.

The two starved children clinging to her skirts, dazed with excitement, only dimly realized their good fortune by the envious glances of the others.

"Thirdly, I come to tell you," the letter

went on, "white bread and meat I eat every day just like the millionaires.

"Fourthly, I have to tell you that I am no more Gedalyeh Mindel — *Mister* Mindel they call me in America.

"Fifthly, Masheh Mindel and my dear children, in America there are no mud huts where cows and chickens and people live all together. I have for myself a separate room with a closed door, and before any one can come to me, I can give a say, 'Come in,' or 'Stay out,' like a king in a palace.

"Lastly, my darling family and people of the Village of Sukovoly, there is no Czar in America."

My father paused; the hush was stifling. No Czar—no Czar in America! Even the little babies repeated the chant: "No Czar in America!"

"In America they ask everybody who should be the President, and I, Gedalyeh Mindel, when I take out my Citizens papers, will have as much to say who shall be the next President in America, as Mr. Rockefeller the greatest millionaire.

"Fifty rubles I am sending you for your ship-ticket to America. And may all Jews who suffer in Goluth from ukazes and pogroms live yet to lift up their heads like me, Gedalyeh Mindel, in America."

Fifty rubles! A ship-ticket to America! That so much good luck should fall on one head! A savage envy bit me. Gloomy darts from narrowed eyes stabbed Masheh Mindel.

Why should not we too have a chance to get away from this dark land? Has not every heart the same hunger for America? The same longing to live and laugh and breathe like a free human being? America is for all. Why should only Masheh Mindel and her children have a chance to the new world?

Murmuring and gesticulating the crowd dispersed.

Each one knew every one else's thought: How to get to America. What could they pawn? From where could they borrow for a ship-ticket?

Silently we followed my father back into the hut from which the Cossack had driven us a while before.

We children looked from mother to father and from father to mother.

"Gottuniu! The Czar himself is pushing us to America by this last ukaz." My mother's face lighted up the hut like a lamp.

"Meshugeneh Yidini!" admonished my father. "Always your head in the air. What — where — America? With what money? Can dead people lift themselves up to dance?"

"Dance?" The samovar and the brass pots rang and reëchoed with my mother's laughter. "I could dance myself over the waves of the ocean to America."

In amazed delight at my mother's joy we children rippled and chuckled with her.

My father paced the room — his face dark with dread for the morrow.

"Empty hands — empty pockets — yet it dreams itself in you America."

"Who is poor who has hopes on Amcrica?" flaunted my mother.

"Sell my red quilted petticoat that grandmother left for my dowry," I urged in excitement.

"Sell the feather beds, sell the samovar," chorused the children.

"Sure we can sell everything — the goat and all the winter things," added my mother; "it must be always summer in America."

I flung my arms around my brother and he seized Bessie by the curls, and we danced about the room crazy with joy.

"Beggars!" laughed my mother, "why are you so happy with yourselves? How will you go to America without a shirt on your back — without shoes on your feet?"

But we ran out into the road, shouting and singing: "We'll sell everything we got — we'll go to America."

"White bread and meat we'll eat every day — in America! In America!"

That very evening we fetched Berel Zalman, the usurer, and showed him all our treasures, piled up in the middle of the hut.

"Look, all these fine feather beds, Berel Zalman," urged my mother; "this grand fur coat came from Nijny itself. My grandfather bought it at the fair."

I held up my red quilted petticoat, the supreme sacrifice of my ten-year-old life.

Even my father shyly pushed forward the samovar. "It can hold enough tea for the whole village."

"Only a hundred rubles for them all," pleaded my mother; "only enough to lift us to America. Only one hundred little rubles."

"A hundred rubles? Pfui!" sniffed the pawnbroker. "Forty is overpaid. Not even thirty is it worth."

But coaxing and cajoling my mother got a hundred rubles out of him.

Steerage — dirty bundles — foul odors — seasick humanity — but I saw and heard nothing of the foulness and ugliness around me. I floated in showers of sunshine; visions upon visions of the new world opened before me.

From lips to lips flowed the golden legend of the golden country:

"In America you can say what you feel — you can voice your thoughts in the open streets without fear of a Cossack."

"In America is a home for everybody. The land is your land. Not like in Russia where you feel yourself a stranger in the village where you were born and raised — the village in which your father and grandfather lie buried."

"Everybody is with everybody alike, in America. Christians and Jews are brothers together."

"An end to the worry for bread. An end to the fear of the bosses over you. Everybody can do what he wants with his life in America."

"There are no high or low in America. Even the President holds hands with Gedalyeh Mindel."

"Plenty for all. Learning flows free like milk and honey."

"Learning flows free."

The words painted pictures in my mind. I

saw before me free schools, free colleges, free libraries, where I could learn and learn and keep on learning.

In our village was a school, but only for Christian children. In the schools of America I'd lift up my head and laugh and dance — a child with other children. Like a bird in the air, from sky to sky, from star to star, I'd soar and soar.

"Land! Land!" came the joyous shout.

"America! We're in America!" cried my mother, almost smothering us in her rapture.

All crowded and pushed on deck. They strained and stretched to get the first glimpse of the "golden country," lifting their children on their shoulders that they might see beyond them.

Men fell on their knees to pray. Women hugged their babies and wept. Children danced. Strangers embraced and kissed like old friends. Old men and women had in their eyes a look of young people in love.

Age-old visions sang themselves in me — songs of freedom of an oppressed people.

America! — America!

## HOW I FOUND AMERICA

### PART II

BETWEEN buildings that loomed like mountains, we struggled with our bundles, spreading around us the smell of the steerage. Up Broadway, under the bridge, and through the swarming streets of the ghetto, we followed Gedalyeh Mindel.

I looked about the narrow streets of squeezed-in stores and houses, ragged clothes, dirty bedding oozing out of the windows, ash-cans and garbage-cans cluttering the side-walks. A vague sadness pressed down my heart—the first doubt of America.

"Where are the green fields and open spaces in America?" cried my heart. "Where is the golden country of my dreams?"

A loneliness for the fragrant silence of the woods that lay beyond our mud hut welled up in my heart, a longing for the soft, responsive earth of our village streets. All about me was the hardness of brick and stone, the stinking smells of crowded poverty.

"Here's your house with separate rooms like

in a palace." Gedalyeh Mindel flung open the door of a dingy, airless flat.

"Oi weh!" my mother cried in dismay. "Where's the sunshine in America?"

She went to the window and looked out at the blank wall of the next house. "Gottuniu! Like in a grave so dark . . ."

"It ain't so dark, it's only a little shady." Gedalyeh Mindel lighted the gas. "Look only" — he pointed with pride to the dim gaslight. "No candles, no kerosene lamps in America, you turn on a screw and put to it a match and you got it light like with sunshine."

Again the shadow fell over me, again the doubt of America!

In America were rooms without sunlight, rooms to sleep in, to eat in, to cook in, but without sunshine. And Gedalyeh Mindel was happy. Could I be satisfied with just a place to sleep and eat in, and a door to shut people out — to take the place of sunlight? Or would I always need the sunlight to be happy?

And where was there a place in America for me to play? I looked out into the alley below and saw pale-faced children scrambling in the gutter. "Where is America?" cried my heart.

My eyes were shutting themselves with sleep. Blindly, I felt for the buttons on my dress, and buttoning I sank back in sleep again — the deadweight slcep of utter exhaustion.

"Heart of mine!" my mother's voice moaned above me. "Father is already gone an hour. You know how they'll squeeze from you a nickel for every minute you're late. Quick only!"

I seized my bread and herring and tumbled down the stairs and out into the street. I ate running, blindly pressing through the hurrying throngs of workers — my haste and fear choking each mouthful.

I felt a strangling in my throat as I neared the sweatshop prison; all my nerves screwed together into iron hardness to endure the day's torture.

For an instant I hesitated as I faced the grated window of the old dilapidated building — dirt and decay cried out from every crumbling brick.

In the maw of the shop, raging around me the roar and the clatter, the clatter and the roar, the merciless grind of the pounding machines. Half maddened, half deadened, I struggled to think, to feel, to remember — what am I — who am I — why was I here?

I struggled in vain — bewildered and lost in a whirlpool of noise.

"America — America — where was America?" it cried in my heart.

The factory whistle — the slowing-down of the machines — the shout of release hailing the noon hour.

I woke as from a tense nightmare — a weary waking to pain.

In the dark chaos of my brain reason began to dawn. In my stifled heart feelings began to pulse. The wound of my wasted life began to throb and ache. My childhood choked with drudgery — must my youth too die — unlived?

The odor of herring and garlic — the ravenous munching of food — laughter and loud, vulgar jokes. Was it only I who was so wretched? I looked at those around me. Were they happy or only insensible to their slavery? How could they laugh and joke? Why were they not torn with rebellion against this galling grind — the crushing, deadening movements of the body, where only hands live and hearts and brains must die?

A touch on my shoulder. I looked up. It was Yetta Solomon from the machine next to mine.

"Here's your tea."

I stared at her, half hearing.

"Ain't you going to eat nothing?"

"Oi weh! Yetta! I can't stand it!" The cry broke from me. "I did n't come to America to turn into a machine. I came to America to make from myself a person. Does America want only my hands — only the strength of my body — not my heart — not my feelings — my thoughts?"

"Our heads ain't smart enough," said Yetta, practically. "We ain't been to school like the American-born."

"What for did I come to America but to go to school — to learn — to think — to make something beautiful from my life . . ."

"Sh-sh! Sh-sh! The boss — the boss!" came the warning whisper.

A sudden hush fell over the shop as the boss entered. He raised his hand.

Breathless silence.

The hard, red face with pig's eyes held us under its sickening spell. Again I saw the Cossack and heard him thunder the ukaz.

Prepared for disaster, the girls paled as they cast at each other sidelong, frightened glances.

"Hands," he addressed us, fingering the gold watch-chain that spread across his fat belly, "it's slack in the other trades and I can get plenty girls begging themselves to work for half what you're getting — only I ain't a skinner. I always give my hands a show to earn their bread. From now on, I'll give you fifty cents a dozen shirts instead of seventy-five, but I'll give you night-work, so you need n't lose nothing." And he was gone.

The stillness of death filled the shop. Each one felt the heart of the other bleed with her own helplessness.

A sudden sound broke the silence. A woman

sobbed chokingly. It was Balah Rifkin, a widow with three children.

"Oi weh!" She tore at her scrawny neck. "The blood-sucker — the thief! How will I give them to eat — my babies — my babies — my hungry little lambs!"

"Why do we let him choke us?"

"Twenty-five cents less on a dozen — how will we be able to live?"

"He tears the last skin from our bones!"

"Why did n't nobody speak up to him?"

"Tell him he could n't crush us down to worse than we had in Russia?"

"Can we help ourselves? Our life lies in his hands."

Something in me forced me forward. Rage at the bitter greed tore me. Our desperate helplessness drove me to strength.

"I'll go to the boss!" I cried, my nerves quivering with fierce excitement. "I'll tell him Balah Rifkin has three hungry mouths to feed."

Pale, hungry faces thrust themselves toward me, thin, knotted hands reached out, starved bodies pressed close about me.

"Long years on you!" cried Balah Rifkin, drying her eyes with a corner of her shawl.

"Tell him about my old father and me, his only bread-giver," came from Bessie Sopolsky, a gaunt-faced girl with a hacking cough.

"And I got no father or mother and four of them younger than me hanging on my neck." Jennie Feist's beautiful young face was already scarred with the gray worries of age.

America, as the oppressed of all lands have dreamed America to be, and America *as it is*, flashed before me — a banner of fire! Behind me I felt masses pressing — thousands of immigrants — thousands upon thousands crushed by injustice, lifted me as on wings.

I entered the boss's office without a shadow of fear. I was not I — the wrongs of my people burned through me till I felt the very flesh of my body a living flame of rebellion.

I faced the boss.

"We can't stand it!" I cried. "Even as it is we're hungry. Fifty cents a dozen would starve us. Can you, a Jew, tear the bread from another Jew's mouth?"

"You, fresh mouth, you! Who are you to learn me my business?"

"Were n't you yourself once a machine slave — your life in the hands of your boss?"

"You — loaferin — money for nothing you want! The minute they begin to talk English they get flies in their nose. . . . A black year on you — trouble-maker! I'll have no smart heads in my shop! Such freshness! Out you get . . . out from my shop!"

Stunned and hopeless, the wings of my courage broken, I groped my way back to them — back to the eager, waiting faces — back to the crushed hearts aching with mine.

As I opened the door they read our defeat in my face.

"Girls!" I held out my hands. "He's fired me."

My voice died in the silence. Not a girl stirred. Their heads only bent closer over their machines.

"Here, you! Get yourself out of here!" The boss thundered at me. "Bessie Sopolsky and you, Balah Rifkin, take out her machine into the hall. . . . I want no big-mouthed Americanerins in my shop."

Bessie Sopolsky and Balah Rifkin, their eyes black with tragedy, carried out my machine.

Not a hand was held out to me, not a face met mine. I felt them shrink from me as I passed them on my way out.

In the street I found I was crying. The new hope that had flowed in me so strong bled out of my veins. A moment before, our togetherness had made me believe us so strong — and now I saw each alone — crushed — broken. What were they all but crawling worms, servile grubbers for bread?

I wept not so much because the girls had deserted me, but because I saw for the first time how mean, how vile, were the creatures with whom I had to work. How the fear for bread had dehumanized their last shred of humanity! I felt I had not been working among human beings, but in a jungle of savages who had to eat one another alive in order to survive.

And then, in the very bitterness of my resentment, the hardness broke in me. I saw the girls through their own eyes as if I were inside of them. What else could they have done? Was not an immediate crust of bread for Balah Rifkin's children more urgent than truth — more vital than honor?

Could it be that they ever had dreamed of America as I had dreamed? Had their faith in America wholly died in them? Could my faith be killed as theirs had been?

Gasping from running, Yetta Solomon flung her arms around me.

"You golden heart! I sneaked myself out from the shop — only to tell you I'll come to see you to-night. I'd give the blood from under my nails for you — only I got to run back — I got to hold my job — my mother — "

I hardly saw or heard her — my senses stunned with my defeat. I walked on in a blind daze — feeling that any moment I would drop in the middle of the street from sheer exhaustion.

Every hope I had clung to — every human stay — every reality was torn from under me. I sank in bottomless blackness. I had only one wish left — to die.

Was it then only a dream — a mirage of the hungry-hearted people in the desert lands of oppression — this age-old faith in America — the beloved, the prayed-for "golden country"?

Had the starved villagers of Sukovoly lifted above their sorrows a mere rainbow vision that led them — where — where? To the stifling submission of the sweatshop or the desperation of the streets!

"O God! What is there beyond this hell?" my soul cried in me. "Why can't I make a quick end to myself?"

A thousand voices within me and about me answered:

"My faith is dead, but in my blood their faith still clamors and aches for fulfillment — *dead generations whose faith though beaten back still presses on — a resistless, deathless force!*

"In this America that crushes and kills me, their spirit drives me on — to struggle — to suffer — but never to submit."

In my desperate darkness their lost lives loomed — a living flame of light. Again I saw the mob of dusty villagers crowding around my father as he read the letter from America — their eager faces thrust out — their eyes blazing with the same hope, the same age-old faith that drove me on —

A sudden crash against my back. Dizzy with pain I fell — then all was darkness and quiet.

I opened my eyes. A white-clad figure bent over me. Had I died? Was I in the heaven of the new world — in America?

My eyes closed again. A misty happiness filled my being.

"Learning flows free like milk and honey," it dreamed itself in me.

I was in my heaven — in the schools of America — in open, sunny fields — a child with other children. Our lesson-books were singing birds and whispering trees — chanting brooks and beckoning skies. We breathed in learning and wisdom as naturally as flowers breathe in sunlight.

After our lessons were over, we all joined hands skipping about like a picture of dancing fairies I had once seen in a shop-window.

I was so full of the joy of togetherness — the great wonder of the new world; it pressed on my heart like sorrow. Slowly, I stole away from the other children into silent solitude, wrestling and praying to give out what surged in me into some form of beauty. And out of my struggle to shape my thoughts beautifully, a great song filled the world.

"Soon she's all right to come back to the shop — yes, nurse?" The voice of Yetta Solomon broke into my dreaming.

Wearily I opened my eyes. I saw I was still on earth.

Yetta's broad, generous face smiled anxiously at me. "Lucky yet the car that run you over did n't break your hands or your feet. So long you got yet good hands you'll soon be back by the machine."

"Machine?" I shuddered. "I can't go back to the shop again. I got so used to sunlight and quiet in the hospital I'll not be able to stand the hell again."

"Shah! — Shah!" soothed Yetta. "Why don't you learn yourself to take life like it is?

What's got to be, got to be. In Russia, you could hope to run away from your troubles to America. But from America where can you go?"

"Yes," I sighed. "In the blackest days of Russia, there was always the hope from America. In Russia we had only a mud hut; not enough to eat and always the fear from the Cossack, but still we managed to look up to the sky, to dream, to think of the new world where we'll have a chance to be people, not slaves."

"What's the use to think so much? It only eats up the flesh from your bones. Better rest . . ."

"How can I rest when my choked-in thoughts tear me to pieces? I need school more than a starving man needs bread."

Yetta's eyes brooded over me. Suddenly a light broke. "I got an idea. There's a new school for greenhorns where they learn them anything they want . . ."

"What — where?" I raised myself quickly, hot with eagerness. "How do you know from it — tell me only — quick — since when — "

"The girl next door by my house — she used to work by cigars — and now she learns there."

"What does she learn?"

"Don't get yourself so excited. Your eyes are jumping out from your head."

I fell back weakly: "Oi weh! Tell me!" I begged.

"All I know is that she likes what she learns better than rolling cigars. And it's called 'School for Immigrant Girls.'"

"Your time is up. Another visitor is waiting to come in," said the nurse.

As Yetta walked out, my mother, with the shawl over her head, rushed in and fell on my bed kissing me.

"Oi weh! Oi weh! Half my life is out from me from fright. How did all happen?"

"Don't worry yourself so. I'm nearly well already and will go back to work soon."

"Talk not work. Get only a little flesh on your bones. They say they send from the hospital people to the country. Maybe they'll send you."

"But how will you live without my wages?"

"Davy is already peddling with papers and Bessie is selling lolly-pops after school in the park. Yesterday she brought home already twenty-eight cents."

For all her efforts to be cheerful, I looked at her pinched face and wondered if she had eaten that day.

Released from the hospital, I started home. As I neared Allen Street, the terror of the dark rooms swept over me. "No — no — I can't yet go back to the darkness and the stinking smells," I said to myself. "So long they're getting along without my wages, let them think I went to the country and let me try out that school for immigrants that Yetta told me about."

So I went to the Immigrant School.

A tall, gracious woman received me, not an employee, but a benefactress.

The love that had rushed from my heart toward the Statue in the Bay, rushed out to Mrs. Olney. She seemed to me the living spirit of America. All that I had ever dreamed America to be shone to me out of the kindness of her brown eyes. She would save me from the sordidness that was crushing me I felt the moment I looked at her. Sympathy and understanding seemed to breathe from her serene presence.

I longed to open my heart to her, but I was so excited I did n't know where to begin.

"I'm crazy to learn!" I gasped breathlessly, and then the very pressure of the things I had to say choked me.

An encouraging smile warmed the fine features.

"What trade would you like to learn — sewing-machine operating?"

"Sewing-machine operating?" I cried. "Oi weh!" I shuddered. "Only the thought 'machine' kills me. Even when I only look on clothes, it weeps in me when I think how the seams from everything people wear is sweated in the shop."

"Well, then" — putting a kind hand on my shoulder — "how would you like to learn to cook? There's a great need for trained servants and you'd get good wages and a pleasant home."

"Me — a servant?" I flung back her hand. "Did I come to America to make from myself a cook?"

Mrs. Olney stood abashed a moment. "Well, my dear," she said deliberately, "what would you like to take up?"

"I got ideas how to make America better, only I don't know how to say it out. Ain't there a place I can learn?"

A startled woman stared at me. For a moment not a word came. Then she proceeded with the same kind smile. "It's nice of you to want to help America, but I think the best way would be for you to learn a trade. That's what this school is for, to help girls find themselves, and the best way to do is to learn something useful."

"Ain't thoughts useful? Does America want only the work from my body, my hands? Ain't it thoughts that turn over the world?"

"Ah! But we don't want to turn over the world." Her voice cooled.

"But there's got to be a change in America!" I cried. "Us immigrants want to be people —

not 'hands'—not slaves of the belly! And it's the chance to think out thoughts that makes people."

"My child, thought requires leisure. The time will come for that. First you must learn to earn a good living."

"Did I come to America for a living?"

"What did you come for?"

"I came to give out all the fine things that was choked in me in Russia. I came to help America make the new world.... They said, in America I could open up my heart and fly free in the air—to sing—to dance—to live—to love.... Here I got all those grand things in me, and America won't let me give nothing."

"Perhaps you made a mistake in coming to this country. Your own land might appreciate you more." A quick glance took me in from head to foot. "I'm afraid that you have come to the wrong place. We only teach trades here."

She turned to her papers and spoke over her shoulder. "I think you will have to go elsewhere if you want to set the world on fire."

## HOW I FOUND AMERICA

### Part III

BLIND passion swayed me as I walked out of the Immigrant School, not knowing where I was going, not caring. One moment I was swept with the fury of indignation, the next moment bent under the burden of despair. But out of this surging conflict one thought — one truth gradually grew clearer and clearer to me: Without comprehension, the immigrant would forever remain shut out — a stranger in America. Until America can release the heart as well as train the hand of the immigrant, he would forever remain driven back upon himself, corroded by the very richness of the unused gifts within his soul.

I longed for a friend — a real American friend — some one different from Mrs. Olney, some one who would understand this vague, blind hunger for release that consumed me. But how, where could I find such a friend?

As I neared the house we lived in, I paused terror-stricken. On the sidewalk stood a jumbled pile of ragged house-furnishings that looked familiar — chairs, dishes, kitchen pans. Amidst bundles of bedding and broken furniture stood my mother. Oblivious of the curious crowd, she lit the Sabbath candles and prayed over them.

In a flash I understood it all. Because of the loss of my wages while I was in the hospital, we had been evicted for unpaid rent. It was Sabbath eve. My father was in the synagogue praying and my mother, defiant of disgrace, had gone on with the ceremony of the Sabbath.

All the romance of our race was in the light of those Sabbath candles. Homeless, abandoned by God and man, yet in the very desolation of the streets my mother's faith burned — a challenge to all America.

"Mammeh!" I cried, pushing through the crowd. Bessie and Dave darted forward. In a moment the four of us stood clinging to one another, amid the ruins of our broken home.

A neighbor invited us into her house for supper. No sooner had we sat down at the table than there was a knock at the door and a square-figured young woman entered, asking to see my mother.

"I am from the Social Betterment Society," she said. "I hear you've been dispossessed. What's the trouble here?"

"Oi weh! My bitter heart!" I yet see before me the anguish of my mother's face as she turned her head away from the charity lady.

My father's eyes sank to the floor. I could feel him shrink in upon himself like one condemned.

The bite of food turned to gall in my throat.

"How long have you been in America? Where were you born?" She questioned by rote, taking out pad and pencil.

The silence of the room was terrible. The woman who had invited us for supper slunk into the bedroom, unable to bear our shame.

"How long have you been in America?" repeated the charity lady.

Choked silence.

"Is there any one here who can speak?" She translated her question into Yiddish.

"A black year on Gedalyeh Mindel, the liar!"

my mother burst out at last. "Why did we leave our home? We were among our own. We were people there. But what are we here? Nobodies — nobodies! Cats and dogs at home ain't thrown in the street. Such things could only happen in America — the land without a heart — the land without a God!"

"For goodness' sakes! Is there any one here intelligent enough to answer a straight question?" The charity lady turned with disgusted impatience from my mother to me. "Can you tell me how long you have been in this country? Where were you born?"

"None of your business!" I struck out blindly, not aware of what I was saying.

"Why so bold? We are only trying to help you and you are so resentful."

"To the Devil with your help! I'm sick no longer. I can take care of my mother — without your charity!"

The next day I went back to the shop — to the same long hours — to the same low wages — to the same pig-eyed, fat-bellied boss. But I was no longer the same. For the first time in my life I bent to the inevitable. I accepted my defeat. But something in me, stronger than I, rose triumphant even in my surrender.

"Yes, I must submit to the shop," I thought. "But the shop shall not crush me. Only my body I must sell into slavery — not my heart — not my soul.

"To any one who sees me from without, I am only a dirt-eating worm, a grub in the ground, but I know that above this dark earth-place in which I am sunk is the green grass — and beyond the green grass, the sun and sky. Alone, unaided, I must dig my way up to the light!"

Lunch-hour at the factory. My book of Shelley's poems before me and I was soon millions of miles beyond the raucous voices of the hungry eaters.

"Did you already hear the last news?" Yetta tore my book from me in her excitement.

"What news?" I scowled at her for waking me from my dreams.

"We're going to have electricity by the machines. And the forelady says that the new boss will give us ten cents more on a dozen waists!"

"God from the world! How did it happen — electricity — better pay?" I asked in amazement. For that was the first I had heard of improved conditions of work.

But little by little, step by step, the sanitation improved. Open windows, swept floors, clean wash-rooms, individual drinking-cups introduced a new era of factory hygiene. Our shop was caught up in the general movement for social betterment that stirred the country.

It was not all done in a day. Weary years of struggle passed before the workers emerged from the each-for-himself existence into an organized togetherness for mutual improvement.

At last, with the shortened hours of work, I had enough vitality left at the end of the day to join the night-school. Again my dream flamed. Again America beckoned. In the school there would be education — air, life for my cramped-in spirit. I would learn to form the thoughts that surged formless in me. I would find the teacher that would make me articulate.

Shelley was English literature.

So I joined the literature class. The course began with the "De Coverley Papers." Filled with insatiate thirst, I drank in every line with the feeling that any minute I would get to the fountain-heart of revelation.

Night after night I read with tireless devotion. But of what? The manners and customs of the eighteenth century, of people two hundred years dead.

One evening after a month's attendance, when the class had dwindled from fifty to four and the teacher began scolding us who were left for those who were absent, my bitterness broke.

"Do you know why all the girls are dropping away from the class? It's because they have too much sense to waste themselves on the 'De Coverley Papers.' Us four girls are four fools. We could learn more in the streets. It's dirty and wrong, but it's life. What are the 'De Coverley Papers'? Dry dust fit for the ash can."

"Perhaps you had better tell the board of education your ideas of the standard classics," she scoffed, white with rage.

"Classics? If all the classics are as dead as the 'De Coverley Papers,' I'd rather read the ads in the papers. How can I learn from this old man that's dead two hundred years how to live my life?"

That was the first of many schools I had tried. And they were all the same. A dull course of study and the lifeless, tired teachers — no more interested in their pupils than in the wooden benches before them — chilled all my faith in the American schools.

More and more the all-consuming need for a friend possessed me. In the street, in the cars, in the subways, I was always seeking, ceaselessly seeking, for eyes, a face, the flash of a smile that would be light in my darkness.

I felt sometimes that I was only burning out my heart for a shadow, an echo, a wild dream. But I could n't help it. Nothing was real to me but my hope of finding a friend.

One day my sister Bessie came home much excited over her new high-school teacher. "Miss Latham makes it so interesting!" she exclaimed. "She stops in the middle of the lesson and tells us things. She ain't like a teacher. She's like a real person."

At supper next evening, Bessie related more wonder stories of her beloved teacher. "She's so different! She's friends with us. . . . To-day, when she gave us out our composition, Mamie Cohen asked from what book we should read up and she said, 'Just take it out of your heart and say it.'"

"Just take it out of your heart and say it." The simple words lingered in my mind, stirring a whirl of hidden thoughts and feelings. It seemed as if they had been said directly to me.

A few days later Bessie ran in from school, her cheeks flushed, her eyes dancing with excitement. "Give a look at the new poem teacher gave me to learn!" It was a quotation from Kipling:

"Then only the Master shall praise us,
And only the Master shall blame,
And no one shall work for money,
And no one shall work for fame;
But each for the joy of the working,
And each in his separate Star,
Shall draw the thing as he sees it
For the God of things as they are."

Only a few brief lines, but in their music the pulses of my being leaped into life. And so it was from day to day. Miss Latham's sayings kept turning themselves in my mind like a lingering melody that could not be shaken off. Something irresistible seemed to draw me to her. She beckoned to me almost as strongly as America had on the way over in the boat.

I wondered, "Should I go to see her and talk myself out from my heart to her?

"Meshugeneh! Where — what? How come you to her? What will you say for your reason?

"What's the difference what I'll say! I only want to give a look on her . . ."

And so I kept on restlessly debating. Should I follow my heart and go to her, or should I have a little sense?

Finally the desire to see her became so strong that I could no longer reason about it. I left the factory in the middle of the day to seek her out.

All the way to her school I prayed: "God — God! If I could only find one human soul that cared . . ."

I found her bending over her desk. Her hair

was gray, but she did not look tired like the other teachers. She was correcting papers and was absorbed in her task. I watched her, not daring to interrupt. Presently she threw back her head and gave a little laugh.

Then she saw me. "Why, how do you do?" She rose. "Come and sit down."

I felt she was as glad to see me as though she had expected me.

"I feel you can help me," I groped toward her.

"I hope I can." She grasped my outstretched hands and led me to a chair which seemed to be waiting for me.

A strange gladness filled me.

"Bessie showed me the poem you told her to learn . . ." I paused bewildered.

"Yes?" Her friendly eyes urged me to speak.

"From what Bessie told me I felt I could talk myself out to you what's bothering me." I stopped again.

She leaned forward with an inviting interest. "Go on! Tell me all."

"I'm an immigrant many years already here, but I'm still seeking America. My dream

America is more far from me than it was in the old country. Always something comes between the immigrant and the American," I went on blindly. "They see only his skin, his outside — not what's in his heart. They don't care if he has a heart. . . . I wanted to find some one that would look on me — myself . . . I thought you'd know yourself on a person first off."

Abashed at my boldness I lowered my eyes to the floor.

"Do go on . . . I want to hear."

With renewed courage I continued my confessional.

"Life is too big for me. I'm lost in this each-for-himself world. I feel shut out from everything that's going on. . . . I'm always fighting — fighting — with myself and everything around me. . . . I hate when I want to love and I make people hate me when I want to make them love me."

She gave me a quick nod. "I know — I know what you mean. Go on."

"I don't know what is with me the matter. I'm so choked. . . . Sundays and holidays when the other girls go out to enjoy themselves, I walk around by myself — thinking — thinking. . . . My thoughts tear in me and I can't tell them to no one! I want to do something with my life and I don't know what."

"I'm glad you came," she said. And after a pause, "You can help me."

"Help you?" I cried. It was the first time that an American suggested that I could help her.

"Yes, indeed! I have always wanted to know more of that mysterious vibrant life — the immigrant. You can help me know my girls."

The repression of centuries seemed to rush out of my heart. I told her everything — of the mud hut in Sukovoly where I was born, of the Czar's pogroms, of the constant fear of the Cossack, of Gedalyeh Mindel's letter and of our hopes in coming to America.

After I had talked myself out, I felt suddenly ashamed for having exposed so much, and I cried out to her: "Do you think like the others that I'm all wrapped up in self?"

For some minutes she studied me, and her

serenity seemed to project itself into me. And then she said, as if she too were groping, "No — no — but too intense."

"I hate to be so all the time intense. But how can I help it? Everything always drives me back in myself. How can I get myself out into the free air?"

"Don't fight yourself." Her calm, gray eyes penetrated to the very soul in me. "You are burning up too much vitality. . . .

"You know some of us," she went on — "not many, unfortunately — have a sort of divine fire which if it does not find expression turns into smoke. This egoism and self-centeredness which troubles you is only the smoke of repression."

She put her hand over mine. "You have had no one to talk to — no one to share your thoughts."

I marveled at the simplicity with which she explained me to myself. I could n't speak. I just looked at her.

"But now," she said, gently, "you have some one. Come to me whenever you wish."

"I have a friend," it sang itself in me. "I have a friend."

"And you are a born American?" I asked. There was none of that sure, all-right look of the Americans about her.

"Yes, indeed! My mother, like so many mothers," — and her eyebrows lifted humorously whimsical, — "claims we're descendants of the Pilgrim fathers. And that one of our lineal ancestors came over in the Mayflower."

"For all your mother's pride in the Pilgrim fathers, you yourself are as plain from the heart as an immigrant."

"Were n't the Pilgrim fathers immigrants two hundred years ago?"

She took from her desk a book called "Our America," by Waldo Frank, and read to me: "We go forth all to seek America. And in the seeking we create her. In the quality of our search shall be the nature of the America that we create."

"Ach, friend! Your words are life to me! You make it light for my eyes!"

She opened her arms to me and breathlessly I

felt myself drawn to her. Bonds seemed to burst. A suffusion of light filled my being. Great choirings lifted me in space.

I walked out unseeingly.

All the way home the words she read flamed before me: "We go forth all to seek America. And in the seeking we create her. In the quality of our search shall be the nature of the America that we create."

So all those lonely years of seeking and praying were not in vain! How glad I was that I had not stopped at the husk — a good job — a good living — but pressed on, through the barriers of materialism.

Through my inarticulate groping and reaching-out I had found the soul — the spirit — of America!

## THIS IS WHAT $10,000 DID TO ME

I WAS VERY POOR. And when I was poor, I hated the rich. Now that I too have some means, I no longer hate them. I have found that the rich are as human as any of us.

When I lived in Hester Street, I could feel life only through the hurts and privations of Hester Street. Why were we cramped into the crowded darkness of dingy tenements? Because the heartless rich had such sunny palaces on Fifth Avenue. Why were we starving and wasting with want? Because the rich gorged themselves with the fat of the land.

And then it happened. I who thought myself doomed to Hester Street had the chance to move myself up to Fifth Avenue. And now where are the horns and hoofs that I always seemed to see at the sight of the well-fed, the well-dressed? Where's the righteous indignation that flared up in my breast when I saw people ride around in limousines? Where's the hot sureness with which I condemned as criminals those who dared to have the things we longed to have but never could hope of having—furs and jewels and houses?

It began five years ago, just a few days before Christmas. Shivering with cold, I walked up and down the shopping district of Fifth Avenue. I caught a glimpse of myself in the mirror of a passing shop window. What a pinched, starved thing! Worried, haunted eyes under a crumpled hat. Faded, ragged old coat. Over-patched shoes, pulling apart at the patches.

All about me fine ladies, sleek and warm in fur coats, stepping in and out of their cars. All about me shop windows glittering with ball gowns and gorgeous wraps. Riches and luxury everywhere, and I so crazed with want!

In one window a dazzling Christmas tree blinded me with rage. Why should there be Christmas in the world? Why this holiday spirit on Fifth Avenue when there's no holiday for Hester Street? Why these expectant, smiling faces of the shoppers buying useless presents for each other, when we didn't know from where would come our next meal?

I had been writing and starving for years. My stories, which appeared in the magazines from time to time, had been gathered together and published in a book called *Hungry Hearts*. Although reviewers praised it, my royalties were so small that it brought me little money and almost no recognition. People who read a book little know what small reward there is for the writer while he is still unknown—of his often solitary, starved existence. A book read in one evening may have taken the author years and years of the most agonizing toil to create.

On and on I walked through the gay street, shoved and elbowed by the hurrying crowd. Wild thoughts raced in the corner of my brain. If I could only throw a bomb right there in the middle of Fifth Avenue and shatter into a thousand bits all this heartlessness of buying and buying! The slush of the sidewalk creeping into the cracks of my shoes made me feel so wretchedly uncomfortable. Exhausted with the bitterness and hatred of my thoughts, my futile rebellion gradually settled into a dull melancholy. If I could only kill myself as a protest against the wrongs and injustices I had suffered! I did not really want to die. But I did so much want to shock the world out of its indifference.

Almost a sense of exaltation stole over me as I went on imagining the details of my death. I could see the beautiful limousine wrenched to a sudden stop. The pale chauffeur lifting my crushed, bleeding body in his arms. The whole world crowding around me, dumb, horrified. Then a voice breaking the hush of the crowd:

"This was the author of *Hungry Hearts,* and we left her to anguish and die in want!"

Already I saw the throngs mobbing the bookstores for my book. My last letter and my picture in the front page of every newspaper in the country. Everywhere people reading and taking *Hungry Hearts*. The whole world shaken with guilty sorrow for my tragic death—but too late!

Yes, on that dark day there seemed no way to take revenge for the cruel neglect of a heartless world but to blow out my brains or plunge under the wheels of the crowded traffic. My last letter was already shaping itself in my head as I hastened back to my room to write it.

How I dreaded to meet the landlady on the stairs! I could not bear to hear her nagging for the rent in my last tragic hour. Trembling with fear, I sneaked into my room.

There on the table lay a little yellow telegram!

I stared at it. Who in the world would send me a telegram?

I tore it open and read uncomprehendingly. It was from a well-known moving picture agent, saying that he could get for the film rights of my book the unheard of sum of ten thousand dollars.

In a flash the whole world changed! And I was changed. It changed still more when, after negotiations for the book had been made, they offered to send me to California to collaborate on the screen version of *Hungry Hearts*.

There followed a wonderful trip across the continent, in a private compartment. I had to pinch myself to make sure that I was not dreaming when I entered the diner and ordered roast duck, asparagus, endive salad and strawberries with cream. I could treat myself with a full hand because a millionaire corporation was paying the bills.

"And this is no accident of good fortune, no matter of luck," I kept telling myself. "*Hungry Hearts* has earned it for me."

Arrived in Los Angeles, I was greeted with overwhelming friendliness by a representative of the company. In a gorgeous limousine, one of those limousines that I always condemned as a criminal luxury of the hated rich—in one of these limousines I was driven to a hotel.

Flowers filled my room. Flowers for me! I looked around, dazzled out of my senses. Luxurious comfort beyond dream all about me. I felt dizzy drunk with this sudden plunge into the world of wealth.

For the first day I stayed in my room struggling to pull together my bewildered wits. I wanted to let go and be happy. But I could not let go, nor be happy. All my Hester Street past rose up in arms against me. "Betrayer! Deserter!" my soul that once was cried accusingly.

The following morning a limousine called to take me to the studio in Culver City. A private office and a secretary were assigned to me. And that secretary! I wondered, would I have to get myself new clothes to match up to her style?

I suddenly became aware of my frumpy, old-fashioned dress against her youthful grace and up-to-dateness. I had heard of newly rich people who were always scared that their servants would look down on them out of the corners of their eyes. And I wondered, would I too let myself get shamed out of being what I am by the proud condescension of my grand secretary? Before I could finish my thought, Julian Josephson, that great scenario man, came in. One look of his eyes, the smile on his face, and I felt at home, among my own. Then other members of the scenario department joined us to discuss the plot for *Hungry Hearts*.

The minute we got busy, I was myself again. Happy for the first time since my good luck. *Ach,* what a heart-filling thing is work! In poverty or wealth, work has been to me the one escape from the storms of the soul within or the struggles with the world without.

At luncheon time I met the "eminent authors" that were working about the lot—Rupert Hughes, Gertrude Atherton, Leroy Scott, Alice Duer Miller, Gouverneur Morris and many others. What a thrilling experience it was to see them for the first time face to face, to talk to them as they were eating luncheon, just as if they were plain human beings!

One of the "eminent authors" invited me to dinner at his house that evening. Such things as dinner clothes or evening clothes never came into my mind. It seemed to me even if I had such fancy things I'd never know how to wear them. I stayed around the lot that afternoon, visiting the different sets. Before I knew it, it was time to go.

Again the company's limousine drove me to the place. A grave, dignified butler opened the door for me. Through the hall beyond I saw ladies almost half naked, in what seemed to me dressy, gay-colored night-gowns, and all the men in wedding suits.

"So these are evening clothes!" I pondered.

I wanted to rush back to my hotel, but my host saw me as he passed the hall and hastened over to welcome me.

"I might as well stay and see how 'eminent authors' dine," I thought. "How do they behave themselves at a party, these shining lights of the world?"

Upstairs, a fancy maid in a black uniform helped me take off my things. She gave me one look that said as plain as words, "From where do you come? You here—among 'eminent authors'?"

But the "eminent authors" themselves were such lively, plain people. They greeted me with such natural friendliness that I almost forgot I was different.

Cocktails were served. And then we seated ourselves about the table. Such a millionaire wedding feast! And that's what "eminent authors" called just dinner.

Four butlers were busy waiting on a dozen guests. Champagne—it would be impossible to count the bottles. As one rich dish after another was served, I thought of the people in Hester Street, starving, thrown in the street for unpaid rent. The cost of the champagne for that one dinner would be enough to feed a whole tenement house full of people . . . I remembered the picture of Nero fiddling before the fall of Rome. I had touched the two extremes of life—Hester Street—Hollywood.

At first there was a lot of educated talk about literature, art, Freud and other high things over my head. Then, warmed by the champagne, they began to talk about other authors. I felt happy just as if I were among my own people in Hester Street. Of course they didn't yell and holler or get excited like the people in Hester Street. They sat quite still in their chairs—ladies and gentlemen. But by the tones in their voices, the looks in their eyes, I saw again the tenants sitting on the stoop, tearing their neighbors to pieces behind their backs. These two "eminent" evening gowns were like those two girls with uncombed hair and flashing eyes fighting over some man. And that grand author lady, so proud of her best-selling books, made me think of that frowzy herring woman with a shawl over her head, nodding and talking behind her hand what was cooking in the neighbors' pots.

In the morning, still elated with the gay party of the night before, I awoke to the delicious feel of my soft, smooth bed. Such fresh, clean-smelling sheets! Warm, wool blankets finer than silk. Fresh air and sunshine flooded my room.

How far away was that dark hole in the tenements whence I came—six lodgers on one hard mattress on the floor, and the landlady with all her children in that narrow bed!

At the push of a button, a Japanese maid brought me my breakfast on a silver tray. Hothouse grapes—great purple ones, big as plums they looked to me. And the smell of that coffee in that silver pitcher and the fresh, buttered toast!

I laughed aloud at myself—crazy from Hester Street! You playing lady? You breakfasting in bed? You served on a silver tray? . . . Well, I'm only finding out how it feels. I'm only doing it for experience.

The limousine called to take me to my office. I felt so fine, so in love with the whole world as I relaxed against the cushions of the car. How much more comfortable than the crowded trolley! Would I ever be able to stand the elevated or subway after this?

My secretary was waiting for me as usual. I greeted her gaily.

"Don't you love it out here?" I laughed.

"Love it! When they don't pay me enough to live?" Then she poured out to me her bitter story. "In my home town in Iowa I got thirty-five a week. But I was crazy to work with the movies. I left a good job to come here. And all they pay is twenty-five dollars a week. I asked for a raise of five dollars. They refused it. It's impossible to get along on my wages. But a lot they care. It's take it or leave it with them. A dozen girls are ready to step into my job."

At every word my spirits sank. The joy over my good luck was over. In the next few days I met other stenographers, clerks, readers, stage hands. So many were horribly underpaid. The "eminent authors," the screen stars, the directors got fortunes for their work; the others drudged from morning till night for less than their bread.

Like a ghost at a feast, my secretary, and behind her the whole army of under-dogs at the studio, rose up before me every time I stepped into the limousine. There was no peace for me at my hotel.

I could stand it no longer. At the end of the week I went to the president of the company. "I'm so miserable in this grand hotel," I said.

"What? Aren't you comfortable?"

"I'm too comfortable—so comfortable—it makes me nervous. I've got to live plain like I'm used to. How much does it cost the company to keep me here?"

"About two hundred a week."

"Good heavens!" I cried. "Seven families with a dozen children each could live on that sum. Give me that money. I can live like a queen on fifty a week."

I left Hollywood a few months later, a tortured soul with a bank acocunt. I had the money now to live securely for a few years. Security buys peace of mind to develop a soul. And here I was losing the very soul that my security was giving me. For now I was a capitalist—one of the class that I hated.

The moving picture company saw in my sudden fortune a good human interest story for the papers, to advertise *Hungry Hearts* throughout the country without cost. And I, new to the game of publicity, gave out one interview after another. And every interview was twisted and distorted. Soon the ten thousand dollars for the picture rights of *Hungry Hearts* grew to twenty-five thousand. The two hundred a week I was paid while assisting on the scenario became two thousand. And then from lips to lips it leaped to ten thousand a week. Such were some of the headlines in the ghetto papers—"From Want to Wealth—From Hester Street to Hollywood."

People who have been always comfortable can't know what it means to come into sudden wealth. My mail was full of begging letters. Poor relatives besieged me for money. And my conscience told me that if I were true to my soul I'd give all. I had hated the rich because they kept their wealth and refused to share it with the rest of the world. But how was I to begin to share?

Ten thousand dollars seemed a fairy tale when I was starving poor, but a few months at Hollywood had so changed me that it did not seem much now. Just about enough to keep me till I wrote my next book.

As the demands for money became more insistent, I grew resentful. "I've slaved and starved and risked all to write something real. I've earned what I've got. What right have they to it? Let them produce *Hungry Hearts*. Let them suffer and agonize for every little word as I suffered and agonized."

The more I tried to make myself feel right, the more uneasy I was. My self-defense turned in upon me like an accusation. I knew the pain of the unjustly condemned and the guilt of those who had committed a crime.

To end the turmoil and confusion of my soul, I took a trip to Europe. As I traveled from city to city and saw the crooked little alleys where the poor huddled on top of each other worse than in Hester Street, I wanted to atone for the luxury of my trip by going back steerage.

I had come steerage to America twenty years ago. Why should I not be able to return the same way? I felt that only by going back to my own people could I hope to regain my lost soul—my soul that I had lost with my sudden good luck.

I stood it one day only, in the steerage. The dingy, crowded, smelly berths, the coarse food, the thick, ugly dishes and the lack of table service that had become a necessity to me.

I realized that you can't be an immigrant twice.

When I returned to New York, I moved boldly into a hotel on Fifth Avenue.

I didn't have time now to hate the rich. I had to use my energies to make myself a better writer, to keep up with the cost of my new standards of living. Here I came in contact with other capitalists, other conspirators of wealth. I discovered they were not ogres, heartless oppressors of the poor. They were as human as other folks.

Now, as I sit alone in my room, watching the wonder of the sunset, I look back and see how happy I ought to have been when I was starving poor, but one of my own people. Now I am cut off by my own for acquiring the few things I have. And those new people with whom I dine and to whom I talk, I do not belong to them. I am alone because I left my own world.

## WILD WINTER LOVE

THIS IS A STORY with an unhappy ending. And I too have become Americanized enough to be terrified of unhappy endings. Yet I have to drop all my work to write it.

Ever since I read in the papers about Ruth Raefsky, I've gone around without a head. I can't pull myself together somehow. Her story won't let me rest. It tears me out of my sleep at night. It leaps up at me out of every corner where I try to hide.

And it's dumb. Dumb. Words only push back the spirit of what I feel about her. The facts that I know so well dwindle into nothing. Only a piece of her life here, and a piece there—the end, the middle, and the beginning rush together in broken confusion.

The first thing that flashes to my mind is her outburst of impatience with the monotonous theme of love in American magazines. "You pick up one magazine after another, and it's all love-stories. Life isn't all sex. Why are they writing only about love, as if there was nothing else real to write about?"

How much she had learned of the realness and unrealness of love before she was through!

It was in the Bronx, the up-town ghetto, that I first met her. Even before we met, her neighbor's whisperings excited my interest.

"Imagine only—such a woman—a wife of a poor tailor—a house and a baby to take care of—and such a madness in her head—goes to night-school—wants to write herself a book of her life."

Her neighbor's voice was high-pitched with indignation. "The husband sweats from early morning till late at night, stitching his life away for every penny he earns. And she is such a lady, when she goes to the market, she don't bargain herself to get things cheaper like the rest of us. She takes it wrapped up, don't even look at the change. Just like a Gentile."

I had just moved in. It was one of those newly built five-story tenements with four three-room flats on each floor. She lived in the front and I in the rear. But it was weeks before I got on friendly terms with her.

All the other women sat around together with their baby-carriages in the sun, darning and mending, discussing what was cooking in the neighbors' pots. But she and her baby carriage were always off by themselves.

She seemed wrapped up inside herself. Not seeing, not hearing anything around her.

Sometimes she'd take up some pages and pencil from under the baby's pillow, jot down something. Then sit back very still, as if she were all alone, looking far out at the top of the world.

But when I met her in the store, or on the stairs, she looked like a neat, efficient, business-like person with a busy concentrated expression on her face. She answered my "good morning" and "good evening" with a nod and a smile, but no more.

Gradually her life pieced itself together out of the fragments of conversation we had.

She had met Dave, her husband, in the same

shop where she had worked. He was a tailor, she a finisher.

The sudden urge to write did not begin till after she was married.

"We were so happy in our little flat, all to ourselves. At first Dave wanted me to fix up a 'parlor like by other people.' But I wanted a plain living room like in the settlement.

" 'And why not?' he humored me. But I could see it wasn't because he thought the plain things I liked beautiful, but that he wanted me to have what I wanted.

"And so it was when I told him I had to write the story of my life. He hadn't much use for books. He only read the 'Vorwarts' and the 'Socialist Call.' He looked a little doubtful. But he loved me so, and he was so good and kind. He shrugged away his doubt. 'If you'll have from it pleasure, go ahead.'

"And so I began to go to nightschool to learn how to write my life. But in a class of fifty, how much time can the teacher give to me?

"I didn't realize when I began how long it would take, how I'd have to tear my flesh in pieces for every little word. I am only just feeling out the beginning of my story. But now I can't stop myself."

I glanced up at her. Under that look of neat businesslike efficiency, a consuming passion flared up in her eyes. Her baby two years already. Writing every day since her marriage, and only just at the beginning.

"If I could only do it by myself! It's having to go to these teachers for help that kills me. Every evening this week they were reading in my class how Washington crossed the Delaware. Here I'm burning up with the crossing of my own Delaware. And I have to choke down my living story for a George Washington, dead a hundred years. All that waste, only to get the teacher's help for a few minutes after the class."

Her tightly clenched hands trembled with nervousness. I've seen the dumb who wanted to say something, but were too confused to know what they wanted to say. Here were brains and intelligence. Here was a woman who knew what she wanted to say, but was lost in the mazes of the new language. And more than the confusion of the new language was the realization that she was talking to strangers, to whom she always felt herself saying too much, yet not enough. To cold hard-headed Americans she was trying to make clear the feverish turmoil of the suppressed desire-driven ghetto.

One evening, several months later, I heard through the open air-shaft window loud quarreling in the Raefsky flat.

"Come to bed already. I waited up for you long enough. It's time to sleep."

"Oh, Dave! Stop bothering me. I only just got started. Why can't you go to sleep without me?"

No sound for a while.

"*Nu?* Not yet finished?"

"Let me alone, can't you? I've scrubbed and cooked and washed all day long. Only when the baby is asleep that I take to myself."

"*Gewalt!*" Dave's voice, raw with hurt, rose into a shriek. "There's an end to a man's patience.

My gall is bursting. You're not a woman. I married myself to a *meshugeneh* with a book for her heart."

"God! What does that man want of me?"

"You know what I want. I want a home. I want a wife."

"Don't you have the things you like to eat? Was there ever a time that you did not have your clean shirt, your darned socks?"

"Oi-i-i! If you had flesh and blood in you, you wouldn't talk that way. What for did you marry me? So you could have a fool of a slave to give you everything, while you go on with your craziness?"

They drifted further and further apart. Whenever I entered their flat, I felt the cold chill that comes to you when you enter a house where the man and woman live under one roof yet live apart. It was only the love for their child that held them together in spite of the growing chasm between them.

As she became more and more consumed with her story, she grew impatient with the little special help she could get out of the night-school. She sought the club-leader of the settlement, a college student, the druggist on the corner, the doctor on the block. Anyone she met with a gleam of intelligence in their eyes, she would stop and make them listen to some little scene in her story that she happened to be working on. Their comments somehow helped her get a truer word, a deeper stroke in her picture.

And so the book built itself up piece by piece through the years.

I lost track of her for a long while when they moved away.

One day the club-leader of the settlement told me the exciting news that Ruth Raefsky had come through with her book, *Out of the Ghetto*.

Breathlessly I read the enthusiastic reviews of great critics who hailed Ruth Raefsky as the New Voice of the East Side.

So she got there at last! What a titanic struggle! With all her dumbness, her fearful unsureness of herself—to have pressed on and on—

beaten out a voice in so much that was dumb. . . . The steerage ship on its way to America—Cherry Street. The sweat shop. The boss. The "hands." The landlord. The rag peddler. The pawnshop. The art theater. Dreams and the brutal battle for bread. Greed and self-sacrifice. The dirt and the beauty seething in the crowded ghetto—to have caught it all—framed it between the covers of a book!

How will she look released from that terrible burden? Would having reached her goal wipe away the tortured driven look on her face? What will she do with herself now? Can she pick up again the relationships she broke to pursue her dream?

I went to see her. I found her already famous. People whose names I read in the magazines were now among her guests for tea.

Success had not yet worked any miracles in her appearance. Though she was excited and elated, the tired strained expression was still on her face. Sleepless nights and tortured days still cried out of her eyes.

"How does it feel to be a famous living author?" I whispered.

"Will I ever be able to do my next thing? This is my worry now."

I wondered why she did not rejoice more in her good luck. Then Dave, grimy from his work in the shop, came in.

He tried to slip away. But Ruth pulled him forward. "Come, Dave. I want you to meet some of my friends."

He bowed awkwardly, hiding his dirty hands in his pockets. Everyone in the room felt the pain of his self-consciousness. As soon as he could, he shrank into a corner and didn't say a word till they had left.

Then he burst out: "My home is no more mine. I come tired from the shop. All I want is peace—and my house is crowded with strangers. Why didn't you tell me you'd have them here?"

"Why hide yourself from people?"

"They're not my people. But what's the difference? What do I count in this house?

To a writer, what is a husband?"

"Oh, Dave!" Her voice was sharp with jangled nerves. "Don't let's go over all that again. My writing is no crime."

"Sure it's a crime," he cried, his eyes blazing. "The pleasures of writing is for millionaires. What right has a poor man's wife to give in to herself? Suppose it willed itself in me to write a book, who'd give you bread? I have to be a tailor, so you could shine in the world for a writer. Somebody's got to work for the rent."

I went away. I thought of an evening years ago, when I first knew them. Dave had come in from work, with eager shining eyes and a package in his hand. It was his wife's birthday. He had saved for months to surprise her with a Hungarian peasant shawl that he had seen her admire in a shop window. How he drank in pleasure out of his wife's delight as he wrapped the shawl around her! And now—the cold looks, the harsh voices with which they pushed one another away.

Some months later we made an appointment to meet for lunch. When the day came, I received word that she was ill. I went to see her. I found her prostrate with a headache.

She looked frightfully old. Her features stood out sharply. Her eyes seemed to have gone deep down into her head. She sat up in bed with a little jerk. Bright red spots burned on her cheeks. She barely stopped to greet me. She began talking at once, as though carrying on a conversation with herself.

"I'm a woman without a country. I'm uprooted from where I started; and I can't find roots anywhere. I've lost the religion of my fathers. I've lost the human ties that hold other women. I can only live in the world I create out of my brain. I've got so that I can't live unless I write. And I can't write. The works have stopped in me. What will be my end?"

Her reserve had unloosed through exhaustion. I never heard her talk so much. It was a torrent of high-pitched nervous words.

"My writing began with my love for Dave. But I've gone on only in my brain. I've gone too far away from life. I don't know how to get back.

"I have so much more to give out than ever before. But something has stifled this giving-out power. My terrible inadequacy is killing me. What is the agony of death to this agony I now suffer—to feel, to see, to know—and to wither in sight of it all—stifled—dumb."

Soon after this, a nervous breakdown forced her to give her daughter to board, and she went away for the first vacation in her life.

I was seeing Dave, off and on, whenever I needed my clothes to be repaired.

"How's Ruth?" I asked toward the end of the summer.

"Now she's come back with a new craziness in her head. She's got to live alone. Such selfishness—" He stopped suddenly.

I was too embarrassed to press him for details. I hurried to see her at her new address. I expected her to be in a worse mental state, now that she was living the hermit. But she was radiant. Her face, her figure, her eyes, had a verve, a sparkle, a magnetism, that I never saw in her before.

"What has happened to you?" I cried. "You look a million years younger."

A light from away inside flashed up in her face. "I'm seeing for the first time how glorious it is just to be alive. Beauty is all about us—only I was too blind to see it till now. What is that verse in the Bible—'all things work together for good to them that love God'?"

I listened in amazement. I couldn't take my eyes away from her shining face.

"Solitude has done you good."

"Solitude is only an empty cup. I have rich red wine to fill my solitude."

Now I knew what had happened to her. Who? Who is it? You—at forty-seven, in love?"

"Yes. And with a man even older than I. What does youth know about love? What can youth bring to love, but the inexperience, the unripeness of youth?"

For a moment I looked beneath the radiance of her face into the battle-scarred, life-worn lines that the years had dug into her throat and about her eyes. In that moment she was all of her forty-seven years old. But it was only for a moment. I was caught up again by the rich warmth of her voice, the inexhaustible energy that poured out of her as she talked.

"Outwardly, my lover is one of those cold reasonable Anglo-Saxons. A lawyer. A respectable citizen. Devoted to his wife. Adores his children. We're drawn to each other by something even more compelling than the love of man for woman, and woman for man. It's that irresistible force as terrible as birth and death that sometimes flares up between Jew and Gentile."

The resonance of her own voice was like fire that fed her. She looked far out—stern forehead, exultant eyes—seeing prophecies.

"These centuries of antagonism between his race and mine have burst out in us into this transcendent love. A love that burns through the barriers of race and class and creed.... Since Christ was crucified, a black chasm of hate yawned between his people and mine. But now and then threads of gold have spun through the darkness—links of understanding woven by fearless souls—Gentiles and Jews—men and women who were not afraid to trust their love."

"Mad-woman—poetess!" In a kind of envy I laughed aloud. But she was too inspired to hear me.

"It's because he and I are of a different race that we can understand one another so profoundly, touch the innermost reaches of the soul, beyond the reach of those who think they know us.

"When I talk to him, it's like traveling in foreign countries. He excites my imagination and releases my imagination. . . .

"My writing is but a rushing fountain of song to him. I pour myself out at his feet, in poems of my people, their hopes, their dreams. He listens to me with the wonder of a child listening to adventure. It's all so fresh and new to him, my world, that it becomes fresh and new to me. . . .

"In some way I do not understand I've been the means of bringing release to him too. I've awakened in him a new worship of life and beauty that none of the women of his class can ever dream is in him."

She threw back her head gloriously. Her laughter was a chant of triumph. "The wonderful way that man looks at me! It's like bathing in sunshine. . . . Dave has driven into me all these years that I'm a criminal. That fire in me, that makes me what I am—a crime. And this man washes away, as in healing oil, the guilt and self-defense with which my flesh and spirit is scarred. To him I can be just as I am. He wants me as I am."

The starved tailor's wife! How it had gone to her head, the little bit of love! But what wonder? For the first time in her life, she found a lover, an inspirer, and an audience all in one—a man of brains who understood the warm rich muddle of her experience.

I was all curiosity to see the man who had so changed this lonely ghetto woman. I got to watching for them. Walking the streets where they were likely to pass. At last I saw them. It was like seeing black and white, so intense, so startling was the contrast between them. His calm Anglo-Saxon face was like a background of rock for her volatile, tempestuous, Slavic temperament.

They lit up the street with their happiness. The world seemed to sweep away before their completeness in each other. And yet, he seemed quite an old man. No different from hundreds of other plain lawyers. She, for all the fire and vivacity that lighted up her face was unmistakably middle-aged. How could they let themselves be so wrapped up in each other? How shameless, at their age, to get so lost in their love!

But a rich power for work was that love. It put a new appeal, deeper humanity, into her writing. Her stories became the fad of the hour. Her stepping up into the world of success, while I was still low down in the struggle, gradually cut us off one from the other.

It was over three years that I had not seen her. By degrees I became aware that she appeared less and less in the public eye. I began to wonder what she was doing.

A sudden desire to see her swept me. But I

pushed back the impulse. . . . What can we talk about now, when she's so happy? . . .

One morning I opened the newspaper as I sat down to breakfast. Ruth Raefsky's picture! Under it, in big letters—Suicide! I read on. But I was too shaken to take in anything. My brain was paralyzed by that one word—suicide.

Ruth Raefsky! So rich with life! So eager to live! She—of all people! I had to know the truth of what had happened. Suicide. That word meant nothing. What led to it, was her story.

I called on her relatives, her friends—on anyone who might know.

"Well, what can you expect? Left her husband, her child, for an affair with a married man," said her next-door neighbor.

And each one had something different to say.

"Such a haunted face as she had the last time I saw her! Poor thing! She looked so unhappy."

"You can't blame the man. The wife and daughters got wind of the affair. He wouldn't let them be hurt. Why should the innocent family suffer? So Ruth Raefsky had to go."

"He had a sense of duty to the community,

if she didn't. I admire him for being strong enough, in the end, to do the right thing."

"How she must have suffered! She shut herself away from all of us. She wouldn't let any of us try to help her."

So their words fell about her—smug or compassionate.

How could they know the real Ruth Raefsky? Those years of toil by day and night, tearing up by the roots her starved childhood, her starved youth, trying to tell, in her personal story, the story of her people. How could they understand the all-consuming urge that drove her to voice her way across the chasm between the ghetto and America?

A lonely losing fight it was from the very beginning. Only for a moment, a hand of love stretched a magic bridge across the chasm. Inevitably the hand drew back. Inevitably the man went back to the safety of his own world.

In the fading of this dazzling mirage of friendship and love, vanished her courage, her dreams, her last illusion. And she leaped into the gulf that she could not bridge.

## ONE THOUSAND PAGES OF RESEARCH

EVERY TIME I walked along Upper Broadway, I saw them. Old men and old women, in their seventies, like me, seated side by side on the park benches set up by a benevolent city on the traffic islands dissecting the main roadway. Every time I passed those benches, stationary amidst the moving cars, I thought about how many more old people there must be all over the city, killing time, waiting for death.

Then one day it came to me. Right here in New York handicapped veterans were being trained for a new life; the blind were being taught skills; why couldn't the old be rehabilitated? After all, we still had much to give. We all had experience and many of us had professional training. Why was all this going to waste?

The idea took hold of me, and I decided to do something about it. I went to the university nearby. I talked. They listened—patiently, but helplessly. I was passed from one department to another. The Rehabilitation Department was only for young veterans. The Adult Education Department was mildly interested, but saw no way of adopting my idea. I persisted. At last I was directed to a psychologist—let us call him Professor Sidney Stone—who specialized in the "learning abilities of adults." I made my speech:

"We want to be of use. There are recreation centers for 'senior citizens' to keep them off the streets, to keep them from going mad in their lonely rooms. But I speak for the old who have brains and intelligence. We are not interested in finger painting and other childish hobbies. We don't want to kill time; we want to use it."

Professor Stone gave me a long, reflective look and said that he was trying to develop an intelligence test for older people. He suggested that if I could get together a group of women around my own age, we might start a "workshop on aging."

It takes six simpletons and one zealot to start a movement. I began recruiting among my friends and fellow has-beens, acquaintances from the reading room of the Public Library, from the cafeterias and the park benches—wherever lonely old people begin talking to one another without introductions. Some had pensions, annuities, social security; one had a family inheritance; a few existed on dwindling savings and others on public welfare. Their enthusiasm was almost unanimous.

We gathered for our first seminar with name tags pinned to our shoulders, looking up at the professor like children on their first day of school. "You are an unusual group of women," he began. "You have the intelligence to voice your own problems and to help us understand the old who cannot speak for themselves. You can throw light on one of the major dilemmas before us today—how to use the potentialities of the old." He was a plump, middle-aged man with a fringe of graying hair around his bald spot, but to us he represented youth, charm, the opportunity to work and live again.

He leaned back in his chair, stroking his lapels. "Many approaches have been made to the problem of aging, but this discussion group is unique. It is to be a study of the old by the old. It is something new to meet a new need of our time. Science has salvaged scrap metal and even found vitamins and valuable oils in refuse, but old people are extravagantly wasted."

Charlotte Hicks, the ex-school teacher among us and the only one who had a notebook, was writing down everything the professor said. The rest of us could only look at him, devouring his words. They were like a bell, calling us to prayer; his genial smile made us feel he saw something special in each one of us. "We cannot tell in advance whether we can solve your personal problems right now," he concluded. "We cannot promise you anything except the satisfaction of working together for something that concerns us all."

The professor rose and the first seminar was concluded. We followed him from the room like a dutiful congregation after an inspiring sermon. Things were indeed looking up. I flung my arms around dour Mrs. Monahan.

Our second session began with questionnaires—age, family history, former occupation, education, how do you feel about growing old? I sat with the blank forms in front of me, thinking about the past. I grew up at the turn of the century, before child labor laws or compulsory schooling. Brief night-school courses in English had only sharpened my hunger for education. Then (could it have been forty years ago?) I stumbled into writing—novels about my experiences in the sweatshops of the Lower East Side. A brief, incredible success in Hollywood was followed by long years of groping, trial and error, and finally silence. Suddenly, shocked, I found that old age was upon me. Editors who had encouraged me were dead. My stories had faded into period pieces. A new generation of writers was creating a new literature.

We handed in our questionnaires. Professor Stone turned on the tape recorder and leaned back in his chair. He talked into a tiny microphone: "When does old age begin?"

Charlotte Hicks, sixty-nine and the youngest

of the group, was the first to speak. She hadn't felt old, she explained, until she applied for a tutoring job at a teacher's agency and was told to say she was fifty instead of sixty-five. Charlotte snatched off her glasses. She was in a rage. "That man told me to lie!"

Kathleen Monahan, who had the worries of the world in her wrinkled face, was incredulous. "Holy Mother! What's a few lies? I tell 'em every day. Is there anyone in this room who doesn't? When my social worker comes snooping around, asking how I spend my money, can I tell her everything?"

The professor did his best to restore order and bring the ladies back to the subject. I said that feeling old was not a matter of years and Rose agreed by defining old age as the time where there is nothing left to look forward to.

Kathleen Monahan eyed Rose's blue cashmere sweater and expressed the view that those who had gone through the hell of home relief probably had less time to feel sorry for themselves.

Alice, the oldest, intervened as peacemaker.

She had outlived the doctors with whom she had worked, outlived what the depression had left of her family fortune. Nearly eighty, she had been forced to go on relief.

"I wasn't aware of age," she said with a slight smile, "until I was seventy-nine and walked up the stone stairs of the Welfare Office to apply for Old Age Assistance. I worked for the poor all my life. But not until I was one of them did I see what goes on under the name of charity."

We did not look at one another. The only sound was the mechanical purr of the tape recorder. Professor Stone watched us in silence.

Alice turned to Kathleen. "You know that Old Age Assistance provides hardly enough for food and rent. The morning paper, news of what's going on in the world, is as necessary to me as coffee for breakfast. I made ten dollars knitting a sweater and was so proud of it I showed the case worker the money I earned. The next month ten dollars was deducted from my check."

Derisive laughter at Alice's innocence was

followed by a storm of indignation. We all began to talk, outshouting each other.

"Ladies! Please!" Professor Stone called us to order. "Pensions are not the subject here. We're wasting time." He paused. "Instead of dwelling on your grievances, have you ever thought of volunteering your services to your neighborhood community center, church, or hospital? In helping others we touch something greater than ourselves."

Anger and disappointment were in every face but Alice's. No one spoke. The closing bell put an end to the embarrassing silence.

In the street I burst out. Was our work than worth nothing? Why should we volunteer? Just because we're old? The very thing we needed was the self-respect that comes with getting paid for working.

At our next session, Professor Stone picked up a glass, partially filled it at the water tap and opined that there were negative and positive ways of looking at everything. The glass, for example, could be considered either as half empty or as half full. It was up to us. Even if this country abolished forced retirement and prejudice against the old, what would each of us then be able to do?

Alice was the first to see what he meant. "I could be a clinic receptionist as long as I didn't have to stand. Or I could work in a doctors' telephoning service."

The other ladies took up the cry. Kathleen could still "cook in six different languages," and even the usually silent Rose Broder debated her chances of becoming a chaperone or housekeeper.

"When you think of your positive assets, you conquer your prejudices against old age," Professor Stone continued. He turned to Charlotte, whose face had grown fixed and still while the others were talking. "Miss Hicks! What are your positive assets?"

"My thirty-five years of teaching," Charlotte retorted in her clipped schoolteacher's voice. "Methods of teaching change, of course, and my eyesight isn't as good as it used to be. But what made me a good teacher is still in me.

My age is the one unpardonable sin."

Minerva Neilson stood up and sorrowfully took the floor. "I was a columnist for thirty years. My column in our hometown paper was the first thing anybody read. When the editor died, his grandson took over. 'We need a change,' he said. 'We want something new.'" She wiped her eyes with her knuckles like a child. "The young have overrun the world."

"All that you ladies have said only accentuates the importance of thinking positively," the professor concluded. "The body weakens with the years, hearing, sight and speed lessen, but the power to serve is ageless. . . ."

And so we went from week to week. Professor Stone would open every session with a smile, greeting us approvingly, secure in the confidence that our project was the opening wedge in an entirely new approach to the problems of old age. He reassured us that as a result of the facts that were being recorded, a revolution against compulsory retirement would be initiated. Facts, the professor said, "have a power and vitality of their own." By way of reply, Minerva Neilson stood up one day in class, her scarf as usual thrown with studied artlessness over her shoulders, and told the professor that if she did succeed in getting a book published, she'd dedicate it to him. Grateful and embarrassed, the professor seized his brief-case and dismissed us five minutes early.

The tape recorder never stopped purring. What is "intelligence in the old"? What is "creative maturity"? How can we learn to "think constructively"? Our discussion trailed off into abstractions and the professor's words sailed higher and higher over our heads. If we could only stop talking, I thought sometimes, and meet in silence as the Quakers do, then maybe he would finally understand.

The dreaded last day of the seminar came. Professor Stone walked in, smiling as always. "Are old people too close to death to be able to talk about it freely?" he began. "A social worker told me to avoid the subject when speaking to the aged. But your attitude toward death is an important aspect of our inquiry, so I deferred the question until we had the broadest possible orientation."

As usual, Charlotte Hicks, the youngest, was the first to speak. "I could die tomorrow. It wouldn't matter. Nobody needs me; nobody would care." She was suddenly on her feet. "I just can't stand the sight of old people! Why don't they just finish us off quickly, instead of prolonging our uselessness!"

The professor's pencil point broke with a loud snap. It was out at last! An odd, reckless excitement possessed the room. At last, after all those months of talking, somebody had said what we all felt. (Were we jealous of Charlotte's comparative youth? Were we glad to discover that she was in the same boat with the rest of us? Perhaps—but there was more to it than that.) Charlotte snapped off her glasses and tapped them lightly against her hand. "From childhood on I was taught to save—to save for a rainy day, to save for the future. Well, now I've got my pension—but what's the use of living without being able to work?"

Kathleen Monahan had the final say. "I can't quite imagine myself under the sod, not yet. There's an old saying: the young may die, the old must die—but not me." Why are we wasting time talking about death, I wondered. *How are we going to live until we die?*

Professor Stone fumbled with his papers, his face gray and tired as if all the old women in the room had inflicted their impotence on him. There was, regrettably, no time to answer these questions, he said. The fact that we could still ask them, though, was encouraging. He glanced at his watch, took a deep breath, and offered us his concluding remarks. We had started something that, developed and expanded, might lead to great changes in ways of dealing with the problem of old age. Our discussions and case histories were only the first of a series, and these already comprised over a thousand pages of data. When these were analyzed and collated, a report would be drawn up that would no doubt be of great benefit to future students of gerontology. This was only the beginning. He thanked us for the insights he had gained from our seminar and expressed the hope that it had been "a profitable year for us all." One by one we bade the professor goodbye, and filed out.

Unwilling, or afraid, to disperse, we made

our way as a group to the school cafeteria. We sat around a table, mute as mourners, sipping tea. "We talked our heads off—for what?" asked Kathleen Monahan.

"For a thousand pages of research," I replied.

"He had a job to do and he did it," said Alice, calmly.

"So our seminar was only a job to him?"

"We were only statistics to him," said Charlotte Hicks. "Dots on a graph." Methodically she began tearing the pages from her notebook, watching them flutter to the ground.

"His heart," said Minerva Neilson, "is wired to a tape recorder."

Kathleen Monahan stood up and took hold of her shopping bag. "What dopes we were. A whole year wasted, only to find out the professor don't know nothing."

"What did you want him to do?" Alice asked. "Be God? Make us young again?"

"Where do we go from here?" I asked.

# AFTERWORD

THE ORIGINAL edition of *Hungry Hearts*, the first book Anzia Yezierska wrote, is republished here sixty-five years after its initial appearance. Added to it in this new volume are three unusual, uncharacteristic stories of hers, never reprinted or collected in a book before, which reflect on the beginning and end of Yezierska's career.

Houghton Mifflin first published *Hungry Hearts* in 1920, after one of its stories, "'The Fat of the Land,'" appearing in a magazine the year before, was named the Best Short Story of 1919 by Edward J. O'Brien. *Hungry Hearts* earned for Anzia, who was my mother, an overnight fortune (more than $10,000, a dazzling sum in those days) when it brought her to Hollywood to work on the silent film Samuel Goldwyn's company made from her book. Her second book, *Salome of the Tenements*, also sold to the movies—for a larger sum, $15,000.

For the next ten years, during which she wrote four more books, Anzia was a celebrity. Newspapers frequently retold the fairy tale of how my mother rose from New York's Lower East Side ghetto to literary stardom. But with the Depression of the 1930s, she lost her audience and her money as well. In 1950 her seventh book, *Red Ribbon on a White Horse*, restored to her a small measure of literary recognition; and thereafter she wrote a striking group of stories and essays about old age—among them, the last story in this book, "One Thousand Pages of Research." They were not much noticed then; they are getting more attention today along with the rest of her writing.

Anzia has been rediscovered by feminists and social historians during the past ten years. As her daughter, I regret that this began to happen only after her death in 1970, but I experience a continuing and pleased surprise that she is turning out to be so contemporary. This first book of hers went out of print in the original edition about fifty years ago. Although some of its short stories (for instance, "How I Found

America" and "'The Fat of the Land'") have been reprinted in new anthologies throughout the succeeding years—so many times as to become classics—and although a few libraries preserved the original edition with rebinding, it has been virtually unknown to most readers for half a century. The three stories added here show what happened to Anzia after the publication of *Hungry Hearts*.

"This Is What $10,000 Did to Me" was published in the October 1925 issue of *Cosmopolitan* magazine five years after *Hungry Hearts* appeared, three years after its movie. Anzia tells in that story the consequences of making so much money from the book. She never overcame her guilt for having become rich by writing about the poor, nor her tragic sense of loneliness because she had changed her circumstances so drastically:

> Now . . . I look back and see how happy I ought to have been when I was starving poor but one of my own people. Now I am cut off by my own for acquiring the few things I have. And those new people with whom I dine and to whom I talk, I do not belong to them. I am alone because I left my own world.

"Wild Winter Love," which Anzia wrote at the height of her own success, about an author whose love and work had failed, appeared in the February 1927 issue of *The Century Magazine*. It is written with the intensity of emotion which had attracted the readers of *Hungry Hearts*, but also, I think, with a superior, confident craftsmanship which Anzia had gained in six years' time. She was by then an experienced writer, much in demand. The real-life model for this story, with whom Anzia felt a close connection, was Rose Cohen, the author of *Out of the Shadows*. That book about the hardships of Cohen's life in the New York ghetto was published two years before *Hungry Hearts*, arousing Anzia's admiration and envy. (In 1918, she was collecting only rejection slips.) But *Out of the Shadows*, Cohen's only book, did not receive the acclaim that *Hungry Hearts* received. Four years after her book was published, Rose Cohen attempted suicide by jumping into the East River. She was rescued and disappeared from public notice thereafter.

"One Thousand Pages of Research," published by *Commentary* in July 1963, shows the difference of thirty-five years in its tone. Anzia was about eighty-two years old in 1963, still writing social protests—in this case, against society's exclusion of the old—but the story is almost drained of emotion, detached. It is a report on a project she initiated at Columbia University: she persuaded a psychology professor and a group of elderly women to join in a seminar about old age. Narrating the results, she became, for the first time in her writing career, a cynic.

She continued, in her eighties, to write stories in this dispassionate vein. In 1962 and 1965 the National Institute of Arts and Letters presented her with awards of $500 each, stating: "This is given you in recognition of your distinction as a writer." These tributes from other writers, a few years before her death, briefly pierced the obscurity to which she had long since returned.

*Louise Levitas Henriksen*

# *VIRAGO MODERN CLASSICS*

The first Virago Modern Classic, *Frost in May* by Antonia White, was published in 1978. It launched a list dedicated to the celebration of women writers and to the rediscovery and reprinting of their works. Its aim was, and is, to demonstrate the existence of a female tradition in fiction which is both enriching and enjoyable. The Leavisite notion of the 'Great Tradition', and the narrow, academic definition of a 'classic', has meant the neglect of a large number of interesting secondary works of fiction. In calling the series 'Modern Classics' we do not necessarily mean 'great' — although this is often the case. Published with new critical and biographical introductions, books are chosen for many reasons: sometimes for their importance in literary history; sometimes because they illuminate particular aspects of womens' lives, both personal and public. They may be classics of comedy or storytelling; their interest can be historical, feminist, political or literary.

Initially the Virago Modern Classics concentrated on English novels and short stories published in the early decades of this century. As the series has grown it has broadened to include works of fiction from different centuries, different countries, cultures and literary traditions. In 1984 the Victorian Classics were launched; there are separate lists of Irish, Scottish, European, American, Australian and other English speaking countries; there are books written by Black women, by Catholic and Jewish women, and a few relevant novels by men. There is, too, a companion series of Non-Fiction Classics constituting biography, autobiography, travel, journalism, essays, poetry, letters and diaries.

By the end of 1986 over 250 titles will have been published in these two series, many of which have been suggested by our readers.